Praise for

"The Ethnic Eats series is too good to miss a single book!"
—Fresh Fiction

"Kylie Logan's *French Fried* is a delightfully jam-packed
novel of both mystery and emotion."   —Criminal Element

"[A] fun and intriguing read . . . Cannot wait for the next
in this series."   —Open Book Society

"[A] delightfully entertaining debut to a series that I hope
is here to stay."   —Dru's Book Musings

More praise for Kylie Logan

"Logan has fun with this unusual story, intimate setting,
and feisty characters, and readers will, too."
—*Richmond Times-Dispatch*

"One of my favorite cozy mystery writers . . . What great
characters Kylie Logan has created."   —Fresh Fiction

Italian Iced

KYLIE LOGAN

BERKLEY PRIME CRIME
New York

BERKLEY PRIME CRIME
Published by Berkley
An imprint of Penguin Random House LLC
375 Hudson Street, New York, New York 10014

Copyright © 2018 by Connie Laux
Penguin Random House supports copyright. Copyright fuels creativity, encourages
diverse voices, promotes free speech, and creates a vibrant culture. Thank you for buying
an authorized edition of this book and for complying with copyright laws by not
reproducing, scanning, or distributing any part of it in any form without permission.
You are supporting writers and allowing Penguin Random House to continue to
publish books for every reader.

BERKLEY is a registered trademark and BERKLEY PRIME CRIME and the B colophon
are trademarks of Penguin Random House LLC.

ISBN: 9780425274903

First Edition: July 2018

Printed in the United States of America
1 3 5 7 9 10 8 6 4 2

Cover art by Tom Foty
Cover design by Sarah Oberrender
Book design by Kelly Lipovich

*For you, the readers who make it possible
for me to have the best job in the world.*

Acknowledgments

Who doesn't love Italian food?

When I was searching for an idea for the third book in the Ethnic Eats series, I knew I couldn't pass up the chance to explore Italian cuisine. Some Italian dishes are easy to prepare. All are wonderfully delicious.

So is the support I receive from family and friends.

Thank you all for helping out with ideas and advice. Special thanks to my brainstorming group, Shelley Costa, Serena Miller, and Emilie Richards, and to Mary Ellis and Peggy Svoboda, who are always willing to listen.

Chapter 1

The sound didn't make any sense.

Plink. Plink, plink.

I squeezed my eyes shut, willing myself to go back to sleep, reminding myself that tomorrow (which was technically today, because before I could tell myself not to, I glanced at the clock and saw it was four in the morning) was the first day we'd feature Italian foods on the menu at Sophie's Terminal at the Tracks. Italian food is always popular. We'd be slammed, and I needed to be at the top of my restaurant manager/menu planner/ staff cheerleader game.

I would be, too, I told myself.

If only I could get back to sleep.

Plink. Plink, plink.

I groaned, but not too loudly. At my side, Declan Fury, he of the overwhelming Irish family, with the sometimes annoying tendency to try and do my thinking for me and—not coincidentally—the sexiest guy I'd met in as long as I could remember, slept quietly, his breaths even, that chipped-from-granite chest of his rising and falling to a rhythm so relaxing, it was hard to imagine that just a few hours ago, he'd made my blood sing, my temperature soar, and every inch of me glad that I'd gone out on the proverbial limb (not an easy thing for a woman who'd grown up in the foster system) and let him know that I was as crazy about him as he was about me. I can't say if it's true that Declan's family was involved in the local Irish mob, but I do know one thing—he's something of a thief himself. In the year since I'd arrived in Hubbard, Ohio, he'd stolen a heart I wasn't sure I had before I arrived.

Plink. Plink, plink.

I propped myself up on my elbows and cocked my head, listening at the same time I tried to make sense of the noise.

The tapping sound wasn't inside Pacifique, the house I'd recently inherited from a dear friend. It was outside, rapping on the windows, each little knock sounding like something quick and hard against the glass.

Plink. Plink, plink.

Reality hit and just like that, I sat up like a shot and I was already out of bed and reaching for my clothes when Declan rolled to his side.

"What's going on?" He didn't look like an attorney, or like the manager of his family's Irish gift shop, for that matter. His hair was always a little too shaggy, and now it drooped over his forehead. He pushed it back with the same hand he used to rub the sleep out of his eyes. "Laurel, what are you doing?"

"I have to get outside!" Well, at least that's what I meant to say. The fact that I was jumping up and down on one foot then the other, tugging on my jeans, made it come out sounding more like, "Ihatogetside!"

To Declan's eternal credit, this did not stop him from sitting up and swinging his long legs over the side of the bed. "What wrong?"

I had already tugged a sweatshirt over my head and poked my feet into my slippers and I darted out into the hallway. "Ice! There's an ice storm!"

I wasn't surprised that by the time I got down to the kitchen, he was right beside me. When it came to loyalty, love, and offering a helping hand, Declan could move pretty fast.

He finished tugging his sweater over his head, peered over my shoulder, and saw the same thing I'd seen when I looked out the window of the back door: there was already a thin sheen of ice covering the glass, and more pellets plinked down by the second. *Plink. Plink, plink.* Like rifle shot.

It had been a warm spring, and hey, I was a California girl. Though I'd been warned by Sophie, Declan, and everyone else who'd seen me in my aqua Windbreaker the past week that spring in Ohio could be fickle, I'd already sent my heavy winter coat to the cleaners. With no choice, I shrugged into the Windbreaker and frantically searched the floor, my voice bumping to the same staccato tempo as my heart.

"My boots! What did I do with my boots?"

I didn't wait for my brain to kick in and provide the answer. I grabbed a pile of newspapers that I'd set on the kitchen table, ready to put in the recycling bin, and raced out the back door in my slippers.

A wicked wind slapped my face. Insult to injury, because cold seeped through my jacket, mud spurted around my slippers with every step I took, and the relentless, icy pellets tapped against my cheeks and hair. I squinted against the onslaught and raced toward the barn.

A little background and geography might be in order.

Pacifique was an idyllic farm and once the home of Raquel Arnaud—Rocky, as her friends called her—a woman who had built a reputation as the area's purveyor of the finest produce. Rocky grew vegetables and herbs and provided them to restaurants and discerning chefs all over northern and eastern Ohio, and when she was murdered the fall before, I had inherited the house and the farm. My background? I was once the personal chef of Meghan Cohan, Hollywood superstar. I knew plenty about cooking food, and nothing about growing it, but in Rocky's name and in honor of her memory, I was sure going to try.

Which explains the order of tomato plants that had arrived just the day before.

Which explains why, in my gardening naïveté and my belief that mild temperatures meant that winter was over for good, I'd never thought to haul them under cover, but left them out in the pool of sunshine against the side of the barn.

Yeah, that golden pool of sunshine.

The one that was now a quagmire of mud and icy slush.

I slogged through it, cold mud seeping through my slippers and squishing between my toes, and I closed in on the three dozen heirloom tomato plants that I'd been so proud of such a short while before.

Then, they'd been tall and leafy.

Then, they were the perfect fresh green that held the promise of spring and a summer to follow.

Then, each and every plant was a sign, at least to me. They reminded me of my commitment to Pacifique. They were living proof of the dream I had to provide fresh vegetables for the restaurant, just as Rocky had, food I'd worked to bring alive with my own two hands.

I took one look at those tomatoes now getting flogged by the ice and I swear, I heard each and every one of them scream in pain.

"I've got to save them!" I wailed, and I would not be deterred, even when behind me, Declan said something that sounded way too much like *too late*. Like the deranged, determined farming maniac I'd suddenly become, I grabbed the sheets of newspaper, one after the other, and laid them over the plants.

"It's not going to help." Declan took my arm, but I was not about to be put off. I pulled away from him and peeled off sheet after sheet of newspaper, each page quickly turning the consistency of oatmeal as the sleet rained down, and laid them over the tops of the plants.

"That's what they say to do," I said, and I'm not sure if I was trying to convince Declan or myself that it might actually help. "In all the gardening articles online. That's what they say to do if there's going to be frost. You have to cover the plants with newspaper."

"You *had* to cover the plants with newspaper." I did not fail to miss his use of the past tense. "And that only applies to frost, anyway. Even if you had the plants covered, that wouldn't have protected them from this. Now that they're already covered with ice—"

"They'll be fine, as soon as the sun comes up, they'll warm right up and perk right up, and—"

Who was I kidding?

I blinked away the icy drops that clouded my vision and stared down at the blanket of newspapers quickly turning to mush.

As fate would have it, Meghan Cohan's face stared back at me.

For a moment, I forgot the cold and the ice and even the tomato plants. Here I was in the middle of the night, muddy and defeated. And there was Meghan's picture on the front page of the Entertainment section. She looked like a million bucks (make that two, because Meghan never did anything small) in a gown cut up to here and down to there, on the red carpet at the Tribeca Film Festival.

"Laurel?" When Declan put an arm around my shoulders, I jumped.

"Sorry." I tried not to, but I couldn't help myself. In spite of the heat of Declan's body against mine, I shivered. With one trembling finger, I pointed toward Meghan's picture. "The face that launched a thousand career disappointments."

"You're going to launch a thousand cold germs if we don't get out of the cold and inside quick."

I wasn't about to argue with him.

I'd like to say we raced back to the house, but by this time, racing was out of the question. Wet through to the skin, mud up to our ankles, frozen to the bone, we plodded back to the house through a curtain of ice. I kicked off my slippers at the door and dropped them right in the trash and it wasn't until I dragged into the kitchen that I realized the wetness on my cheeks wasn't ice, it was tears.

I sobbed. "I took all the time to do my research. I ordered the tomatoes I thought would do best in our climate and our soil. I found recipes that I can use them in. I was so proud of them when they arrived. They were perfect. And now . . ." I burst into tears. "I killed them!"

Declan pulled me into a quick hug. Since he was as soaked as I was, I didn't even flinch when his wet jacket pressed against mine. "Hey, you've never been a farmer before. You didn't know."

I sniffled. "I should have. I did my homework. I read that the last frost date around here is in the middle of May. But it's been so beautiful, I just figured winter was over. And no one warned me about ice storms."

"See? That proves it."

I wasn't sure what it proved, but that would have to wait since Declan slipped off my jacket, took off his own, and disappeared upstairs. He came back to the kitchen carrying my terry cloth robe and a change of clothes for himself.

"Come on." He urged me with a wave of one finger. "Get out of those wet clothes before you catch your death."

Sure, I was feeling like a drowned rat, but that didn't erase the memory of everything we'd done since Declan arrived at Pacifique: I made dinner, we shared a bottle of wine and more than a few laughs, and—

Tomato killer that I was, I still somehow managed a smile. "If I get out of my wet clothes, will you keep me warm?"

He'd already peeled out of his sweater and jeans and tossed them into the kitchen sink and he poked his feet into the legs of flannel lounge pants and pulled a sweatshirt over his head. Declan didn't live at Pacifique with me; he had a house in Hubbard near the gift shop he managed and the Terminal at the Tracks, where I worked. But he kept some things at the farm, things like a shaving kit and clothes, for just-in-case times like this.

He gave me a lopsided smile. "I will not keep you warm. Not like I did last night, anyway. Because it's nearly five and if we start what you want to start—what I want to start—you're going to be late getting to the restaurant." He motioned again for me to disrobe. "But I will make coffee. How does that sound?"

Not nearly as good as what I had in mind, but I knew he was right. I was too wet and too cold and feeling too guilty to do anything but give up without a fight.

While Declan made coffee and popped English muffins into the toaster, I got out of my clothes and into my robe.

The warmth was heavenly, not to mention therapeutic. By the time I sank down into a kitchen chair, I felt better. Not a lot better, but better.

At least until Declan sat down in the chair across from mine.

"So did you mean that?" he asked. "Are you really disappointed Meghan Cohan ruined your brilliant Hollywood cooking career and you ended up here?"

I was just taking a swallow of coffee and it stuck behind the lump in my throat. "That's not what I said."

"It's what you implied."

"Stop acting like a lawyer." Across the table I made a face at him, hoping it would lighten the mood. Since he jumped up to fetch the English muffins along with the butter and raspberry jam that were in the fridge, I wasn't sure it worked.

"You know what I meant," I told him after he sat down, but not until I'd taken a bite of my muffin. "When I first got here, yeah, I was plenty disappointed that Meghan accused me of leaking gossip to the paparazzi when it wasn't true. I was devastated when she fired me and used her chops to make sure no other celebrity would hire me."

"And now?"

I reached across the table and folded a hand over his. "You know how I feel now. Pacifique . . ." I glanced around the kitchen. When Rocky lived there, the house was a combination of museum, showroom, and carnival. Rocky was a firm believer that if she saw something she liked, she had to own it. And if she liked it and owned it, she needed to enjoy it. And if she was going to enjoy it, she had to have it out on display. All the time.

Rocky had eclectic tastes, and many beautiful and interesting things, but back when she was in residence at Pacifique, I sometimes found it hard to breathe in a house chockablock with porcelain figurines, paintings, fabric draped over furniture, silk flowers, and peacock feathers.

Over the last months, I'd pared down most of the clutter. I'd given some of Rocky's mementos to Sophie, the sister of my foster mother and the owner of the Terminal at the Tracks, because Rocky and Sophie had been friends since college and I knew no one treasured Rocky's memory like Sophie did. Other things—mountains of lace tablecloths, piles of linen napkins, stacks of floral handkerchiefs—I'd offered to Inez and Dolly, the waitresses over at the Terminal, and to Declan's various sisters, sisters-in-law, and cousins because really, there was only so much I needed and I figured I might as well spread the beauty. The parlor where Rocky had died I'd completely redone; I'd bought new furniture, painted the walls, switched out the area rug Rocky loved so much—one with a white background decorated with huge pink and blue roses—for a tasteful Oriental in shades of maroon, tobacco, and sage. The bedrooms that had been packed with gorgeous things, artsy things, whimsical things, were pared down to the essentials. The kitchen . . .

Well, I'd been busy at the Terminal, and I hadn't gotten to the kitchen yet. It wasn't a big room, but Rocky had made sure to pack as much of her French heritage as she could into every corner. Whitewashed cupboards, a floor made of wide, oak planks, walls covered with things like a Grateful Dead poster, a painting of chickens in a farmyard, and a framed photograph of Julia Child. Autographed, no less.

Declan knew how I felt. But I guess it never hurt to remind him once in a while.

"This is home," I told him.

"I just always wondered . . ." He shrugged his wide shoulders in a sort of uncertain movement that didn't mesh with his intelligent, take-charge personality. "I guess I'm just worried that one day you're going to wake up and realize that life on a farm in Ohio is nothing like life in Hollywood."

"Thank goodness!" I said it and I meant it. While I was at it, I gave his hand a playful little slap. "You're falling down on the job." I held my coffee cup out to him. "How about a refill?"

"Yes, ma'am." He got up and filled my cup and his own then came back to the table. "You know . . ." He held out my cup to me. "As long as you're planning to stick around . . ."

I knew what he was going to say. He was going to ask me to marry him. Again. And this time, like every one of the other times, I was going to be tempted to say yes.

Until I remembered that I was not the marrying kind.

"We've been through this," I reminded him. "You know what I'm going to say."

"You're going to tell me that growing up in the foster system, you never had a really good role model as far as what happy families are like. That's why the Fury clan is here, you know." He gave me a broad wink. "To show you how it's done."

I couldn't leave it at that. "You know how I feel about you."

He sipped his coffee before he said anything. "Exactly why it's maddening."

"It's just as maddening for me! Maybe if I was on more stable footing when it comes to relationships—"

"Maybe you just need to give it a chance. You know, step out of your comfort zone. Take a chance. Try something new."

My wet clothes might have been discarded, but my hair was still soaked and a giant drop of water plopped on the table between us. "Something new? You mean like growing my own tomatoes? You see how successful I've been at that."

"I see that you're the type of woman who's determined enough to try again."

He was right. I was, and I would order more tomato plants, and I would plant them after the middle of May, and I would make sure I got tomatoes from them if it was the last thing I did.

But growing tomatoes and getting married—those were two different things.

Chapter 2

I might not know squat when it comes to tomatoes, but I was right about the Terminal—the first day we featured Italian specials on the menu, we were slammed.

This, of course, is a very good thing. Before I'd arrived from California and had the brainstorm of featuring a new ethnic food each month, the Terminal was, to put it kindly, floundering. There are only so many folks in Hubbard, Ohio who enjoy old-fashioned foods like fried baloney and onions, meatballs over rice, and tuna casserole. To please them, we still kept those dishes on the menu, but these days, we featured new foods, new recipes, innovative combinations. It hadn't exactly put the Terminal on the map when it came to up-and-coming trendy restaurants, but it brought in a steady stream of customers and, truth be told, that was fine by me.

Ever since I'd left Meghan's Malibu mansion in the middle of the night, I'd been flying under the radar, culinary-wise. I didn't want publicity or the high life. I'd found a home in Hubbard and friends I could share my life and my dreams with (and Declan, of course!) and that had made me realize I didn't need the prestige of A-listers drooling over my vanilla bean crème brûlée and swooning like they did the time they showed up in the wee hours after the Oscars presentation and I was so bold as to serve peanut butter and jelly sandwiches along with Argentine Torrontés.

These days, I was happy providing good food to nice people. Yeah, I know, it sounds corny and a year ago, I wouldn't have believed it myself, but the truth is, it was enough for me.

In the Terminal kitchen, I considered the thought as I paged through the cookbook I'd used to take bits and pieces of one recipe, dribs and drabs of another, and come up with a recipe for tagliatelle pasta with asparagus and marjoram. It was a popular menu item and sold well all day and I'd use the recipe again later in the month, so I stuck the piece of paper where I'd scrawled my version of the recipe in the book and tucked the cookbook in a drawer rather than put it back on the shelf. The orecchiette with broccoli, chili, and anchovy sauce . . . well, I thought it was as delicious as it looked in the picture in the other cookbook I put back on the shelf, but it hadn't gone over so well. Something about anchovies just turns people off.

Finished reshelving, I took a quick look around the kitchen. The Terminal wouldn't close for another hour and a half and if that day was like every other Thursday, orders would be slowing down, but that didn't mean customers would stop coming, or that we would stop working. There were still enough breadsticks, I could see that, and a big bowl of salad that could be dished out as it was ordered.

"Got everything you need?" I asked George, our cook.

George is a man of many tattoos, a lot of muscle, and few words. He grunted, nodded, and went back to stirring a pot of minestrone.

That was good enough for me. I pushed through the swinging kitchen door. Right outside it was our overflow area and I was pleased to see that two of the tables there were occupied. We'd need to push all four tables in that area back against the walls the next day when Luigi Lasagna and His Amici (yes, I know, corny name for a band but they were actually pretty talented) would play and our customers would take to the small dance floor like they did every weekend we featured ethnic music. On my way through, I checked the tables to make sure they all had centerpieces of tiny Italian flags stuck into mason jars filled with dried pasta and headed into the fifteen-by-fifteen entryway, where I assured the two groups of customers waiting to be seated that we'd be right with them, gave them menus so they could start looking over our selections, and slipped behind the front counter, where Sophie Charnowski, wearing a green, white, and red scarf, was seated on a high stool and ringing up sales.

"We're having a good night." She gave my arm a squeeze. "Everyone's thrilled about this month's menu. They say it's the best Italian food they've ever had and they're going to tell all their friends and they can't wait to come back again."

Sophie was older than middle-aged, rounder than plump, and so in love with the Terminal, her eyes glowed with excitement. She leaned nearer to me. "You're a genius."

"Not so much," I told her. "It's just that everyone loves Italian food."

"It sure was good!" A young couple and their two kids strolled up to the register and handed Sophie their ticket. "Even the kids liked the pasta."

"I'll take that as a compliment," I said, and while Sophie took care of the sale, I went into the main part of the restaurant, stopping to chat with customers, making sure our waitresses had everything they needed.

As its name implies, the Terminal at the Tracks is housed in an old train station. Before I'd arrived and taken over management of the place for Sophie when she had knee-replacement surgery, the decor had been . . . ahem . . . well, if Sophie knew what I really thought, it would break her heart and I adore her too much to let that happen. Let's just say the decor was *homey* and as long as I'm saying that, let's add that I don't mean that in an especially complimentary way.

Sophie's was a wonderland of old posters, old teddy bears (most of them wearing Victorian outfits), and old lace.

Lots and lots of old lace.

Sure, the decor fit in with a building that had been erected more than one hundred years earlier, but lace and greasy spoon restaurants are not exactly a good combination, aesthetics-wise or when it comes to cleaning.

Little by little, I'd gotten rid of most of the bears and all of the lace, and if Sophie minded—or if she even noticed—she didn't say a word. I have a feeling she'd been wanting to purge the place of its flamboyant decorations for years but never found the time and never had the energy. I'd left the old railroad photographs in place— timetables and pictures of hulking old engines and the crews of hardy men who ran them—because trains were one of the things people loved about the Terminal. Heck, six times a day, a train still rolled by outside the back windows and shook the old place to its foundation, and every single time, customers stopped eating and talking and just oohed and aahed and watched in wonder.

Here in the main part of the restaurant, we had eight tables lined up against the far wall next to the windows that looked out over the railroad tracks and more tables on the other side of the jut-out wall that marked the back of the waiting area.

There was a man, alone, at one of the tables. Though he was concentrating on the newspaper in front of him and his head was down, I could see that he had bulging cheeks and although it was still nasty outside after the morning's ice storm, it was comfortable enough inside the Terminal that I was surprised to see him wearing a tattered gray overcoat dotted with raindrops. His black fedora looked like it had seen better days, too, and there were smudges of mud from his shoes on the floor near his table. He had nothing in front of him but that newspaper and a cup of coffee.

"Inez!" When our waitress breezed by, I buttonholed her and lowered my voice. I glanced at the man. "I haven't seen him in here before."

She shook her head. "New one."

"Did he order dinner?"

"Just coffee."

"Did he even look at a menu?"

Another shake of her head made Inez's dark curls gleam in the light. She looked where I was looking, then pulled me farther from the table. "I'm thinking homeless."

"I'm thinking hungry." My mind made up, I zipped back to the kitchen and when I came out again, I was carrying a plate of tagliatelle.

"Excuse me." I stopped at the man's table. "I wonder if you could help me out."

The man didn't look up at me. Instead, he tucked both his hands in his lap and glanced to his side just enough for me to see that he wore dark-rimmed glasses and behind them, his eyes were rheumy. His eyebrows were dark and bushy and one corner of his mouth twitched. His voice sounded like tires crunching over gravel. "Whaddya want?"

"Some help." I gave him a smile I was pretty sure he couldn't see since he refused to make eye contact. "You see, this is our first day of featuring Italian foods on our Ethnic Eats menu and—"

He sniffled and wiped his nose on his sleeve.

I kept on smiling and while I was at it, I lied like a pro. "I'm developing this recipe, you see. For pasta with asparagus and marjoram. And I'm anxious to include it on our menu but I'm not sure it tastes exactly right. I was wondering if you'd try it out for me."

"You wan' me to—"

"Eat the pasta, yes." I set the plate down in front of him.

"But I . . ." He kept his gaze on the steaming plate in front of him. "See, I'm not very hungry and—"

"And you really would be helping me out. I know I'm being pushy, but I get really nervous when I'm try-ing out a new recipe. Oh, it's not like I'm going to charge you for it!" I pretended this had just occurred to me. "I'm asking you as a favor, so your meal is on the house. Won't you give it a try? You don't even have to eat the whole thing. Just a few bites. And when you're done, let me know what you think, okay?"

Rather than make him feel even more uncomfort-able, I turned and went back up front and when I did I saw that the entire Thursday-night bowling league from over at Bowladrome Lanes in Struthers was waiting for tables. After that, things got a little hectic, what with dishing up fourteen salads and popping more bread-sticks into the oven and helping George plate ten ta-gliatelle, two liver and onions, a hamburger, and a fried baloney (and not one orecchiette). I never even thought of the man in the fedora again until we were just about to close. That's when I was going to duck into the office to look over the day's receipts and saw him peeking into the window in the kitchen door.

"Hi!"

At the sound of my voice, the man winced. He wasn't quite as tall as me and when he turned around, he didn't look up, so pretty much all I could see was the top of his hat.

He scraped one shoe against the wooden floor. "I was uh . . . That is, I, uh . . ."

I hoped my voice was enough to convey my smile. "So how did you like the pasta?"

"That's what I come to tell you. To find you. To tell you, yeah, I wasn't hungry or nothin', but it was ah . . . it was pretty darned good."

And with that, he darted around me and took off and I watched him dash out the front door.

"Well, that was weird."

"Weird?" Dolly, our newest staff member, had bleached-blond hair that she wore piled on top of her head and a love of red lipstick and sparkly earrings. She was short and stocky and she'd been a waitress since forever so I wasn't surprised when she said, "I've seen it all. That one, at least he was pleasant."

"Was he?" I craned my neck to try and get a better look out the front windows, but the man was long gone. "He seemed pretty sullen to me."

"Chatted up a storm with me!" Dolly was efficient and never backed down from a job, no matter what I asked her to do so I cut her some slack when it came to the fact that she thought herself the world's greatest waitress. "It's all on account of my gift, I suppose. I could make that there wall talk if I had a mind to. It's a talent, you know. After you've been serving people as long as I have, oh yes, it's a talent you develop, all right."

This I did not dispute. Besides, she was right. I hadn't gotten Mr. Fedora to say more than a couple of words at a time. If she'd gotten him to open up and brightened his evening, three cheers for her.

I left her and Inez to the last of the cleanup and went into the office, where Sophie already had her butt down in the desk chair and her feet on the guest chair.

"What a day!" Her sigh was monumental, but then, so was her smile. "Laurel, you're the best thing that ever happened to this place."

"I seriously doubt it." When she swung her feet off the guest chair, I sat down and while I was at it, I rubbed a fist to the small of my back.

"If it wasn't for the ethnic foods—"

"I never would have had a chance to put ethnic foods on the menu if it wasn't for you keeping this place going over the years," I reminded her. "Speaking of which . . ." With one hand, I urged her to get up and get moving. "You won't be around to keep it going for more years if you don't get home and get some rest. It's late. Go ahead. Go! I can take care of counting out for the day."

She did her best to look uncertain at the same time she reached for her purse. "You're sure?"

"I'm sure. Just make sure George and the girls are gone and everything's locked up when you leave. I'll be done in another hour."

"And then you're going home?"

It wasn't what Sophie said, which was, on the face of it, an innocent-enough question.

It was the way she said it.

With that little lilt to her voice, the one she used when she was poking around, looking for answers even though she figured she already knew them.

It was the way she tilted her head so that her shaggy bangs fell into her eyes.

It was that smile of hers, small and bright and knowing.

"Sophie!"

"I didn't say a thing, did I?" She jumped out of her chair with far more energy than a woman of her age should have had at the end of a long day. "I just asked if you were going home."

"Yes." I grabbed the pile of receipts on the desk and started flipping through them. "I'm going home."

"Alone?"

When I looked up, it was to find Sophie with her mouth pursed, staring up at the ceiling.

"The innocent act isn't going to work," I told her.

She wrinkled her nose. "It's not an act."

"And it isn't innocent, either."

"Oh, come on!" She flopped back down in the chair, the better to look me in the eye. "I know Declan's been going home with you most nights."

"He's got inventory at the Irish store tonight."

"Now who's acting innocent?" She squealed out a laugh. "I didn't ask about inventory."

"Technically, you didn't ask about anything else, either."

"Except you know I'm dying to know. You and Declan . . . you're getting along?"

That was putting it mildly. Since there was no sense in sending Sophie's imagination soaring any further than the stratosphere where it already was, I simply concurred. "We're getting along."

"He's spending a lot of time at Pacifique."

"He is."

"And you're getting along."

"We're getting along."

"He's a good man."

"He is."

"And he'd make a great husband."

"Sophie, out!" I pointed toward the door and for once, Sophie knew she'd crossed the line. After a quick "See you tomorrow," she was on her way.

I was left shaking my head. At Sophie. At Declan. At the fact that people just couldn't be happy with things the way they were, even when things were fine.

I guess that's what I was still thinking about an hour and a half later when I drove home to Pacifique. The farm is in Cortland, about thirty minutes northwest of Hubbard, and by the time I got home, it was long past dark.

"Inventory." I breathed the word while I parked my car near the barn where Rocky used to pot up fresh herbs that she'd sell at farmers' markets, and when I stepped through the mud to the house, I realized how much longing there was in my voice. If Declan didn't have to finish inventory at Bronntanas, the store no one could remember the name of and simply called *the Irish store*, we'd share a late-night glass of wine and stories about what we'd done that day and then—

The heat that built in my stomach at the thought dissolved in an instant.

My back door was open.

No sooner had the thought hit like the punch of a heavyweight champ than I heard the squeal of tires on the driveway and saw the pulsing blue and red of police car lights. A second later, the squad car screeched to a stop next to me and Tony Russo jumped out of the car. I'd met Tony during the investigation of Rocky Arnaud's death a few months before and I knew he was an honest, dependable, steady sort of cop.

I did not realize he was also telepathic.

I stammered, "But how did you . . . ? Where did you . . . ? How could you . . . ?"

The answers to my questions arrived along with Otis Greenway, my nearest neighbor, who came huffing and puffing through the copse of maple trees beyond the barn.

"Sorry! Sorry, I had to leave." Otis is middle-aged, middle height, and paunchy. Even in the thin light that flowed from my open back door, I could see that his face was the same vivid red as the lights on Tony's squad car. Automatically, I grabbed his arm and piloted him to the bench just outside the back door.

"What's going on?" I asked no one in particular.

While Otis fought to catch his breath, Tony stepped up beside me. "Mr. Greenway here called 911 just a few minutes ago."

"That's right." Otis nodded and pulled in a breath. "Minnie and I . . ." Minnie was his wife. "We . . . we were out for a little walk and that's when I saw it. I . . . I knew it just didn't look right. I knew I had to call the police. But then Minnie . . . well, you know how it is, Laurel. You know how she can wander off. And she started off toward home and I couldn't wait around here for the cops to arrive. I had to get her home and now . . ." He pressed a hand to his heart. "Now I'm back."

"So go over it again, Mr. Greenway." Like I said,

Tony was the steady sort. He knew the last thing Otis needed was excitement and he took it slow and easy. "What exactly did you see?"

"Well, we'd just come around the barn." As if we'd forgotten where it was, Otis looked that way. "And I saw that the light was on in Laurel's kitchen. But I didn't see her car, and I thought that was strange. And that's when I saw him."

"Him?" The single word stuck in my throat.

Otis dipped his head. "A man. He walked out your back door. And it's not the man I've seen around here so many times before, not Declan."

I refused to let my cheeks heat up, even when Tony gave me a knowing look.

"This was another man, one I'd never seen. He walked out of your house and he looked all around like he wanted to make sure no one saw him. I knew it wasn't right. So that's when I called."

"And you did the right thing, Mr. Greenway." Tony bent so he could look Otis in the eye. "Can you tell me what the man looked like?"

"Sure." Otis thought about it, but not for long. "He was a short fellow, kind of thin. Of course it's dark and I couldn't see really clear, and the second he saw me he jumped in a car that was parked down the driveway, but I can tell you he was wearing glasses and a gray coat. And a hat. Yeah. A black fedora."

Chapter 3

"It had to be the same man."

This was so obvious, I wasn't at all sure why Declan had an expression on his face that reminded me of a thundercloud. We were in the office at the Terminal, me perched on the desk and him, over near the door, his arms crossed over that broad chest of his and his feet slightly apart.

Maybe he hadn't heard me.

"The guy I told you about? The one I gave dinner to last night here at the restaurant. The way Otis described him, it had to be the same guy he saw running out of my house."

Declan stalked to the other side of the office. Just for the record, this did not take long because the office isn't very big. Maybe the narrow room and the high ceiling

explained why when he finally spoke, his voice sounded
so loud.

"Why didn't you call me?"

I tossed my hands in the air. "I did call you. I called
you this morning. And I told you I didn't call you last
night because I knew you were doing inventory and—"

"And what? Laurel, somebody breaking into your
house is a pretty big deal. You could have gotten hurt."

"No, I couldn't have. Like I told you when you
walked in here, thanks to Otis, Tony was there practically before I was. And another cop showed up right
after. It's not like I walked in and looked over the place
all by myself. And when they did walk through the
house—"

"Yeah, yeah. I know. They checked out everything
and no one was there."

"Which is why I didn't want to bother you. The excitement was all over. There didn't seem to be much
point in—"

"Sharing big, scary news with the one person you
should want to share it with more than anyone else?"

His words slammed into me like a punch to the solar
plexus and I sucked in a breath. "When you put it that
way—"

"There's no other way to put it!" He scraped a hand
through his dark hair. I'd called him as I drove to the
Terminal that morning and told him what had happened the night before and no sooner had I parked in
the lot at the side of the building than he came racing
over from the Irish store across the street. Then I would
have described his hair as tousled. Now it looked more
as if the shock of all I'd told him had run through him

like an electrical current, taking that gentle tousling to the nth degree. In a flash, he was back across the office and standing right in front of me. He put his hands on my shoulders and bent so he could look me in the eye.

"You're impossible! You think you can take on the world, all alone. All by yourself."

"That's because I can."

I didn't mean to stiffen at his touch, but I guess he noticed because he dropped his hands.

"But you don't have to! Don't you get it? That's why I'm here."

"And I appreciate it. I do."

"You're not supposed to appreciate it. I'm not looking to play the hero or to make you feel obligated in any way. You're just supposed to accept it. It's something I want to do for you. Something I need to do for you. I love you and it's my way of showing you that. If you're just going to reject me every time I try to—"

"So now I'm rejecting you because I didn't want to bother you when I knew you had a lot of work to do?" Really, he could sometimes be as maddening as he was usually wonderful. "It was late. I knew you were busy. Tony checked the house and he assured me I was safe. I didn't need you racing over to Cortland in the middle of the night like the cavalry in some old western. For one thing, I'd worry about you driving too fast and getting into an accident. And for another, there was nothing you could do at that point. Everything was under control."

"Except for the fact that some random guy was in here last night eating your food and then drove thirty minutes to Cortland and broke into your house to go through your things."

"Yeah, my things." Thinking about it, a chill scraped up my spine and I wrapped myself in a hug. "The house is a mess."

He slanted me a look. "A mess I could have helped clean up."

He was doing his best to smooth over our harsh words and even if he wouldn't have believed it, I did appreciate that. I gave him a playful boff on the arm. "You can still help me clean up. I didn't touch a thing last night. I was too tired to even try. And anyway, Tony wants me to look through everything carefully so I can tell him if anything is missing."

"And is there?"

Because I didn't like to be indecisive, I hated shrugging, but sometimes, it's the only way to handle a question. "Hard to tell. The kitchen . . ."

I made a face. "Every single one of my cookbooks is off the shelf, the drawers are open and emptied. Upstairs is a mess, too. It's going to take days to get it all back in order."

He dared a step closer. "I've got days."

"And I . . ." Since it wasn't easy for me to admit I couldn't carry the weight of the world on my shoulders and my shoulders alone, I swallowed around the words. "I'd love your help. You're familiar enough with the house. Maybe you'll notice something I won't. Something missing. Something broken."

He cocked his head, wrinkled his nose, and gave me a look. "So why would some stranger eat here, then break into your house? And how did he know where you live?"

I plopped back against the desk. "I wish I knew. I guess it would be easy enough to find me—it's not like I'm trying to hide my identity or where I live or anything. But why . . . why would he care? He was . . ." In my head, I pictured the man I'd offered dinner to the night before. "There was something off about him. He wasn't filthy, exactly, but he was tattered. Like his clothes were tired. And he wouldn't look me in the eye."

"Well, maybe he has a conscience and he was feeling guilty about what he was planning after dinner."

A thought hit. "Or maybe he didn't want me to get a good look at his face," I suggested.

Declan's dark brows rose. "You mean you think it was someone you know?"

I thought about it. But not for long. "No. No way. He's certainly not a regular. Inez and Dolly didn't know him, either. Still . . ." Forcing myself to think, I took a deep breath and tried my best to settle my mind. "There was something about the way he sat there. He was hunched over the table, reading the newspaper, but if I did that . . ."

Since it was hard to explain, I demonstrated. I stepped forward so Declan had to step back, then I pulled out the chair and sat down facing the desk.

"Say this is the table out in the restaurant." I tapped the desk. "And here's my newspaper." I pulled over a sheet of paper as a substitute. "And I'm just sitting here casually reading it and drinking coffee and . . ." Just to prove it to myself, I took a careful look at how I was seated. My shoulders were rolled forward, my elbows were on the desk. I had one hand around a pretend coffee cup and the other resting against that faux newspaper.

"That's exactly how he was sitting," I told Declan. "Until I walked up. Then he tucked his hands in his lap."

It was his turn to shrug. "So?"

"Oh, I don't know!" I grumbled. "It's just something I remember, that's all. It doesn't mean a thing." Because one grumble didn't help, I grumbled some more.

"So I guess yesterday wasn't a good day, huh? I mean what with your house getting broken into, and you giving a free dinner to the guy who did it, and you killing all those tomato plants."

Black humor, yes, but he was doing his best and in spite of myself, I smiled. "No, not a good day."

"Which means today is bound to be better."

"Yeah." I stood up so I could give him a peck on the cheek. "Today is bound to be better and—"

"Oh!" The office door opened and Sophie let out a little squeak of surprise. Her cheeks shot through with color. "I didn't mean to interrupt."

"You're not," I assured her. "Declan just stopped by to make sure everything was okay."

"You mean about your house last night." Sophie tossed her purse on the desk and pulled off her blue Windbreaker. "He called me." She gave Declan a look that wasn't necessary since I knew who she was talking about as soon as she mentioned *he*. "You really should have called me, Laurel."

My sigh pretty much said it all.

Sophie puffed out a little breath of annoyance. "Well, you shouldn't have stayed by yourself last night."

"There's no use fighting with her," Declan told Sophie, and a shake of his head left his hair more disheveled than ever.

"Exactly! And I'm fine. So neither one of you needs to worry." I pushed past them and toward the door. "So let's get to work."

That would have been easier if Inez and Dolly and George weren't right outside the office door.

"Heard!" Inez grabbed my arm.

"Terrible." Before I could fend her off, Dolly pulled me into a hug.

"What do we need to do?" George asked.

What was all that about me being self-sufficient, independent, and fearless?

Before I could even try to stop it, my eyes filled with tears.

"You're all . . ." I looked from coworker to coworker, and I sniffled a little, too. "Thank you. All of you. Declan . . ." I grabbed his arm and pulled him to my side. "Declan is going to be in charge of cleanup at my house. There's no use even worrying about it this weekend, we'll be too busy here. How about Monday after work? Since Declan's in charge . . ." The smile I gave him was the sweetest I could muster. "He'll make all the plans and have dinner arranged for all of us, too."

Hey, Declan wanted responsibility, right?

I gave him a *gotcha!* smile and went into the kitchen to get ready for the day. Fridays are always busy and with spaghetti and meatballs, fire-roasted pizza, and eggplant parmigiana on the menu, that one was no exception. By the time Luigi Lasagna and his band were into their final set, playing wonderful and corny old standards like "Arrivederci, Roma" and "Volare" and

"O Sole Mio," there were still eight groups of customers waiting to be seated for dinner and six to-go orders on the front counter for pick up.

Just for the record, in all that commotion, there was no sign of the man in the fedora.

Earlier in the day, I'd promised myself I wouldn't think about him and I'd been pretty successful (well, except for the time when I was making the morning coffee, the few minutes it took me to put out the day's menus, when I seated the first lunch customers, when I rang out the first dinner customers, and a couple of times in between). This time, like all those other times I pictured the man, a prickle traced along my skin. I reminded myself he wouldn't have the nerve to come back to the Terminal, but that hardly helped; I glanced over my shoulder.

And found a skinny woman with a hunched back looking up at me.

"Welcome to the Terminal." My greeting was as automatic as a smile. "We'll have a table for you in just a minute."

In spite of the fact that it was considerably warmer than it had been the day before, the woman had a red knitted cap pulled down over her ears. She wore a black cloth coat and a pair of those knitted mitts that cover a person's hands, but not their fingers, and her shoes were sturdy and had thick heels. She wore a pair of enormous round glasses with brown plastic frames that sat crookedly on her face thanks to the bulge on the bridge of her nose. Behind her glasses, her face was as wrinkled as a baked apple.

"Ladies' room," she croaked.

I pointed her in the proper direction and got back to work and never thought a thing of it until an hour later.

"Knitted mitts when the weather is warm," I mumbled to myself. "And a man who tucked his hands in his lap when I came by to talk to him."

What did it mean? I had no idea, but I promised myself I'd think about it the moment I had the chance.

Two hours later, I turned off the last of the lights and locked the front door only to find Declan out on the sidewalk waiting for me.

He kissed me hello. "I'm coming home with you."

Not something I was going to argue with. Oh, I wasn't looking for a watchdog, but after a long day at the restaurant, a little TLC sure wouldn't hurt.

"I can drive," I said, and he didn't argue, but then, his vintage motorcycle was parked behind the Irish store and there was a nip in the night air. As soon as we were in the car, he pulled a sheet of folded papers out of the pocket of his jacket.

"I've got three places for you to look into," he said.

I was negotiating a turn so I couldn't give him more than a glance. "For . . . ?"

"A security system, of course. You had one put in Sophie's house for her, but you never got one for Pacifique." He poked a finger at the list on the page. "I'd go with this one. Owned by an Irishman."

"And a relative, no doubt."

"Liam is a trustworthy businessman."

I plucked the paper from his hand and set it on the seat between us. "Are you telling me what to do?"

"I wouldn't dream of it."

"Good."

"Except you know, you could drive a little slower."

THE NEXT MORNING, Saturday, I dropped Declan off at Bronntanas, then parked and went around to the front door of the Terminal.

I can't say I knew something was wrong. Not exactly.

I can say I felt that something was wrong.

Just like I can say that the moment I felt it, I knew I was being too imaginative.

"Get over it," I told myself, poking my key in the lock, swinging the door open, and letting go a breath I hadn't realized I was holding.

Everything inside the Terminal waiting area looked exactly the way it should have.

"No boogeymen with or without fedoras," I reminded myself, and strolled to the kitchen, where I pushed open the door and stopped cold.

My cookbooks were all over the floor. The fridge was open. Pots and pans were scattered all around, along with loaves of bread, cooking utensils, and just about every piece of cutlery we owned.

I don't know if I screeched, then grumbled.

Or if I grumbled, then screeched.

I do know I made two phone calls, the first one to the cops and the second one to Declan.

DETECTIVE GUS OBERLIN is apparently not a morning person.

Then again, in the course of investigating a couple of murders, I'd run into Gus in the afternoon, the evening, and the nighttime, too.

Maybe he's just not an any-time person.

He took a long slurp of coffee from the paper cup he'd brought into the Terminal with him, stretched his six-foot-four-inch frame, scraped a hand over his bulging belly, and burped.

"Who the heck would want to trash the Terminal?" he asked.

"If I knew that, maybe I'd also know who broke into my house."

As I've mentioned, the Terminal is in Hubbard and Pacifique is in Cortland, out of Gus's jurisdiction.

That would explain why his shaggy eyebrows rose a fraction of an inch.

Declan had his arm around my shoulders and before I could say another word, he gave me a little squeeze. "Friday night," he told Gus. "You can get the report from Tony Russo."

"A break-in here and a break-in there?" Gus scratched one meaty finger behind his ear. "Ain't that strange!"

"And annoying," I remarked.

"And troubling," Declan added. "If someone has it in for Laurel—"

This was not something I wanted to think about so I dragged away from Declan's protective hold and grabbed the closest cookbook off the floor.

"Uh-uh." Gus wagged a finger in my direction. "Let us get some pictures before you start picking things up."

"But we're going to open soon and—"

Gus rolled the toothpick he was chewing on from one corner of his mouth to the other. "How about you hang a sign out front that says you'll be delayed an hour or so? That will give us time to dust for prints, and you're going to need time to clean up."

He was right.

I put the cookbook right back where I'd found it, grabbed a piece of paper, and scrawled *Opening Today at Noon* on it, and Declan volunteered to hang the sign on the front door.

"So . . ." Gus gnawed the toothpick in his mouth. "This is crazy, huh?"

"You could call it that." I leaned against the stainless steel counter where I thought I'd be prepping salads that morning, not looking at so much of a mess. "And we're extra busy because of the Italian food."

"Italian food." Gus said the words like he could taste them. "Had some of that . . . what do you call it? . . . gelato once when I was in Vegas. Mighty good stuff." His look was pure innocence. "I don't suppose you're serving gelato?"

He was about as subtle as a clap of thunder. "Pistachio or chocolate?" I asked him.

"Oh, chocolate. And maybe a scoop of pistachio, too."

I went to the freezer to get the gelato.

Like most restaurants, the Terminal has a walk-in freezer. Ours isn't huge, but it's got plenty of shelf space and George is meticulous about keeping everything on them nice and orderly.

That meant there was always plenty of space on the floor.

Except that day.

The freezer door open, my jaw slack, and my heart in my throat, I gurgled out something that might have been "Gus!" or maybe it was just a half-formed scream.

"What?" He ambled over.

"There's a—" I dared a step inside, closer to the woman who lay on her back with her arms splayed out at her side, her legs bent, and her red knitted cap askew.

"She's dead!"

I don't think I had to tell Gus. He could see she had a bruise on the side of her head and that she wasn't breathing, just as well as I could. I could also see—

My heart started up again with a thump that pounded my ribs.

The woman's glasses were off. And remember that bulge on the bridge of her nose? It was gone, too, a piece of actor's putty that had come off to reveal a nose that launched a thousand cosmetic surgeons' dreams.

"It's . . ." My breath caught. My blood whooshed inside my ears. "It's the lady who was here last night." I gasped. "And the lady who was here last night is Meghan Cohan!"

Chapter 4

"So what was a Hollywood superstar like Meghan Cohan doing dressed up like an old lady and eating in your restaurant?"

I was listening to Declan, honestly I was, it was just that I was having a little trouble concentrating at the moment. I mean, what with the kitchen of the Terminal trashed and the body of my former employer in the freezer.

"I don't think she was just the old lady eating in the restaurant last night." The thought rose out of the fog inside my head. "I think she was the old man with the fedora, too."

At this, Declan sat up and pulled back his shoulders. We were in the Terminal office along with Gus and Sophie, George and Dolly and Inez, and, believe me, it was more than a little crowded in there. Since I was the one who'd stumbled on Meghan's body, I'd been given the chair by the desk. Everyone else was packed into every other inch of the room: Sophie in the guest chair, Declan sitting on the desk, Inez and Dolly hanging on to each other near the door, George looking even more gloomy than usual with his back up against the filing cabinets, and Gus Oberlin pretty much taking up the entire center of the room.

"Wait a minute!" Gus waved a hand and the murmur of conversation that started up when I made the comment cut off in a jiffy. "What do you mean he's . . . that is, she's . . . what are you talking about?"

"I'm talking about her hands." Declan and I exchanged looks and he knew exactly what I meant. That's why he gave me a nod. The rest of them didn't have a clue what I was talking about, so I explained. "When the old guy with the fedora was here, he didn't want me to see his hands. Last night, the old woman . . . well . . . er . . . Meghan, she wore fingerless gloves. So you see, I couldn't see either of their hands."

"But why . . ." I couldn't blame Sophie one bit for being upset. A body in the freezer is not a daily occurrence. She sniffled and sipped the coffee George had been kind enough to pour for everyone before we started this powwow.

"Because Meghan is a . . . well, she was a skilled actress. She knew how to choose clothes to disguise herself. I'll bet the clothes she wore as the old man were stuff she bought at Salvation Army or Goodwill. I remember thinking how tired they looked. And she's had enough experience with makeup to know how to create an illusion and fool the eye. The glasses, the hats, the putty she used to make the old lady's nose look big and bumpy. But your hands . . ." I held mine out and looked at them and automatically, everyone else did the same.

"It's harder to disguise hands," I told them. "And believe me when I tell you I know Meghan has . . . had . . . hands that were pampered to the max. Massages, manicures, hand soaks, seaweed wraps. She had beautiful skin and beautiful nails."

"And that's the kind of thing that's harder to camouflage." Gus nodded knowingly.

"Exactly. My guess is she never thought about it until she was dressed as the old man and in here reading the newspaper. When I walked up and started talking to her, she realized her hands were a giveaway. That's why she hid them and why she was wearing mitts last night even though it wasn't all that cold out. The old lady she wanted me to believe she was wouldn't have such gorgeous hands."

"So that explains that." Declan crossed his arms over his chest and sat back, careful not to squish the computer monitor. "But it doesn't explain what she was doing here in the first place."

"Or why she broke into Pacifique," Sophie pointed out.

"Or what she's doing dead in our freezer," Inez said.

"Dead! In our freezer!" As I might have mentioned, Dolly is the newest member of the Terminal staff. She hadn't been here back when the Lance of Justice, a local TV reporter, was killed in our dining room. I couldn't blame her for sounding a little breathless and looking a little green. She hiccuped, clapped her hand over her mouth, mumbled, "Be right back!" and rushed out of the room.

"You don't suppose she's going to quit?" Sophie asked no one in particular.

This, I couldn't say, so I kept my mouth shut. At least until an idea hit.

"Meghan was looking for something," I said. It seemed like a no-brainer so I was grateful no one pointed that out. In fact, they actually looked interested in my theory.

"I mean, she must have been," I said. "She broke into Pacifique and trashed the place, and my guess is she didn't find whatever it was she was looking for because she came here last night and looked again."

"And while she was here," Gus said, "somebody else showed up, knocked her unconscious, and dragged her into the freezer and she froze to death."

It was too horrible to even think about.

Before I could hug my arms around myself, Declan came over and draped an arm over my shoulders. It helped ease the tattoo of panic that started up inside my rib cage. At least a little.

I looked at Gus. "So there's another question we need to ask. Not only what was Meghan doing here and what was she looking for, but who wanted her dead?"

Gus is not the thinking type. He rolled his toothpick through his mouth a time or two before he made up his mind, then clapped his hands together, and we all jumped. "All right! I'm going to want to talk to each and every one of you in the next couple hours, but for now, Sophie, you and George and Inez, you can go into the kitchen and see if my guys are done in there. If they are, you might as well start cleaning up."

"We're going to need someone to handle the media."

The very thought made my stomach swoop. "Talk
about a feeding frenzy! Meghan wasn't just a star, she
had a host of charities she raised money for, her work
as a director, her line of clothing . . ." If I didn't already
have a headache, I would have had one now.

"I'll take care of that." I had no doubt of it, though
if Gus would do it with any finesse at all was another
matter altogether. "For now . . ." He made a shooing
motion with his hands, and Sophie, George, and Inez
filed out of the office. Once they were gone, Gus gave
Declan an evil-eye stare. "I'll talk to you later, Fury.
Laurel will be along in a minute."

"You're forgetting . . ." Declan stood. He was nearly
as tall as Gus, but not nearly as bulky. Still (and I might
be just a tad prejudiced here), he was an imposing figure, especially with his head held high and his shoulders thrown back and that stony expression on his face,
the one that said he wasn't going to put up with any
nonsense, not from Gus, not from anyone. "I'm Ms.
Inwood's attorney," he said. "I'm not going anywhere."

In all the time I'd known him, Gus had never had a
good thing to say about Declan or his Irish Traveller
family. He claimed it was because the Fury family—
and all their relatives, which, as far as I could see, num-
bered in the hundreds—were nothing but frauds and
cheats and involved with the local Irish mob, too. It
may have been true in the past, but it sure wasn't now,
and what Gus didn't know was that thanks to Declan,
his Uncle Pat's ill-gotten money (which Declan handled
as business manager for his family) was being put to
good use in keeping the St. Colman's food pantry open.

Gus's top lip curled. "It's up to Laurel if you stay."

"Of course." I squeezed Declan's hand. "But I'm not sure how much I can tell you that you don't already know, Gus. You were with me in the kitchen when I found the body, and you came right away to see what was going on and—"

The truth of the situation slammed into me, as clear as the stains of raspberry jelly from his morning toast on Gus's green and white tie.

"You think I'm a suspect!"

He rolled back on his heels. "Did I say that?"

I clapped a hand over my heart. I guess I figured that way, neither Declan nor Gus would hear the way it was suddenly pounding. "You didn't have to. You think I could . . . you think I might have . . . Are you saying you think I could have . . . ?"

"All I'm saying is that you knew the deceased. And you're the only one here who did."

"Not exactly accurate," Declan pointed out. "Since just about everyone, everywhere, knew who Meghan was."

"Knew who she was, sure," Gus conceded. "But they didn't know her. Not personally. Not the way Laurel did. The way I recall the story, you worked for her and things didn't turn out so well."

I gulped down my horror. "It's no secret. Meghan, she thought . . . see, she has this son, Spencer. He's maybe . . ." I thought about it for a moment. "I guess he's fourteen or fifteen by now, maybe even older, though he doesn't act like it. And it's not entirely his fault because he's always been coddled and had everything handed to him and he's never been taught about consequences, but Spencer, you see, he's one bad kid. And he's got a serious drug problem."

"The way I remember it, Miss Cohan, she's the one who thought you leaked that piece of information to the press."

I hadn't realized Gus had taken a notebook from his pocket. His pen poised over the page, he waited for me to respond.

I nodded, then realized he needed more than that. "It wasn't true. I'm not the one who told the press, but Meghan . . . well, once she gets something into her head, it's impossible to change her mind. She decided I was the guilty party and that was that. She fired me."

"And you were angry."

Gus's statement hung in the air between us.

In an attempt to steady my erratic heartbeat, I pulled in a breath. "Yes, I was. At first. I mean, who wouldn't be?" I looked to Declan for support and found it there in those amazing gray eyes of his. His look gave me courage. "This whole thing, it blew up in Meghan's home in Malibu. At the time, she told me I could stay on for a few days. You know, long enough to get my things together and figure out what I was going to do although she already knew there was no way I'd find a job with any of her A-list friends. She blackballed me, only I didn't know that at the time. I didn't wait around. I packed up everything I owned that night and jumped in my car and got away from there as fast as I possibly could."

"Were you angry enough to want to hurt Ms. Cohan?"

I shook my head. "Mad, sure. But I've never been violent. You can check the records, Gus. I'm sure the California Department of Social Services has all the files pertaining to my foster care. I could be a real pain in the neck."

"No surprise," Declan muttered.

I made a face at him. "And I could be difficult. But I was never violent."

"You know I have to check," Gus said.

"Go right ahead. Besides, even if I was mad when Meghan sacked me, that was a year ago, before I came to Hubbard. Since then, I've made a home for myself here. And friends. Honestly, Gus, looking back on it, getting fired by Meghan was the best thing that ever happened to me. Why would I still be mad at her?"

Since his shoulders were so big, Gus's shrug reminded me of a glacier inching toward the ocean. "All this time, maybe you did get over being mad. But then out of nowhere, she shows up here in Hubbard and—"

"Why?"

Since he didn't know, he ignored my question.

"She shows up here in Hubbard and my guess is she wants something. That would explain why she went through your house, and the restaurant. She's looking for something, you don't want her to have that something, and—"

"What something?"

This, too, he couldn't answer. "One thing leads to another," Gus said, "and before you know it, Ms. Cohan ends up in the freezer."

"Except I didn't know she was in town. I haven't heard a word from her, not since the night I left her house."

"That's not exactly true. She was here in the restaurant. You said so yourself. You talked to her last night, and the night before."

"I did, but I didn't know it was her. You've seen her in enough movies. Everybody has. Meghan could be petty and vengeful and nasty. But she was also a darned good actress. I worked for her for six years and I didn't know she was the shabby man or the old woman."

"So you say."

This was not the ringing endorsement of my honesty I'd hoped for. I looked to Declan for backup.

"That's all Ms. Inwood is going to say for now," he told Gus. "Of course, she'll cooperate with your investigation as much as she's able."

"Then she can start by telling me where she was last night."

"With me," Declan told him. "All night. We left here, went to Pacifique, had a glass of wine and a snack, went to bed."

"So you're"—Gus pointed one meaty finger in my direction—"his alibi." He swung his finger around to Declan. "And he's your alibi."

"And believe me, we wouldn't be covering for each other," I assured him. "Declan never met Meghan."

"But you knew the victim. You knew her lifestyle and her friends. Who else might want to see Meghan Cohan dead?" Gus asked me.

I couldn't help myself. I burbled out a laugh. "My guess is just about everyone who ever met her, and for sure, just about everyone who ever worked with her."

"Ah, someone who worked with her." Gus threw out the comment, as innocent as can be, but that didn't change a thing.

I knew what he meant, and the realization froze me to the bone.

Yikes! Bad analogy. I mean, considering what had happened to Meghan.

Still, that didn't change the truth and the truth was this—my former employer was dead, and with each passing minute, I was looking more and more like the prime suspect.

THE FORENSIC TEAM finished with the kitchen right before I got in there, which meant it was still as much of a mess as it was when I walked into the Terminal that morning.

I propped my fists on my hips and looked it over. "This is going to take some doing."

"You got that right." George carried an armload of pots and pans over to the sink that Dolly had already filled with hot, soapy water. "But we'll be good to go by lunch."

And we were.

Of course, by lunchtime, the Terminal was also overflowing not only with our usual customers, but with media, Meghan's fans (there were plenty of them and they heaped flowers near our front door), and the curious.

"No order, no eat, no table," I reminded Dolly and Inez because I remembered when the Lance of Justice was killed and how a lot of the media just wanted to camp out and get information.

"I still can't believe it." Since Dolly had a tray of cannoli in one hand and a tray of tiramisu in the other, she couldn't dab at her damp nose so she had to sniffle. "I remember Meghan in *Sunset over Sarasota*. She was so beautiful. And remember that other movie . . . that . . . Oh, I know which one it was. Meghan was a princess who was kidnapped by pirates and there was this tropical island and the dashing pirate and . . ." Her sigh made the tiramisu jiggle.

I remembered that movie, all right. While it was being filmed, I'd spent two months in the Caribbean with Meghan keeping her happy—culinary-wise—while I cooked my way around mosquitoes the size of hummingbirds.

"She married him, didn't she?"

Dolly's question snapped me out of the memory, which was just as well because I was starting to itch.

"She? Married who?"

"Meghan, of course. She married the guy who played the pirate."

"Rolph Longstraw, yes." I didn't bother to mention that Longstraw was the most egotistical, least mature man I'd ever met. There was no use disappointing Dolly. The way her eyes shone, I could tell she still dreamed of that scene with Meghan and Rolph in front of the bonfire on the beach.

"They were married for a while."

"Two years, six months." Dolly's cheeks shot through with color. "At least that's how I remember it." And with that, she raced off to deliver desserts.

I went up front to see if Sophie needed any help at checkout and was just in time to see Declan sidle his way through the crowd waiting to be seated.

"Looks like murder is good for business."

Luckily, he said it quietly enough that no one but me could hear, but just in case he decided to say anything else inappropriate, I crooked a finger and beckoned him to join me in the kitchen. We pushed through the swinging door and the noise of the restaurant receded.

"It's nuts." Not that Declan needed me to tell him that; he'd seen the crowds in the waiting area, the TV trucks out front. "Anybody try to get you to talk?"

"Everybody." When I got bottles of water out of the fridge and offered him one, he took it and cracked it open. "It's mostly the local media now, but I have a feeling the national media is going to be showing up here any minute now. The news is all over TV and the radio."

I leaned back against one of the high stools pulled up to the stainless steel counter and while I was at it and because I knew we were going to need it, I started rolling spoons and knives and forks in paper napkins. "And I don't suppose any one of those news stories can explain what Meghan was doing here in Hubbard."

"Gus is dodging and feinting for all he's worth. So far, he's been pretty successful avoiding the questions."

"That's because he doesn't know the answers. Has my . . ." My throat went dry so I took a long swig of water. "Has my name come up?"

"I'm not going to lie to you. Wish I could. But, yeah, some of the media outlets have gotten hold of the fact that you work here, that you used to work for Meghan, and that you're the one who found the body."

I cringed. "Has anybody decided that I'm the murderer yet?"

"Come on!" Declan pulled me into a brief hug. I have a feeling he might have kissed me, too, if not for the fact that at that moment, George came out of the basement, carrying a case of canned tomatoes. "Nobody thinks you did it," he said.

"Nobody but Gus." I plunked down the newly rolled

silverware in my hand. "You know the only way to prove him wrong is to figure out who really did it."

A smile tickled the corners of Declan's mouth. "I've been waiting for you to say that."

"You'll help?"

He thought it over, but only for a heartbeat. "Of course. Only, where do we start?"

I pushed my hands through my blond hair. That's when I realized it was still down around my shoulders, the way it had been when I walked into the Terminal that morning, and I grabbed a ponytail holder from a nearby drawer and scooped my hair out of the way.

"We have to figure out what she was doing in Hubbard."

"And why she didn't want anyone to know she was here," Declan added.

"And why she was looking through my things." I thought about what I'd told Gus, about the night I hightailed it out of Meghan's grand mansion so I didn't have to face her again the next morning. Though Inez, Dolly, and George had cleaned up all the pots and pans and silverware that had been scattered in Meghan's search of the kitchen, I'd asked them not to touch the cookbooks. Those, I wanted to organize myself since I knew which ones I used most often and which I'd be looking through in the next few weeks for Italian recipes. Automatically, I glanced over them there on the floor.

"My cookbooks at home were a mess, too," I said.

Declan got the message. "You think that's what she was looking for? Cookbooks?"

"Maybe not the cookbooks themselves. Maybe something in them?"

It wasn't much of a plan, but it was the closest we'd come to one and we didn't wait another minute. I cleared off a space on the counter and together, Declan and I retrieved the cookbooks.

Chapter 5

"I don't care what Gus says. If I knew Meghan was in town . . . if I was in touch with her like Gus thinks I might have been . . . then why would she need to wear disguises to come here to the restaurant to see me?"

"Excellent question." Declan scooped up the last of the cookbooks from the floor and plunked them down on the stainless counter. "You know Gus is going to say it's because you and Meghan didn't want anyone to know you were meeting."

"Then why would we do it here at the restaurant? We could have met at Pacifique."

"Playing devil's advocate here." Declan held up both hands, palms out, to distance himself from whatever he was going to say. "You were supposed to meet at Pacifique. Meghan came here disguised as the old guy to get last-minute instructions. Or last-minute directions to your house. She got there before you did and she would have stayed and waited for you if Otis didn't see her and scare her off."

"And she trashed the house as a sort of welcome-home present for me then came back here the next day in a different disguise?"

Honestly, I didn't expect Declan to answer so I didn't even give him a chance. "How did she even know where I live?"

Thinking, Declan pressed his lips together. "As the old guy, she could have asked someone. Everybody around here knows you inherited Pacifique last year. If Meghan knew even that much, it wouldn't have been hard to find you."

I wrapped my arms around myself. "I don't think I like the thought of people talking about me. And I'm sure I don't like the thought of some creepy guy asking where I live and one of our neighbors telling him."

"I have a feeling Meghan would have been a little more subtle than that."

"Maybe," I conceded. From my days of working with Meghan, I knew she didn't have a subtle bone in her body. But then, when you've got the face and the fame and the money, you don't need to be subtle. Disguised as the old man, she might have needed to be more clever to get the information she was looking for.

"Dolly." I groaned. "When I said something about the old man to Dolly, she said he was chatty. He sure wasn't chatty with me."

"You want me to have a talk with her?" Declan asked.

He should have known better. "I can handle Dolly,"

I assured him. "As for all these cookbooks . . ." We both looked over the mountain of books in front of us.

"That's a lot of cookbooks," he mumbled.

"It takes a lot of recipes to keep a restaurant going. I usually make up my own, but sometimes it helps to get ideas from various sources."

"And your cookbooks at home are messed up, too."

"You saw it yourself last night. Except for picking them up off the floor and piling them on the kitchen table, I haven't touched them."

"Maybe that's a good thing. If we don't find anything interesting in this batch . . ."

"I can't imagine what we're even looking for." I couldn't help but sigh. Like Declan, I stepped back and sized up the number of books along with the enormity of the task. "It's not like I tucked one-hundred-dollar bills in the pages to mark them."

"Then we know Meghan wasn't looking for one-hundred-dollar bills."

It was a brilliant deduction that got us nowhere.

"Except . . ." Again, I looked over the variety of titles. Irish cookbooks, French cookbooks, Italian cookbooks, Japanese cookbooks. All used for our Ethnic Eats menus. (And just for the record, sushi did not go over well with the Hubbard crowd.) There were a lot of other, nonethnic titles, too: cooking with cheese, cooking without cheese, vegetarian delights, vegan cooking, desserts, desserts, desserts.

"If Meghan was looking for something, then it must have been something she suspected she'd find in one of my cookbooks."

"Brilliant, Sherlock!" Declan's sour tone negated the message.

"But wait, hear me out. If she was looking for something she suspected might be in one of my cookbooks, maybe it was something she put there. And if she put it there—"

"It would have to be in a cookbook you brought here with you from California!" He got what I was getting at and grinned. "That really is brilliant. So tell me, which of these books moved here with you from sunny California?"

"Not Irish. I hate to wound your ego, but Meghan didn't exactly consider Irish cuisine anything she wanted to serve at dinner parties."

"Her loss."

I picked out those books and set them aside along with the French-inspired cookbooks Rocky Arnaud had loaned to the Terminal when we first discussed featuring the foods of her homeland. "This dessert one is new." I handed it to Declan so he could add it to the pile. "And John and Mike over at the Book Nook got this one on wine pairings for me just a couple of weeks ago." That one, too, got put to the side. "Some of the ones on Italian cooking, yeah, I had those back in California. In fact, I bought a couple of them in Tuscany the last time I was there with Meghan." These I separated into another pile. "And this one and this one and this one . . ." The second pile grew larger. "These are all books I already owned when I worked for Meghan."

"It helps. A little." Declan pulled two of the high stools up to the counter. "Now we go through them."

"So what are you looking for?" Dolly breezed through

the swinging door that led out into the dining room, an empty iced tea pitcher in one hand. "A recipe? Maybe I can help."

I figured this was as good a time as any to clear up the mystery of how Meghan found me. "You can help by telling me what you and the old guy talked about the other night."

"The old guy?" Dolly's eyes went wide. "You mean Meghan! Ohmygosh, if I knew that was her, I would have fainted right there at her table. Imagine, being that close to greatness and not even realizing it. I felt like such an idiot when I found out it was really her in disguise. I mean, I should have known, right? I've seen every one of her movies."

"I worked for her for six years and I didn't know it was her," I told Dolly. "Now, you were saying, about what you two talked about?"

"Well, actually . . ." The sheen of excitement in her eyes never dimmed. "I was thinking about it. You know, after the cops were finished here in the kitchen and we got everything cleaned up and washed up and put back where it belongs. And if that was just any other customer, I wouldn't have cared. But once I knew it was Meghan, well, I didn't want to forget what happened. Not one moment of it. So I was thinking and . . ." She whipped a piece of paper out of her pocket. "I wrote it all down."

I wanted to be sure. "You wrote down what you and Meghan talked about?"

Dolly nodded. "As much as I can remember. You know, for my scrapbook."

"So what did you talk about?"

She set down the iced tea pitcher, the better to consult her notes. "Well, he . . . she . . . she asked for coffee and I said I'd be happy to get her some. And then when I brought it over to the table, I forgot the creamer. See . . ." She pointed to a line on the page. "I said right here that I forgot the creamer and I apologized and went and got some and brought it back to the table. Oh, if only I'd known who it really was sitting right there!" She groaned. "We could have had our picture taken together. I could have gotten her autograph."

"I think the whole point was that she didn't want to be recognized," I said.

"Well, I didn't recognize her. Not for a moment. Which just proves what a wonderful actress she is. I can't believe she never won an Oscar. Can you believe she never won an Oscar?"

"And then what did you two say to each other?" Declan did his best to get Dolly back on track.

Lucky for us, Dolly didn't read the rest of her report word for word. She looked it over. "I asked about the weather. She said it was raining. I said I hadn't seen her at the Terminal before and she said it was her first time. Then she asked . . . well, Laurel . . ." I guess she remembered this part because she didn't have to look at the paper. She clutched it to her chest.

"She asked if you worked here."

"And you told her I did."

"Well, of course." Dolly laughed. "And then she said something about how people don't always live close to where they work."

"And that's how you happened to mention where I live."

"Sure. We were just making small talk. And people love hearing the story about how you inherited that cute little farm of yours and . . ." The smile faded from Dolly's face along with every last little bit of color. "Oh my. They're talking out front. They said they think Meghan's the one who broke into your house. That's how she found out where you live. I . . ." She gulped down a breath. "I told her."

"You did." I was not about to forgive and forget. Not easily. Just so she was sure to get the message, I looked Dolly in the eye. "You made it possible for Meghan to trash my house, and who knows what would have happened if I came home and she was still there."

"Well, nothing would have happened!" I was obviously the biggest dolt in the world to think it might. That's what the look on Dolly's face told me. "Meghan was the sweetest, the kindest, the gentlest soul in the world. She just wanted to see you, that's all. What might have happened!" She chuckled. Then her lower lip protruded. "What happened is what happened to poor, sweet Meghan."

"Which we might figure out if we knew what she was doing here," I mumbled.

"Poor Meghan." Dolly's eyes filled with tears. "She was so beautiful, and so talented, and so young. What a terrible tragedy. I'll bet that detective who was here, I'll bet he asked you if you knew anyone who would like to see Meghan dead."

I sloughed off the question. "It's one of those standard things they always ask."

"Maybe. But you've got the inside track." When she shivered, Dolly's sparkling earrings caught the light and twinkled at me like pink and blue and yellow stars. "You knew Meghan like no one else did. You worked with her." Her sigh heaved the front of her maroon polo shirt with a picture of the Terminal embroidered over the heart. "You were so lucky. You had the best job in the whole, wide world."

At one time, I would have agreed with her. But that was before I found out how demanding and vindictive Meghan could be.

Now, of course, was not the time to mention that. If I needed a reminder, it was the yellow and black crime scene tape slapped over the door of our walk-in freezer.

"I had a lot of good experiences," I told Dolly.

"You should write a book!" The thought hit, and excitement made Dolly's voice rise an octave. She grabbed my arm with both hands. "You could tell stories about Meghan. You know, what it was like working for her, and how she always knew exactly what to wear, and all the guys she dated. You could even include recipes, you know, for the food you served at her elegant parties. Everyone would want to read a book like that."

"Oh, I don't know." The gleam in Dolly's eyes was a little too ghoulish for me; I shrugged out of her grasp. "I have a feeling there are plenty of people who will be telling Meghan's story in these next months."

"They've already started," Dolly assured me. "There's a retrospective of her movies on TCM tonight. I had a friend stop over and set them to record on my DVR. And all the major news networks have picked up on the story. There are reporters out in the restaurant right now."

"Reporters you're not talking to, I hope."

She lifted a shoulder and grabbed the pitcher so she could refill it. "There's nothing I can tell them. But you . . ."

"No." I couldn't be any clearer. "I'm not interested in being interviewed. Or interrogated. Let them get their information somewhere else."

"I'll tell them that."

"Don't tell them anything," I called after her when she headed back into the restaurant. "Say you have no comment."

I could only hope Dolly would listen.

That, and . . . my gaze wandered back to the stack of books in front of me . . . Truth be told, the real thing I wished for was that we knew what we were looking for.

Together, Declan and I began the search, page by page, book by book.

"Here's a receipt for two pints of whipping cream and three quarts of strawberries." Declan plucked the receipt out of one of the cookbooks and waved it in my direction. "Maybe that's what Meghan was looking for."

I'd just finished with a soup cookbook and I slapped it shut and laid it aside and didn't bother to comment. "What we haven't considered is that she found what she was looking for so even if we look, we're not going to find it because it's already gone. Did Gus say anything about what was in her pockets?"

Declan pursed his lips. "Not to me."

"But, of course, even if she found what she was looking for, the person who killed her might have taken it." I stretched a kink out of my back. "If that's the case, then we're wasting our time."

Which didn't mean I was going to give up.

I got up, poured coffee for both me and Declan, and took two slices of Italian sausage/banana pepper/ mushroom pizza George offered so we could eat while we worked.

"Good pizza." Declan chewed the last of his piece and set aside the fish cookbook he'd just finished with. "Anything in that one?"

Since I'd just dripped gooey mozzarella all over a German chocolate cake recipe, I made a face. "Cheese."

"I don't think Meghan was looking for cheese stains."

"Maybe she loved my tagliatelle with asparagus and marjoram so much, she had to have the recipe for herself."

"It was pretty darned good." Finished with another book, Declan set it aside, and his shoulders heaved. "Maybe we're going at this all the wrong way. Maybe we shouldn't care what Meghan was looking for. Maybe we should concentrate on who didn't like Meghan."

I made a face. "A whole lot of people."

"Anybody in particular seem to dislike her more than anybody else?"

I thought about it, but not for long. "Every time she and her current lover broke up . . . well, there's nothing quite as ugly as Hollywood heartbreak."

"So let's start there." Declan stretched out his long legs. "Was she ever married?"

"A bunch of times." I thought about it. "I wasn't around for the first one. That's when she was mar-ried to—"

"Benito Gallo!"

Who knew Dolly had come back into the kitchen? She stood with her back to the swinging door, her eyes sparkling like her earrings. "Ben was Meghan's first husband. Spencer's father." Dolly nodded. "Everyone's heard of Ben Gallo. He's famous. And dreamy. Oooh!" Her eyes went wide and she closed in on me. "I never thought of it. You . . . you've probably met him. I'm telling you, Laurel, you are the luckiest woman in the entire world. You knew Meghan, and I'll bet you knew Benito, too."

"I've met him," I admitted. "He and Meghan were married—"

"Seventeen years ago." Like it was a fact everyone in Hubbard would have at their fingertips, she nodded knowingly. "Of course, that was long before you worked for Meghan."

"It was. I started working for her—"

"When Rocky Stegano walked out on her." It was another one of those tabloid-fueled stories so I wasn't surprised Dolly knew it. Rocky—a mediocre actor who happened to have a better-than-average body and be a better-than-average cook—and Meghan had an affair of epic proportions. Once he moved in with her, he handled all the cooking, and once they had a breakup that was as whopping ugly as any Hollywood had ever produced, Meghan hired me to take over the kitchen duties.

Dolly left the kitchen and I turned back to Declan.

"Benito Gallo. Handsome Italian race-car driver." I repeated the words automatically; anytime Ben's name was mentioned—on the news, on sports programs, in the tabloids—they always were part and parcel of the story. "He's rich, he's charming, he's a daredevil, and he's—"

"Ben and cars! That's what made me think of it."

Since I hadn't been expecting Dolly to be back so quickly, when she shoved open the door and hopped inside the kitchen like her shoes were on fire, I squealed.

She hurried over to where her jacket was hung on a peg next to mine and Sophie's. "I meant to tell you. I mean, because you've been asking questions. Which is perfectly understandable." Dolly added this last little bit almost like an apology. "After all, you and Meghan were good friends."

I would hardly say that, but there was no use mentioning it to Dolly, not when she had the glow of excitement in her eyes. She came over to where Declan and I were standing, her phone in her hand, and whispered like a conspirator. "The cops found the car."

"What car?" No way we could have planned it, but Declan and I asked the question at the same time.

Dolly barked out a laugh. "The one Meghan rented, of course. There had to be a way she got here."

Yes, there had to be, and I gave myself a mental slap for not considering it sooner.

Dolly swiped through the pictures on her phone. "There. See." She turned the phone so I could see the picture that showed a police tow truck just about to hoist a late-model cream-colored Lexus. "I think they think there might be evidence."

I wasn't so sure since the murder had taken place there in the Terminal, not in the car, but I didn't have the heart to squash Dolly's investigative excitement. "Where was it parked?"

She tipped her head. "Just down the street. In back of the Book Nook. They figured it was Meghan's because it was a rental so they took it away, you know, to dust for prints and stuff."

Big points for Declan; he didn't make it sound at all like he wondered how a woman who was so . . . well, so ordinary as Dolly might know all this. "How did you find out?"

She gave him a wink. "Hey, it's a gift! There's plenty you can find out if you just listen, and we've had enough cops and reporters in here all day. I just pay attention, that's all. That's how I knew to get over there and snap a couple pictures before they took the car away."

It was mildly interesting, though how it would lead us to find answers to the question of Meghan's death was beyond me.

Or maybe it wasn't.

"Let me take another look at that." When I pointed, Dolly handed me her phone. I squinted at the picture that showed the sedan from the driver's side door, then came to my senses and hit the screen to make the picture bigger.

"What?" Declan saw what I was doing and came to stand at my side. "What do you see?"

"I'm not sure." I enlarged the photograph just a little more. "It looks like a hotel key. You know, one of those swipe cards."

He took the phone out of my hands and gave the picture a closer look. "It sure does. A Holiday Inn, I think."

"Meghan at a Holiday Inn?" It didn't jibe with everything I knew about the diva of all divas, but hey, I could understand. If Meghan wanted to fly under the radar, it was the perfect choice, somewhere she could slip in and out of where no one would pay too much attention to her.

"What does it tell us?" Declan wanted to know.

I didn't answer. Not right away, anyway. Not until I handed the phone back to Dolly, thanked her, and asked if she'd do me a favor and make sure there was enough rolled silverware on the table outside the kitchen door where we stacked extra supplies.

Once she was gone, I turned to Declan. "I'm not sure she's keeping as quiet about all this as she should with our customers," I told him.

"And you don't want Dolly or anyone else to know our next move."

"Smart as well as handsome." I gave him a peck on the cheek then told George we were going out and we'd be back in a couple of hours. Honestly, I don't think I had to. Just because George is the quiet type doesn't mean he doesn't pay any attention, and the little salute he gave us as we headed out of the kitchen told me he knew exactly where we were going.

It was time to do some serious investigating.

Chapter 6

It was a twenty-minute ride from Hubbard to Austintown where the Holiday Inn was located. Declan and I didn't talk much in the car, but once we arrived at the hotel with its neatly trimmed bushes and flags snapping in the spring breeze from the poles out front, we looked at each other and Declan said what we'd both been thinking.

"Now what?"

"I wish I knew. Even if we had the hotel card key we saw in that picture Dolly took, it wouldn't do us any good since there wouldn't be a room number on it. So we go inside . . ." I looked toward the sliding glass doors at the front of the hotel. "And we ask if Meghan is registered here."

"Only she wouldn't have used her own name. And no one's figured out yet that she was staying here. If they had, this place would be crawling with reporters and TV cameras just like the Terminal is."

"Then we'll . . ." Because I had no idea what we'd do, I got out of the car before I could talk myself out of it, and I strode through those front doors and walked up to the registration desk. Since I'd been told (and not just by Declan) that I am an attractive woman, and since the clerk behind the desk was a kid of maybe nineteen with a shock of badly dyed black hair, sallow skin, and crooked teeth, I was hoping to work a little feminine magic.

"It's Granny," I said, clutching the front of the counter with both hands and adding a little hiccup to the last word along with what I hoped was a convincing sniffle. "She said she was coming in from Buffalo Thursday and checking in here and that she'd be over this morning to babysit, but she never showed up. Something's wrong. I just know it. You've got to help me!"

From behind me, I felt Declan poke me in the back.

I ignored him and kept my a-little-sad-a-little-worried expression firmly in place. The kid might be young, but sooner or later, he was bound to ask for my granny's name and since I didn't know what name Meghan had used to check in, I couldn't let things get that far.

"I've got to find her! She's here, right? Please tell me she is. She's about this high." I demonstrated, one hand out, my palm flat to the floor. "She's got a black coat and she always wears that red hat I knitted for her and—" Since I had to give him a chance to say something, I stopped there, the better to shed a few crocodile tears.

"I . . . I don't see everyone. I'm . . . I'm not always here," the kid stammered, and by way of demonstrating that, in spite of that, he was obviously ready, willing, and able to help, he touched a hand to the computer keyboard in front of him. "If you let me know your grandmother's name, I can check our records and—"

"Oh, I just know something's happened to her!" Stalling for time—and hopefully, information—I spun around and buried my face against Declan's chest. (Just for the record, this is a dandy place to be.)

Good thing I did because when the clerk stuttered, "L-let me g-get the manager," and I moved away from Declan, I got a look over his shoulder down the hallway to our right and the long line of closed hotel-room doors. I was just in time to see one of them swing open.

"I . . . I should have known!" It was my turn to stammer. Right before I took off running down the hallway.

The woman who stepped out of Room 112 had her back to me, and she was busy fumbling with the four suitcases she dragged out of the room. Lucky for me. That gave me the element of surprise when I stopped behind her and said, "Hello, Corrine!"

She froze and I heard her gulp.

"Going somewhere?" I asked her.

Corrine Kellogg was a little shorter than me and a couple of years older. The way I remembered it (and I have a pretty good memory), her hair had always been that shade of blonde that's more dishwater than it is pretty, but somewhere along the line in the year since I'd last seen her, she'd become a redhead. The color did not go especially well with her always too-rosy cheeks, her always too-squint-eyed stare, or the fact that her untamed eyebrows were a mixture of blonde and silver and made her look like there was one fuzzy caterpillar resting over each of her eyes.

"Uh . . . uh . . . hello, Laurel. What are you . . . ?" Corrine squinted past me to Declan and stepped slightly to her left. Yeah, like her skinny little body might actually hide all those suitcases she'd just dragged out of the room. "What are you doing here?"

"Isn't that funny? I was just going to ask you the same thing." I stepped to the side, the better to give Corrine a look at Declan and Declan a look at her. "This is Corrine Kellogg," I told him. "Meghan's personal assistant."

The expression on Declan's face went from confused to *I've got it* in a flash. "It's good to meet you," he told her, shaking her limp hand. "We have a lot to talk about."

"Do we? I wish I had time. My flight out of Pittsburgh is at seven this evening, and I've still got the long drive ahead of me and—"

"The cops in Hubbard are going to be so glad to know you're still here!" I whipped out my phone and paused, a finger poised over the keyboard. "They've got a lot of questions and I bet you're the one who can provide the answers."

Corrine ran her tongue over her thin lips. "Not really."

I glanced at the closed hotel-room door. "Maybe you'd like us to wait here with you until they get here."

Though she worked side by side with one of the most sophisticated and savvy women in Hollywood, Corrine herself had never been very good at playing the part. She shifted from foot to foot, maybe committing the steps to memory, or maybe just tracing the pattern in the green and blue hallway carpeting. "Like I said, I've got a flight to catch and—"

"Detective Oberlin!" Declan, smart guy that he is, had pulled out his own phone and made the call. He turned his back on us and strode down the hallway, his voice just loud enough so that Corrine couldn't fail to hear—and know exactly what he was talking about. "Declan Fury here. I'm in Austintown. Yes, at the Holiday Inn. I figured you'd send someone over here sooner or later, but it's a good thing Laurel and I got here when we did. There's someone here who may be able to provide some information regarding Meghan Cohan's murder and . . ."

While Declan kept talking, I put a hand on Corrine's shoulder. "Maybe we should wait in your room."

She dug her key card out of her purse and when she opened the door, I grabbed two of the suitcases, she lifted the other two, and we went inside. While she peeled off her beige rain jacket, I stationed myself between her and the door. Not that I expected her to make a run for it. In all the years I'd known her, Corrine had never had an original, a daring, or a surprising thought.

"So, what do you think?"

Her tongue flicked out from between her teeth. "You mean about . . ." She cleared her throat. "About Meghan being . . ."

"Dead. You can say it, Corrine. Meghan is dead."

"Yeah. I know." She didn't so much sit down in the gray and black upholstered chair as melt into it. "It's terrible. But I don't see how you think I can tell you anything about it. I didn't even know . . . I didn't even know Meghan was here."

"Oh, come on, Corrine! Number one, you went everywhere with Meghan. Number two, you can't expect me to believe the two of you just happened to end up in Austintown, Ohio, at the same time, independent of each other. And number three, well, how do you think I knew to come here? I saw her key card."

She swallowed hard. "That doesn't mean—"

"Should we look through these suitcases?" I closed in on them. "Because I know Meghan never traveled light. One of them might be yours, but the other three are bound to be full of her stuff. As soon as I see a packet of the Keemun Hoa Ya A tea Meghan always had with breakfast, I'll know the suitcase is hers, and the cops, they're going to wonder why you're so anxious to leave town with a dead woman's possessions."

"No, no. Don't do that!" One hand out to stop me, Corrine popped out of her chair. "You don't need to look. You're right, the suitcases are Meghan's. She was here . . . that is, I was here and . . . and we were here together. We have been since Thursday."

"Why?"

Corrine pressed her lips together. "She didn't say."

"Yeah, because Meghan was so good about keeping her business to herself." She would have had to be unconscious not to catch the note of sarcasm in my voice. "Come on, Corrine, help me out here. I'm trying to figure out who killed Meghan."

"Well, I just sort of figured . . ." She darted me a look and raised her scrawny shoulders. "I just naturally thought it was you."

I barked out a laugh. I'm not sure why because really, it wasn't funny. "I didn't kill Meghan," I told Corrine in no uncertain terms. "I had no reason to kill Meghan."

"She fired you."

"That was more than a year ago."

"You were mad. When it happened. I was there and—"

"Yes, I was mad. It was unfair. And Meghan wouldn't listen to reason. But, news flash, Corrine, I don't care. Not anymore. I'm happy here."

"You're happy . . ." As if she'd just woken up from a long and troubled sleep, Corrine looked around the room with its utilitarian furnishings and its view of the air-conditioning unit out in the parking lot at the side of the building. "You're happy here?"

"I'm happy with my life. With the decisions I've made since I left California. I had no reason to kill Meghan. But someone else must have." I thought back to my trashed house, the trashed restaurant. "Why was Meghan looking for me?" I asked Corrine.

When she shook her head, her hair drooped in her eyes and she pushed it back. For a woman as drab and plain as she was, Corrine had fine-boned hands and long, elegant fingers.

"She never said."

"She dragged you all the way from California to Ohio and she never said why?"

Corrine threw those beautiful hands of hers in the air and paced away from the window, then back again. "You know how she could be, Laurel. She didn't give explanations. Not to anyone. Especially not to me. Last Wednesday we were in Malibu getting ready for our move to Maui for the summer and the next thing you know, we're heading to the airport."

So Meghan's decision was sudden. Maybe that was because she'd just found out where I was.

I tucked the thought away.

"And so you showed up here and Meghan did what?"

Corrine's top lip curled. "We went to a thrift shop. Can you even imagine it? Meghan in a thrift shop?"

"That's where she found the clothes for the man's disguise she wore on Thursday and the old-lady costume she was wearing when she was killed."

"I told her it wouldn't work." I didn't believe this for a moment since in as long as I'd known both of them, Corrine had never even dreamed of contradicting Meghan. Corrine knew that I knew—that would explain why her face flushed with color.

"Well, I didn't exactly tell her it wouldn't work. I just told her to be careful. I reminded her that you knew her well and—"

"So you did know Meghan was here to find me." Big points for me, I did not poke an accusing finger in Corrine's direction and shout *Aha!* "Why, Corrine? Why would she come all this way just to see me?"

"I don't know." Corrine could mewl with the best of them. "She never said. I never asked. No one ever asked Meghan to explain herself, no one but you. It's one of the reasons she dumped you, you know."

"I thought it was because Meghan assumed I'd leaked information about Spencer to the press."

A small, satisfied smile tugged at the corners of Corrine's mouth. "Yeah, that's what she told everyone, but she'd been thinking about getting rid of you long before that bit about Spencer and his addiction showed up on all the cable channels. I knew all about what she was planning. Of course I knew all about it. I knew everything about everything Meghan did."

"Then you know why she wanted to find me."

"I didn't say that. I said—"

"Gads, Corrine, you are so annoying!" The words popped out of me before I could stop them, and listening to them fall flat against the stuccoed ceiling, I realized they were true, and something I'd been wanting to say to Corrine since I'd met her.

"You never just answer a question, Corrine. You waffle and you shuffle and you dodge. You're unorganized. You're scatterbrained. You're not good with people. Why on earth would a high-powered woman like Meghan even want you for a personal assistant in the first place?"

Corrine squared her scraggy shoulders and lifted her pointy chin. "Meghan and I went back a long way. We were friends. Back then . . ." A smile tickled the corners of her mouth. "People have always said that Meghan and I looked enough alike to be sisters." Those people, I decided right then and there, needed glasses, but before I could point this out, Corrine went right on. "We treated each other like sisters, too. Then and now. We were friends, and real friends are loyal to each other."

"Even when one of them isn't very good at her job."

"I'm not the one who got fired."

I told myself I had a snappy comeback to this hurled insult, and actually might have found it if there wasn't a tap on the door. I opened it and Declan stepped into the room.

"So . . ." He looked back and forth from Corrine, who was breathing hard over by the window, to me, and since I could feel the heat in my cheeks I'm sure he knew something was up.

"The police are on their way," he said because he's a smart guy and he knew there was no use asking what was going on. Hey, he has sisters. He knows better than to get between women who are fighting. "They asked us to stay here and wait with you, Corrine."

"That's ridiculous." She huffed to the chair and plunked herself down on it. "There's nothing I can tell them, just like there's nothing I can tell you. I came here because Meghan wanted me to. And when she went out Thursday night—"

"To trash my house."

"Did she?"

Was that a sparkle of amusement I saw in Corrine's dark eyes? Since I didn't want to go another round with her, I ignored it.

"I have no idea where she went or what she did while she was there." Unconcerned, she melted into the chair and let her head rest against the back of it. "The same thing happened Friday when she went out again, and I knew better than to ask what she was up to. Maybe . . ." The thought hit, and just like that, Corrine bolted up, her bottom lip trembling. "Maybe if I asked some questions, maybe if I paid more attention to what was going on, Meghan would still be alive."

"LAUREL, I JUST got a call from the station. There's someone over there and I'd like you to stop by and talk to him."

Since we'd just left Gus at the Holiday Inn with Corrine, I was surprised to hear his voice on the other end of the phone as we drove back to Hubbard.

Instead of having a chance to ask him if he'd gotten any more out of Corrine than we had, all I could say was, "Who?"

"You'll see." The sound of Gus chuckling is reminiscent of chains dragging across a metal sewer grate and always takes me aback. "Just stop in there, all right? It's practically on your way home."

It was, and we were there in only a few minutes and ushered right into Gus's office, where a muscular guy in his forties with a pencil-thin mustache, a bald head, and a sparkling diamond stud in his left earlobe was waiting.

"Jason Fielding." The man stuck out a hand. "I can't tell you how glad I am to finally get to meet you in person."

"Meet . . . me?" Just to be sure, I poked my thumb at my own chest. "I don't get it."

One of Gus's fellow detectives had been waiting in the room with Fielding, and now he stepped back to allow me to take the guest chair in front of Gus's utilitarian gray metal desk. Fielding perched himself on the edge of Gus's desk.

"I feel like we're practically best friends," he said. "After all, I've been looking for you for just about a year."

It took a moment for the words to sink in. When they did, they landed in my stomach with a thud. "You've been looking for me! Because—"

Fielding threw back his head and laughed. "Because Ms. Cohan paid me to, of course." He reached into his back pocket, pulled out a wallet, and took out two business cards. One he gave to Declan, the other to me. "I'm a private investigator."

I could see that. Fielding Investigations had an address in Brentwood, a tony LA suburb.

I eyed up Fielding. His ear stud winked at me.

"Why?" I asked.

When he shrugged his shoulders his black cashmere sweater pulled across his chest. "I don't ask questions. I do what my clients want me to do. I provide results. I get paid. Only you . . ." His smile told me that while the search may have been frustrating, he appreciated the challenge. "You made it tough for me."

"I wasn't exactly living under an assumed name. Or under a rock."

"No, you were not. And that's what had me all confused. See, when Ms. Cohan asked me to take the case, she told me you were a high-end sort of chef."

"Which she is." Declan stood behind me and he put a hand on my shoulder. "Laurel is the best."

"Which is why I never thought I'd find you in a town like this." As bemused now as he must have been when he discovered the truth, Fielding grinned. "It was very clever of you."

"I wasn't trying to be clever. I was trying to make a living."

"Well, whatever you were trying to do, you did it well."

"Then how did you find Laurel?" Declan asked.

"Ah!" Fielding wagged a finger at me. "I don't think I would have except that it looks like you just inherited some property."

"Yes, Pacifique."

"Well, the property records led me to your door, so to speak."

"And you told Meghan where I was."

He pursed his lips. "No crime in that."

"No one is saying there is," Declan said before I could. But before he could ask the questions burning in me, I beat him to them.

"You told her last Wednesday." Okay, so it wasn't exactly a question, but it was a way to worm my way to what I hoped would be useful information.

"I did." Fielding nodded.

"And she showed up here in Hubbard."

"I hear she broke into your house. I just want you to know, Ms. Inwood, I did not help, and I do not condone that sort of behavior. I do everything by the book. Strictly by the book."

"Did she tell you why she was looking for me?"

"It's not my business to ask."

"But you did know she was here."

His eyes narrowed, Fielding gave me a careful look. "You're not saying I might have been involved in Ms. Cohan's murder, are you?"

"I'm saying you seem to be one of the only people who knew she was here in Hubbard."

"Only I wasn't." He pushed off from the desk. "Here in Hubbard, that is. I came into town last week to verify your real estate transaction. I checked out that restaurant where you work to make sure it was really you and just to be sure, I sent Ms. Cohan some pictures."

"You've been following me around? Taking pictures?" The thought made my stomach swoop. So did the cold realization that I'd never known I was being tailed.

"Not to worry," he assured me. "It's all strictly professional and it was only to make sure you were who I thought you were. Ms. Cohan, once she saw the pictures, she said it was you, all right."

"And then she came here."

"Well, obviously, since this is where she died. Only I didn't know that. You see, I called her last Wednesday and gave her the news, and then I left here and drove to Cleveland. I've got relatives there and I've been with them ever since. So if you're thinking I might have had something to do with Ms. Cohan's death . . . well . . ." He sauntered to the door. "Sorry to disappoint you, folks. I may have been following you, but I sure didn't kill anybody, and I've got the alibi to prove it."

Chapter 7

Just as we were getting ready to leave the police station, I got another call from Gus. This time he said he was on his way over to the county coroner's office in Youngstown and he asked us to meet him there. By the time we arrived at the nondescript brick building, Gus was just getting out of his car. He had Corrine Kellogg with him.

Corrine's usually ruddy cheeks were ashy. The moment she spotted me, she rushed over and grabbed my arm with both her hands. "They want me to identify the . . ." She gulped and looked at the building as if it were a snake, reared back and ready to strike.

"Meghan is here." Corrine sniffled. "They want me to identify the body."

"It's just a formality," I assured her. "You were the one who last saw Meghan alive so you—"

"But you did, didn't you? Friday night at the restaurant?"

Had I mentioned that to Corrine? I wasn't sure, and not being sure always has a way of making me suspicious of the facts I'm being fed.

"She called you," I said, and I knew I was right when Corrine's blubbering stopped. "You said you had no idea where Meghan went when she left the hotel Thursday and Friday evenings. But then how did you know she spoke to me at the Terminal on Friday? You wouldn't know, not if she didn't call you and tell you she'd seen me and talked to me."

Her bottom lip jutted out. "She . . . she didn't. You told me."

"I don't think I did."

"Well, you must have." She threw her hands in the air and turned on her heels to follow Gus into the building.

"You're coming, too, right?" Gus asked me and Declan.

I wasn't planning on it, but Declan and I exchanged looks and followed along.

The coroner was expecting us.

Then again, so were the two dozen reporters camped out in the lobby.

"Detective Oberlin!" A man I recognized from the evening network news stuck a microphone in Gus's face. "What can you tell us about the latest developments in the case?"

"No comment." Since Gus's reply accompanied a snarl of epic proportions, the reporter gave up without a fight. He scanned the rest of our little group. Declan and Corrine—lucky folks that they were—were strangers to the media.

Me, not so much.

If I needed any more proof that my name had been mentioned in the media circus and someone had come up with a picture of me to go with it, I found it when the guy pretty much drooled the moment he caught sight of me.

"Ms. Inwood!" He swung the microphone around at the same time he darted in front of me, blocking my progress. "We've been told that you found the body, and our viewers know you knew the victim better than most. It must have been a terrible shock to see Meghan dead."

"No comment." Big points for me since I managed to say this pretty clearly even though my teeth were clenched.

I kept walking and the reporter had no choice but to fall back. Believe me, I knew it had nothing to do with my not-so-intimidating presence; Declan stepped right in front of me, and he moved through the crowd like he did everything else, no messing around. One look at the fire in those incredible gray eyes of his and the crowd parted in front of him and we pushed our way through a set of double doors.

The sheriff's deputy who stepped up behind us made sure those reporters didn't get any farther.

By this time, Corrine wasn't just sniffling, she was outright sobbing. She pressed a hand to her heart. "I don't think I can do this!" she wailed.

"Oh, come on, Corrine. Don't let those jackals out there get to you. You're used to paparazzi." Yeah, I know, Corrine is the last person I should have felt sorry for, but there was something about the sheer terror in her eyes that tugged at my heartstrings. "Just handle them the way Gus and I did."

She swallowed hard. "The reporters . . . they ask so many questions . . . and when they find out I was the one who identified Meghan's body . . ." She stared at the door to our right, the one marked MORGUE. "You have to come with me, Laurel."

"I don't know if Gus wants me to—"

"It's fine." Gus opened the door and stepped back so Corrine and I could go inside. "If it helps Ms. Kellogg relax so she can make the identification, yeah, you can go right ahead."

We were done in a matter of minutes. But then, it didn't take long for Corrine to take one look at the body laid out on a metal slab and dissolve into tears. The heavy stage makeup had been removed from Meghan's face and the wig she'd worn when last I saw her alive was long gone. There on the cold metal table, she looked like the glamorous star so familiar to millions of fans—the porcelain skin, the perfect jawline, the high cheekbones. She seemed to be asleep, and only the wound on her head from the force of a heavy object, said otherwise.

"Poor Meghan." I grabbed Declan's hand and squeezed it, grateful to have him to hold on to at a time like this. "She could be tough to deal with, but she sure didn't deserve this." I cleared away the sudden lump in my throat. "No one deserves to die like this."

"Knocked unconscious and left to freeze." The coroner replaced the white sheet that had been over Meghan's face when we walked into the room. "That's one nasty way to go. It takes someone with a cold, cold heart to commit a murder like this."

Bad pun notwithstanding, I knew he was right.

I also knew that all the while we'd been in the room with Meghan's body, Gus had been watching me carefully. I didn't hold it against him; if I thought I was a murder suspect, I would have been watching me, too.

The convoluted logic made my head spin, and I shook it and gave the detective a look.

"So, you think I'm that coldhearted person?"

Even here in the morgue, Gus had a toothpick in his mouth. He rolled it from one side of his mouth to the other. "I doubt it, but I've seen stranger things. Though now that we know Ms. Cohan was in town with Ms. Kellogg here—"

"You think I killed her?" Corrine spit out the words. "Why would I . . . ? How could I . . . ?" Still blubbering, she pushed out the door and went into the hallway.

Gus rocked back on his heels. "Did I accuse her of anything?"

"Being told you might be a murderer tends to make people feel a little testy," I reminded him.

He had the good grace to look sheepish. Which for Gus with his wide nose, his heavy brows, and his flapping jowls, is no easy thing. "You know I have to cover all my bases," he said. "So let's get something else out of the way. You say you saw Ms. Cohan in the restaurant sometime Friday evening."

"That's right."

"So she either left and came back. Or she hid somewhere and stayed in the restaurant until after the rest of you were gone. So let's look at possibility number one.

If she did come back, how did Ms. Cohan get into the Terminal?"

I slanted him a look. "There were no signs of a forced entry, were there?" I already knew the answer but it doesn't hurt to get official confirmation. "So that leaves possibility number two. She could have—"

"Hidden somewhere and waited until the rest of you were gone for the night?" His lips pursed, Gus nodded. "Exactly what I was thinking."

"We have the rooms upstairs we use for storage," I said to no one in particular since Declan and Gus both knew about the upstairs rooms where we kept things like extra paper products and clean linens. "She could have snuck up there when no one was looking."

All the while we talked, we'd slowly been making our way to the door and once we stepped out into the hallway, I looked at Corrine where she was leaning against the wall, my voice and my look oh so casual. "Did Meghan say anything to you, Corrine? When she called you Friday night?"

"She called you Friday night?" This was news to Gus, and exactly why I mentioned it. "Are you with-holding evidence, Ms. Kellogg?"

In spite of her swollen eyes and her red nose, Corrine looked as pale as death. "Evidence? Me? I don't know a thing. Yes, she called. Meghan called. She told me she'd be back at the hotel in a couple hours and she expected me to have a hot bath run for her and a hot cup of tea made for her and she said she'd let me know when she was on her way."

"Only she never called and told you she was on her way," Declan pointed out.

Corrine nodded.

"And you didn't think that was odd?" I asked her.

"You know Meghan!" She lifted her chin. "I imagined she'd stopped at some dive bar, met some guy. I figured she'd show up sooner or later."

"Only she didn't." Leave it to Gus to point out the obvious.

"No, she didn't." Corrine's shoulders slumped. "Only none of that is evidence, is it? And none of it is important. None of it tells you who killed Meghan so . . . so it's not exactly like I've been withholding evidence because there was nothing to withhold." When she looked up at Gus, her eyes were pleading. "Right?"

Before Gus ever had a chance to respond, a sound rolled our way from the direction of the lobby, where we'd left all those reporters. It wasn't a hum exactly. It was more of a buzz, like the noise made by a swarm of agitated bees.

It didn't start out quiet and gain in intensity. It was loud from the start and soon, it was punctuated by the sound of first one voice, then another, raised to be heard above the din.

Questions.

One after another, the reporters called out questions, and what with all the commotion, I couldn't tell if those questions were getting answered or not.

The next second, the double doors that separated us from all those reporters flew open and a man strode into the hallway with each and every one of those reporters right on his heels. He was dressed in slim-fitting jeans that made the most of his trim body. His golf shirt was as blindingly white as his teeth. The shirt was open

at the neck to reveal a shock of inky chest hair and a
glint of the gold chain he wore around his neck. He had
thick, rugged features, hair that was darker even than
Declan's, and a gleam in his eye that would have ful-
filled any casting director's dreams if that person happened to be looking for someone to play the part of a
handsome Italian race-car driver.

Benito Gallo's gaze swung around touching on Gus
and Declan and moving to Corrine. In the one second
he kept it there, I heard her breath catch, but he didn't
give her a chance to say a word. His gaze moved right
on and his eyes landed on me. He threw his hands in
the air and his voice rang through the hallway.

"Ciao, bella!"

THE DOORS WERE still wide open and all those reporters
were looking at us and all those cameras were aimed at
us when Ben rushed forward and kissed both my cheeks.

"You are here! I am so . . . happy, it is not the word.
Relieved. Yes, yes. I am so relieved!" Just for good
measure—or to make sure the paparazzi got his best
side—he gave my right cheek another kiss. "I am so . . .
how do you say it? . . . comforted. I am so comforted
knowing you, Laurel, are here at Meghan's side at this
difficult moment."

It took a second for me to make my head stop spin-
ning and, believe me, it had nothing to do with Ben
Gallo's kisses. Oh sure, he was gorgeous, successful,
and a household name, at least in those households that
knew anything about auto racing. But he'd also lived in
the good ol' USA for as long as anyone could remember.

Since when had Ben Gallo suddenly become so downright Italian?

The answer hit, and in spite of the time and the place and the reason we were standing outside the door of the morgue, I couldn't help but grin at the audacity of the man. According to the reports in all the tabloids and on all the news channels, Ben had just recently married Italian countess Adalina Crocetti, jet-setting fashionista with a family lineage that went back to the Caesars and a bank account that made even Meghan's look puny.

In his own way, Ben was as much a publicity hound as Meghan ever was. Now that he had an official attachment to Italian aristocracy—not to mention the prestige, the estates, the vineyards, and the fortune—he was going to play up being Italian for all he was worth.

As if to prove what I was thinking, he looped an arm around my shoulders, pasted a sad expression on his face, and posed for one more picture.

That is, before he instructed the deputy to shut the door on the drooling paparazzi.

Once that was done, Ben breathed a sigh of relief.

"I can't believe it. Can somebody explain to me what is going on here? Because I heard the news and I just do not . . . I cannot . . ." He hauled in a breath. "It cannot be true."

"It is, Ben." Corrine stepped forward and touched a hand to his arm. "Meghan, she's . . . it's true. She's dead."

He put a hand over his eyes and his shoulders heaved.

"You're Ben Gallo." Gus spoke the words like he was afraid someone was going to accuse him of being wrong and when Ben looked over at him and nodded, it was Gus's turn to breathe a sigh of relief. "We're going to need to talk to you."

"Of course." Ben slipped his arm off my shoulders and stepped back. "And me, I know what you are going to ask. What am I doing here? I heard, of course. About Meghan. It is all over the news. You must be with the *polizia*." Ben said this last bit to Declan and I wasn't surprised. Even in his jeans and with a plaid button-down open over a dark T-shirt, Declan looked more like a representative of law enforcement than Gus in his ill-fitting beige sport coat, his brown pants, and a cream-colored shirt with gravy stains on it.

Declan pointed a finger at Gus.

Ben didn't apologize. But then, like Meghan, Ben never apologized for anything. "I know you are going to ask about my relationship with Meghan," he said to Gus. "We had our . . . help me out here, Laurel, how do I say this? Differences? Yes, we had our differences." He didn't give me a chance to say that was an under-statement to anyone who ever read the tabloids and es-pecially to me, who over the years had seen Ben and Meghan interact with each other. "But she is the mother of my only child."

"Spencer." Corrine filled in the details.

"Then that's how you know Mr. Gallo." It wasn't really a question, but I couldn't blame Declan for trying to make sense of the situation. He wasn't used to the complexities of Hollywood marriages, Hollywood re-lationships, Hollywood divorces.

"Ben and Meghan were divorced long before I started working for Meghan," I told him. "But we've met."

Ben nodded.

"He used to come to visit Spencer," I said. "So naturally we know each other."

"And you were what . . . just around the corner when you heard about Ms. Cohan's murder?" Gus asked.

Ben's smile was dazzling. "Racing," he said. "Near Pittsburgh, so I was not so very far away. What happened to Meghan, it is *una cosa orribile*, no? When I saw the news on the *televisione* this morning, I could not stay away. I had to be here. I had to know this was real. And if you need someone to identify the body . . ."

"Ms. Inwood and Ms. Kellogg have already taken care of that," Gus told him. "But if you'd like to see Ms. Cohan . . ."

Ben's shoulders rose and fell. "No. No. I do not think so. I had to make the offer, yes? But I am relieved you do not need me. Me, I would rather remember Meghan as she was last time I saw her, so beautiful. So talented. So full of life. What happens . . . what happens now?"

"Well, that all depends on Ms. Cohan's will," Gus said. He looked from Ben to Corrine. "Do either of you know anything about that?"

"Not me." Like someone just yelled, *Stick 'em up!* Ben put his hands in the air.

"It has been many years, Detective, sir, since Meghan shared information of that kind with me."

"She had a will." Corrine stepped forward. "There are copies at home, of course, and Meghan's attorney will have one as well. I can provide you with his information."

"Let's make the call to that attorney now." Gus went down the hallway and stepped into the coroner's office.

Which left me and Declan with Ben.

"So . . ." I knew Ben well enough to know that while he was about as unsubtle as a tornado, he didn't respond well when other people acted the same way. Still, I had to take a chance. "You just happened to be within driving distance when Meghan was murdered?"

He blinked. Pulled back his shoulders. Gave me a careful look.

"What you are saying to me, Laurel?"

I rolled my eyes. "Cut the Italian act! There aren't any reporters around right now and lucky for you, Gus isn't here, either. Would you rather have him ask the question? He's going to, you know. It's his job. You might as well practice your answer on me. So, tell me, did you have any reason to kill Meghan?"

Ben looked as flash-frozen as Meghan had when I found her body that morning.

Well, except for the fact that his jaw flapped open.

"Why would I kill her? We've been divorced since just after Spencer was born, and that was sixteen years ago."

"But once upon a time, you were in love and then you weren't. That kind of closeness breeds plenty of emotions and emotions can turn ugly."

"Don't be so naive, Laurel." Ben's laugh wasn't as pleasant as it was cynical. "You act like Meghan and I are the only two people in the world who've ever gotten divorced. Hey, we were married, and what happens to every marriage? We were crazy in love for a while, we had Spencer. But then she got that role that turned her into a star, and she got wrapped up with her career, and I got busy with mine, and . . ." His shrug pretty much said it all. "We got divorced. End of story."

"But you still keep in touch with your son?"

"Of course." Offended by Declan's question, Ben shot him a look. "Spencer's got some problems. Sure. Everyone knows that. But deep down, he's a great kid. And I've got a good relationship with him. He's my son. I had a great relationship with Meghan, too, just in case you're wondering."

He must have forgotten who he was talking to.

I cleared my throat, the better to get his attention. "That's not exactly how I remember things. The last time I saw you two together in Maui, you fought like you'd been divorced ten minutes, not ten years."

"That was what . . . more than a year ago." Like a magician who could make it disappear, Ben dismissed my observation with a wave of one hand. "You've been out of Meghan's life for a while now, Laurel. You don't know what happened between us since then. We realized we've got Spencer to worry about. He's more important than our squabbling. Ask anyone. Meghan and I, we've been getting along pretty well these days. Ask what's her name, Corrine, she'll tell you."

I couldn't help but remember the backbiting and the bitter fights. Every time Ben showed up to visit Spencer (which actually wasn't all that often), things between Meghan and Ben went from bad to worse—fast. "I've seen you two together. It's pretty hard to believe."

"Yeah, well, I didn't say we were best friends. I said we realized we had to work together if we were going to help Spencer. Truth be told . . ." Again, he looked toward the double doors. They were still closed. "The truth is, it didn't take me and Meghan long after we were married to realize we didn't like each other very much. Meghan was self-centered, egotistical, mean, and stingy."

"You hated her." I knew my observation hit the mark when Ben winced, so I pressed it further.

"Did you hate her enough to kill her?" I asked.

Ben sucked in a breath, then erupted like Vesuvius. Color washed over his cheeks. His hands curled into fists. "How dare you?" he demanded.

Right before he stormed out of the building, muttering in Italian just as he got to those double doors.

Chapter 8

I had a lot to think about.

Corrine.

Ben.

Meghan, of course.

And the fact that though Gus admitted that he didn't really think I'd killed her, it was a very real possibility and he couldn't ignore it completely.

Obviously, my brain should have been working overtime.

It was.

Only not on the mystery.

All that evening back at the Terminal, all I could think about was what Ben had said at the coroner's office.

"And what happens to every marriage? We were crazy in love for a while . . . We got divorced. End of story."

Was that really how love and marriage worked?

I, obviously, was not the one to answer the question, no matter how often or how persistently it pounded through my head. Throughout my time in foster care, I'd been moved from family to family and home to home, and I'd seen it all—squabbles and fights, cold shoulders and hot tempers, resentment and cruelty and greed. I'd never once seen the crazy-in-love part.

Maybe that's because it doesn't exist.

"You look preoccupied." I hadn't heard the door to the Terminal office open, and when Declan walked in, I sat up like a shot and pressed a hand to my heart.

"Sorry." He put a hand on my shoulder. "I should have knocked. Sophie told me you were in here, but I should have known you'd be deep in thought. It's the murder, right? I know, it's got me baffled, too."

Since he had given me the perfect out, it would have been rude of me to point out that Meghan's murder had been the last thing on my mind.

"None of it makes any sense," I told him instead. And who knows, maybe I was still talking about love and marriage!

Declan sat in the guest chair. "You think Ben had anything to do with it?"

Before I'd fallen into a deep reverie about love and marriage, I actually had been thinking about the case, and I touched a hand to the computer keyboard, and the webpage I'd been looking at popped up on the screen.

"Meghan's home page," I said. There was still no announcement of Meghan's death on it, just a picture of her on the red carpet at last year's Academy Awards. She was dressed in gold lace, her hair was perfect, and her smile was dazzling.

She looked nothing at all like the frozen corpse I'd found that morning.

Just thinking about it caused me to shiver, and I wrapped my arms around myself. "It's all the usual PR hype. It does mention that she was once married to Ben, and it mentions Spencer, too. But the rest of it . . ." I made a face. "Not very helpful."

"How about her early life?" Declan leaned closer to get a better look at the computer screen. "Does it say anything about where she was born or where she went to school?"

I went back to the page and scanned it. "All it talks about is a *prestigious New York acting school* and how she went from there to her first big break in *None Are Waiting*."

Declan's top lip curled. "I never liked that movie."

"I've never seen it," I admitted, and as long as I was in confession mode, I added, "I've never seen any of Meghan's movies."

"Really?" He cocked his head and studied me. "How did you get away with that?"

"I saw her every day, in person. In my book, that was enough. Oh, I've seen bits and pieces, you know a clip on a news show, or a scene before she was interviewed by Oprah or somebody like that. But never a whole movie, never on the big screen." I tapped the keyboard and exited out of the page, then sat back. "This is getting us nowhere."

"You know everyone in Meghan's circle. What about Corrine? She strikes me as being pretty sketchy."

"In a completely nonthreatening way. Like I said, Corrine is a little flaky, but I've never known her to be—" As if they'd been snipped with scissors, my words cut off.

"I just remembered," I explained. "Right before I left California. Meghan and Corrine, they had a fight."

"That was a year ago." Declan didn't need to remind me. "What you told Gus about how you feel about getting fired last year applies here, too. Nobody holds a grudge that long."

"Probably not, but hear me out. This wasn't just a fight like Corrine didn't fold the morning paper just right when she brought it up to Meghan in bed. Or Corrine forgot to tell Meghan about a scheduled interview. Corrine did stuff like that all the time and, surprisingly, Meghan never really complained. But that time . . ." Thinking, I squeezed my eyes shut. "It was something more serious than just some slipup. I remember Corrine, she said something to Meghan about how Meghan shouldn't forget the favors Corrine did for her."

"Did she do her favors?"

"Seems to me Meghan was the one doing Corrine the favor. She's not the brightest bulb in the box, and Meghan was hardly patient. Yet Corrine's had her job for years."

"So it sounds like Meghan was the one doing Corrine a favor. But that's not the way you heard it. You heard Corrine say she did Meghan a favor."

"That's right. And the way Corrine said it . . . well, I suppose my imagination is just running wild. I mean, with everything that happened today. But the way I remember it, there was the promise of a threat in Corrine's voice."

"It might mean something." Big points for Declan for

not blowing me off completely. "Let's think about it and see where it gets us. Who else should we be looking at?"

"Well, Ben, I think. Don't they say that when someone is murdered, the police always look at the spouse first?"

"That doesn't mean every marriage is a disaster waiting to happen."

Declan jumped in with the disclaimer so fast, I couldn't help but think he'd been reading my mind. I shifted uncomfortably in my chair. "I'm not talking about every marriage." How's that for a slick way to waffle out of a sticky situation? "I'm talking about Ben and Meghan. He'd come to see Spencer and they'd have epic fights."

"About . . . ?"

"Spencer, for one thing. Ben didn't approve of the way Meghan was raising him. Meghan would say if he didn't like it, Spencer should live with him. Other than that . . ." Thinking, I pursed my lips. "Hard to say. They never had a knock-down, drag-out right in front of me. They were usually behind closed doors and I only heard bits and pieces."

"And both Meghan and Ben have had other relationships since."

I had to admit he was right.

"So who's Meghan's latest main squeeze? Maybe we should be looking at him."

I had to think about it. But then, I'd always pictured Meghan's bedroom as having a revolving door. "There's that What's-His-Name. You know, the guy in the car movies. But . . ." I dismissed the thought with the lift of one shoulder. "I just read somewhere that he up and married some former nun. If anyone was going to be angry about that, it would have been Meghan, not him."

"Okay, then we won't worry about What's-His-Name. Anyone else?"

I didn't mean to, but I rolled my eyes. "Dozens. But let's face it, how many of them are hanging around Hubbard, Ohio?"

"I never expected to see Benito Gallo here."

I barked out a laugh. "I bet Ben never expected to be seen in Hubbard, Ohio. He was on the evening news, you know. Did you catch it? He gave an exclusive interview and talked about how sad he is and how the world has lost a great treasure."

"You think he means it?"

"I think he sees Meghan's death as a great opportunity to get some publicity and no . . ." I looked Declan's way. "Before you can say it, I don't think that would give him reason enough to kill her. Heck, he just married that Italian countess. Their picture is on the front of every magazine and every tabloid around. He doesn't need to get any more publicity for himself."

I'd brought a cup of coffee into the office with me and I took a sip, realized I'd been deep in thought for so long that it was ice cold, and made a face. I glanced at the closed office door.

"Busy out there tonight?" I asked Declan.

"People are disappointed Luigi Lasagna isn't here."

"It didn't seem right having music here tonight, not after what happened to Meghan. We'll have Luigi back next week. So if I go to the kitchen for a cup of coffee, am I going to have to dodge a dozen reporters?"

"More than a dozen. But they're all ordering food."

He was trying to cheer me up with the good news about our bottom line. I was picturing the gauntlet I'd have to get through just to get as far as the kitchen.

Before I could convince myself to have a go at it, Declan popped out of his chair and grabbed my cup. "I'll get coffee, you stay put."

"And when you come back . . ." He went to the door. "You could bring me a slice of pizza."

He pulled open the door. "Your wish is my command! You just stay here."

It was good advice. Too bad I didn't listen. One look at the tables of customers in our overflow area outside the office and I bolted out of my chair, raced into the dining room, and stood at the table nearest the dance floor, where a woman with fine features and silvery hair sat eating with a teenage boy.

"Wilma!" I don't know why I was surprised. Somehow, it seemed as if all of Hollywood had suddenly been transplanted to Hubbard. "Wilma, it is you, and . . ." I looked at the kid who was just about to shove a slice of pizza into his mouth. "Spencer! What are you two doing here?"

"I THINK IT would be best if we didn't look too conspicuous." Wilma said what I would have if I'd been thinking straight. She glanced past me to the packed waiting room, no doubt checking for paparazzi, and with one hand, she patted the tabletop. "Why don't you sit down, Laurel?"

I grabbed the nearest empty chair and pulled it over to the table.

"What are you . . . ?" Like his father's, Spencer's hair was coal black, but he had his mother's fine features, her well-shaped chin, her green eyes, her fine-boned hands. His nose . . .

As always when I thought about it, I was taken aback by Spencer's nose. It was wide and long and so doughy, it gave his face the appearance of having been slapped together by a preschooler with too much clay to play with and no concept that some didn't have to be used. He had a baseball cap on his head, the brim low over his eyes so that most of his face was in shadow.

"I'm very sorry about your mother, Spencer," I said.

He washed down his pizza with a glug of cola. "Whatever. This is where it happened, huh?"

"Yes. I'm sorry about that, too. It can't be easy for you to be here when—"

"We can get another pizza, right?" Spencer looked to Wilma. "I'm starving!"

Her smile was soft. But then, in all the years I'd known Wilma Karlsson—Meghan's longtime housekeeper—I'd never known her to be anything but kind. "You can get anything you like," she told Spencer. "You're a growing boy. You need to eat."

Eat, he did.

While Spencer wolfed down another slice of pepperoni/mushroom/sausage/olive pizza, I scooted my chair closer to Wilma's.

"What are you doing here?" I asked her. "You couldn't have heard what happened to Meghan and gotten here so quickly."

She shook her head. Wilma was a woman of seventy with smooth, clear skin and eyes the color of a summer sky. As always, her hair was pulled back into a severe bun, and every last hair was exactly in place. She'd been born in Sweden and even after years of working in Hollywood, she still had the trace of an accent. It was charming, as were her manners—formal without being off-putting, friendly without being fawning. She was quiet, efficient, and kept Meghan's household running like a well-oiled machine. Meghan could always count on Wilma, and I knew I always could, too. When it came to planning parties, organizing dinners, ordering food, or buying new china, Wilma and I worked hand in hand, and we always got along.

"We had no idea, of course." Wilma's skin was as pale as snow so when two spots of color rose in her cheeks, they were impossible to miss. She glanced at Spencer, but the kid was so busy ogling Inez when she walked by, I got the feeling he didn't know—or care— what we were talking about. "We couldn't have known what was going to happen to Ms. Cohan when we left home on Wednesday."

Wednesday.

The same day Meghan had learned where I was and came looking for me.

"Why?" I asked.

She looked again at Spencer and she lowered her voice. "Spencer heard his mother was leaving and he . . ." Her hands fluttered like butterflies over her plate of untouched pasta. "He wanted to tag along and—"

"Come on, Wilma, get it right." Spencer talked with his mouth full. "I said there was no way in hell she was going to leave without me again."

So Spencer had been listening.

His sneer was a little less threatening than he intended thanks to the pizza sauce in the corners of his mouth. "Go ahead, tell her the whole story. If you don't, I will."

"Well . . ." Wilma cleared her throat. "Spencer asked his mother if he could accompany her wherever she was going, and when she said no, he decided he was going to follow her."

"And I would have done it, too. All by myself if I had to." His top lip curled. "I wasn't going to let that bitch—"

"Now, Spencer." To be sure we hadn't attracted any attention, Wilma glanced around. "You mustn't speak that way. Your dear mother is dead."

"Good riddance." He gulped down the last of his cola and waved to Inez to bring more, and when she was done refilling his glass, he pushed back his chair.

"Going to the head," he said, and he shuffled off in the direction of the men's room.

"Is he all right?" I asked Wilma.

"A little too all right considering his mother's just been murdered." She watched the men's room door slap shut. "Or are you talking about his heroin habit? I assure you, Laurel, he brought no drugs with him on this trip. He's as clean as he's been in the last months."

"I'm glad to hear it." Spencer and I had never had much interaction, and when we did, he always seemed to find a way to reinforce the fact that he was sullen, resentful, and ridiculously spoiled by a mother who provided every physical thing he wanted and none of the affection he craved. His father wasn't much better. Ben buzzed in and out of Spencer's life, and even when he did come and visit, he never stayed long. Every year, he took Spencer "for the summer" and every year, he brought the kid back in less than a week, haranguing Meghan when he did about Spencer's lack of manners, his lack of respect, and his lack of decency.

He was right on all counts.

"This can't be easy for him," I said.

"No. Which is why I told him we shouldn't have even come here tonight. I thought I would call you. I thought if he needed to see the place where his mother died, we might come when it is not too busy. The last thing he needs is to get hounded by the press."

"But you came, anyway."

"He can be so like his mother." Wilma punctuated the observation with a sigh. "It is impossible to say no to the boy, you are aware of that. I knew if I didn't bring him, he'd come alone. It is exactly what happened last Wednesday when Meghan said she was leaving for a few days."

"Did she say where she was going?"

"No. She simply packed up . . . well, Corrine packed up. They packed up and left. We weren't anticipating any trips and Meghan's private jet, it is being serviced. She had to fly on a commercial airliner like any other person. Spencer said he was going to follow her, and I knew he would. Yes, yes, I know, the boy is seventeen. Practically a man. But he's immature. He's never been held accountable for anything and he has no idea how to get along in the real world. I couldn't let him go off like that with no one to care for him so I came, too."

"Were you surprised when you arrived?"

"I was surprised enough to know we were flying to

Pittsburgh. And disappointed that though we were on the same flight, Meghan never realized her son was there. But then, she could be very good about not noticing anyone but herself. Then we drove to a place called Austintown. Meghan and Corrine checked into a Holiday Inn. Can you believe it? Spencer and I waited outside for a while, then we checked in, too, and he staked out the lobby so he could keep an eye on his mother."

"Did he tell you what he saw?"

"He said he didn't see her at all. But then, from what I've seen on TV, Meghan wore a disguise when she came here to the restaurant last night. She must have left the hotel wearing it. Her own son didn't recognize her."

"But why did he want to follow Meghan in the first place?"

"It is like I said, he'd had it with his mother. She was a good employer, you know that, Laurel. Well, you did know it before she turned on you. But I worked for her for years, and I never had any complaints. She let me run the household and she was generous."

True enough. When I worked for Meghan I made more money each week than a month's worth of Terminal profits.

"But when it came to her son, she was a cruel woman," Wilma added. "She never had time for him. She never cared what he was doing or who he was hanging out with. When she should have been giving him hugs, she was throwing money in his direction. The school would call and report trouble, and Meghan would tell them Spencer was a free spirit and they must leave him alone. When he started using drugs, she said it was because he was trying to find himself. I swear, Laurel . . ." Wilma's silvery brows dropped low over her eyes and her voice, always so mild and pleasant, suddenly sounded more like the growl of a mother lion intent on protecting her cub.

"All he ever wanted was for her to notice him. Everything he ever did, he did it to see how she would react, when she would finally pay attention. He wanted nothing more than for her to give him a fraction of the time she gave her career and her lovers and all the drama in her life."

"And she never did."

"It is inexcusable. Look what it has done to the poor child!"

Over the years, I saw exactly what it had done to Spencer, but I'd never realized before what it had done to Wilma.

Maybe she didn't, either.

Breathing hard, her teeth clenched, maybe even she didn't realize she'd grabbed the knife next to her plate, and she was holding on to it like she would have loved to use it as a murder weapon.

.

Chapter 9

I had more suspects than I knew what to do with.

Really. I'm not kidding.

There was Ben, who, in spite of what he said about working closely with Meghan for the benefit of Spencer, could never be in the same room with her without a fight erupting.

There was Wilma Karlsson, who might have been the world's best housekeeper but made no secret of the fact that she thought Meghan was a terrible mother who was shortchanging her son when it came to discipline and good ol' motherly love, and she apparently harbored some nasty feelings because of it.

As much as I hated to even think it was possible, there was Spencer, too. Not exactly the poster boy for a son's devotion to his mother, and he did make it a point to follow her to Ohio.

At the time of the murder, they were all conveniently in or close to a town where they had no business, all with convincing stories, all with alibis.

None of which made me believe any of them.

But wait! As they say on all those commercials, there was even more.

Jason Fielding, for example. Yeah, I know, the PI who'd been looking for me for the last year claimed to have an alibi. That didn't mean I believed him. And who knew what kind of drama had built between him and Meghan in the time he worked for her?

Then there was Dolly . . .

Yeah, I know, just thinking that our newest Terminal waitress might have had something to do with the murder gave me the willies. But Dolly sure did know a lot about Meghan's life, and Meghan's career, and where Meghan had left her rental car. And that couldn't help but make me wonder what else Dolly knew that she wasn't talking about.

Last but certainly not least, there was Corrine.

I had a legal pad on the table in front of me, and I scrawled her name at the bottom of the long list, but no sooner had I written it down than I crossed it out again.

Out of all the people I'd ever seen Meghan deal with, Corrine was the only one Meghan was ever nice to. What reason would Corrine have to kill her employer? She made tons of money in a job she wasn't very good at. She traveled the world. She lived the high life in homes from Malibu to Maui to Tuscany, just as I always had when I worked for Meghan. What reason would Corrine have for wanting Meghan dead?

"Unless the murder had nothing to do with warring personalities or old hatreds. Maybe it was all about money."

I was in the kitchen at Pacifique, just finished with Sunday-night dinner and talking to myself even though Declan was over by the sink putting the dishes in the dishwasher.

"Huh?" was his natural question.

"Just thinking out loud," I told him at the same time I shoved away the legal pad and the less-than-helpful ideas I'd written on it. "Maybe it all comes down to what's in Meghan's will. Gus and Corrine called her attorney. Did Gus say anything to you about what they found out?"

I couldn't blame him for the look he gave me. Quizzical. Amazed. Disbelieving.

"Like Gus would confide in me?"

"I know, I know." I sighed and leaned back in my chair. One of the day's specials at the Terminal had been baked ziti, and we'd brought a portion of it home for dinner and served it along with crispy green salad and a nice Primitivo. I scraped a finger along the rim of my salad bowl and licked the last of the balsamic-rosemary vinaigrette dressing from my finger. "If Gus was smart, he'd realize that we could be a big help to him if he'd share information."

"If he was smart." Declan plucked my salad bowl off the table and put that in the dishwasher, too.

I finished the last of the red Primitivo in my wineglass. "Maybe the problem is I'm just too close to this whole investigation. Too focused on it. If I could get my mind off of it for a while . . ."

When Declan started the dishwasher, then spun to face me, his eyes were bright and his smile was wicked.

"I could help you get your mind off of it for a while. Guaranteed." He grabbed my hand and together, we went upstairs.

DECLAN WAS RIGHT. For the next couple of hours he *was* able to take my mind off murder, and I was grateful (not to mention very happy) by the time he drifted off.

What I wasn't was sleepy.

Careful to be quiet so I didn't wake him, I got up, pulled on my robe, put on the new slippers I'd bought to replace the ones I'd ruined in the ice storm, and left the bedroom. Back when Rocky Arnaud owned Pacifique, she had a library/office of sorts up there on the second floor, and in her honor—and because it didn't make any sense to make wholesale changes to the house when they didn't serve any purpose—I'd put my office in the same room. I'd left the framed botanical prints on the wall and the two chairs on either side of a small table with a stained glass lamp on it. In the center of the room was a large table with a chair pulled up to it, a spot where I imagined Rocky looked over catalogs from seed companies and jotted notes in the journal she kept each year that showed which crops she'd planted, how much she'd harvested, how much she'd sold. Often, I spent time at the table, too, or over at the desk. After a long day at the Terminal, I sometimes brought the day's receipts home so I could enter them in our office management program. Other times, I carried along all the advertisements and mailers that came to the Terminal from places that sold napkins and silverware and dishwasher soap and mops and buckets so I could settle back and wade through them all, compare prices to what our current suppliers charged, and decide if it might be a good idea to make a move.

All of those flyers and samples were stacked on the table in neat little piles, and I bypassed them and sat at the desk. I flicked on the light next to my computer and touched a hand to my keyboard.

My screen popped to life and showed a picture of me and Declan taken at his family Christmas party several months earlier.

He was wearing a charcoal gray suit and a tie with green and red Christmas trees on it. Just for the record, each and every one of those trees was decorated with tiny shamrocks. His hair was tousled, but then, he and his brothers had been roughhousing with the light-sabers the kids had gotten for Christmas. His smile was as bright as the lights on the Christmas tree behind us.

I was wearing black lace, not because I wasn't in the holiday mood, but because the dress with its boat neck and long sleeves was the nicest thing I'd brought with me from California, and my paycheck from the Terminal did not allow for shopping sprees. My hair was pulled back in the elaborate braid Declan's sisters, Bridget and Claire—both of them RNs at the local hospital—had helped me wind into my hair, and like Declan, I was wearing a smile a mile wide.

That day, I'd been surrounded by noise and chaos, kids and wrapping paper and ribbons and food I didn't

have to cook and no one was more surprised than me—
who had always reveled in my aloneness—to admit that
I was deliriously happy with it all.

Happier than I ever remember being on Christmas.

Little did I know when the picture was taken that in
just another half hour or so, Declan was going to propose.

For the first time.

I'd give him that; he was a persistent man. He was
also generous, caring, smart, handsome, funny, and
crazy about me.

What was not to love?

I grumbled—quietly so I didn't make too much
noise—and wondered if it was Declan I was angry at.

Or myself.

What was wrong with me, anyway? The man of my
dreams was sleeping quietly in the next room and here I
was obsessing about all the reasons I couldn't marry him.

Which pretty much boiled down to the fact that I
didn't believe I could make a relationship work.

As if it would somehow prove my determination, I
clicked on the Internet icon and my desktop and that
Christmas picture on it faded away.

For a moment, I sat with my finger poised over the
keyboard, debating about what to do next, where to
start.

There was no use looking at Meghan's home page
again, I told myself, back to thinking about murder now
that Declan wasn't there to distract me in incredibly
interesting ways. I'd read over her website again and
again and knew I'd see nothing there now that I hadn't
seen then.

Instead I looked over the reporting of Meghan's

murder—there was plenty of it—and checked various social media sites to see what her fans were saying about her life and her death. Many of them were calling her the greatest American actress since . . . well, since anybody, and I told myself that someday I'd watch a couple of her movies to see if they were right. I skimmed the messages and wondered where I thought it would get me besides the big ol' nowhere where I already found myself.

Still wide-awake and at a loss for ideas, I sighed, sat back, and checked my e-mail.

There was the usual smattering of junk, and I deleted it without a second thought. I was just about to delete another message from an address I didn't recognize when something stopped me, a little niggling voice inside my head that told me it just might be worth my while to look.

Then again, the subject line was *About M*, and if nothing else, it got my attention.

I clicked on the message.

It was short and sweet, that was for sure—one line with an unmistakable message:

You need to talk to Dulcie Thoroughgood.

"SO WHO'S DULCIE Thoroughgood?"

Declan finished the last bite of his poached eggs (just for the record, he makes the world's greatest poached eggs) and sopped up the yolk swimming on his plate with a piece of toasted wheat bread. "And how did you say you found her?"

"I didn't find her." I finished my OJ, and since he'd

cleaned up the dinner dishes, I took over the task for breakfast. I took my dishes to the sink and came back for his. "I got an e-mail."

"From someone you don't know. You shouldn't have opened it."

"I know. But I did. I just felt . . ." Honestly, I didn't know what I felt, not the night before and not that morning, standing there in the kitchen with Julia Child grinning at me from the photograph on the far wall. I hoped my shrug said it all and because I knew it didn't, I added, "I need to do something. Anything. I feel like we're getting nowhere fast, and I figured it was worth taking the chance."

"And you found out about someone named Dulcie Thoroughgood."

I went back over to the table and pulled out the sheets of paper I'd printed out in the wee hours of the morning.

"I've got a telephone number." I handed the paper to Declan. "But it seems a little weird to just call out of the blue and tell her some anonymous person pointed the finger at her in Meghan's murder."

As if he could look at it long enough to change the basic information on it, Declan stared at the paper in his hands. "Nothing online about where she works? Who she is? How she might be connected with Meghan?"

I pulled over a different sheet of paper and hoped the heat I felt in my cheeks didn't make me look as guilty as I felt. "I logged into the background check site we use at the Terminal to check on new employees and suppliers. I know, I know," I added quickly before Declan could accuse me of exactly what he should have accused me of. "Sophie gets charged every time we do a background check. I'll reimburse her."

"Of course you will." His look clearly said he'd never consider that I'd do anything but what was right. "And the background check told you what?"

"Not a heck of a lot. If she works, her place of employment isn't listed. If she's got family, there are none named. All I've got is the address."

He pursed his lips. "An address is good enough for me."

"You'll come along?"

He pushed back from the table. "You don't think you're going without me, do you?"

Within an hour we were on our way to a little town called Hermitage, Pennsylvania. In case it sounds like a big deal to go from Hubbard to another state, think again. Hubbard is on the eastern boarder of Ohio and the little town of Hermitage, across the state line and into Pennsylvania, was just twenty-five minutes away.

My GPS directed us to an overgrown drive where a painted sign peeked out from bushes that hadn't been trimmed since the day they were planted. And something told me they'd been planted a long time before.

SUNNYSIDE TRAILER PARK.

I consulted the printout from the background check site.

"Looks like the right place," I told Declan, and we drove right in.

From what we'd seen since we'd arrived, Hermitage was a town not unlike Hubbard. Shipshape, simple houses, a smattering of businesses, retail stores, and restaurants. Since it was Monday and still early, it was hard to tell if the community was thriving. Many of the parking lots outside the retail sites were still empty and traffic coming into town was light.

Sunnyside Trailer Park looked like it had been dropped into that neat, unassuming town by someone playing a practical joke. The mobile homes we passed were rusted, and the small lawns outside them that weren't covered with cars up on cinder blocks or kids' bikes and sandboxes and swing sets, had weeds growing on them that were nearly as high as some of the roofs.

"No way we've got the right Dulcie Thoroughgood," Declan said, and I knew exactly what he was thinking.

"No way anyone who lives here could have anything to do with Meghan. That's what you mean, right?"

"Maybe . . ." Declan was driving, and he slowed down enough to check the faded numbers on the nearest trailer. "Maybe we're about to find out."

He stopped the car and even before we climbed three rickety stairs to get to the door, I was sure someone was home; there was a TV on inside the trailer and a familiar voice from it had just called out, "Come on down!"

I knocked.

There was no answer.

The TV was pretty loud, so I tried again.

The front door popped open and I found myself nose to nose with a woman with bleached-blond hair that looked as if it hadn't been conditioned (or washed, for that matter) in a good, long time. She was as skinny as a spaghetti noodle and since she was wearing short, short denim cutoffs along with an army green tank top, her knobby knees showed along with her knobby elbows and a whole host of tattoos.

A mermaid.

A rose.

A star.

Tinker Bell.

I was so busy staring at her right arm and the elaborate red and purple heart with the name *Joachim* in the center of it, I didn't snap to until the woman's voice roused me.

"Whaddya want?"

"Hi." I offered a smile she didn't return and launched into the little speech I'd practiced in the car on the way to Hermitage. "I'm looking for Dulcie Thoroughgood. Are you Dulcie?"

She reached into her pocket, pulled out a pack of cigarettes, and lit one. "Whaddya want?" she asked again, the question seeping out of her along with a long trail of smoke.

I kept my smile firmly in place. "Just to talk. If you're Dulcie."

She had small eyes the color of faded jeans and skin so anemic, I could clearly see the veins in her neck. The fingers in which she clutched her cigarette were bony. Her teeth, surprisingly, were as straight as soldiers, even if they were discolored from the nicotine. She glanced at Declan, who was standing at my shoulder.

"I'm Dulcie," she said. "You cops?"

"We're not." When I felt my smile fade, I stuck it back in place. "But you may recognize me. You might have seen my picture on the news in the last couple days. My name is Laurel Inwood."

The name didn't register. Dulcie continued to puff away and give us the evil eye.

I tried again.

"Like I said, I've been on the news. Well, my picture's been on the news. I don't like being interviewed, but you know how the press can be! They find a way to drag a person into a story whether they want to be there or not."

I gave her time to agree. Or disagree. Or do anything besides just stand there.

When she didn't, I forged ahead.

"But there I was, on TV! Like it or not. And even if you don't watch much TV, I know you've heard the news because everyone's heard the news. The press was talking about me because I once worked for Meghan Cohan."

As if she'd been slapped, Dulcie reared back. After that . . .

Well, after that, I can't say exactly what she did because she slammed the door in our faces.

"So much for that line of questioning."

Since Declan said what I was thinking, I didn't criticize him for it. Together, we turned and trudged down the steps.

"It's pretty strange, though, don't you think?" I commented. "No sooner does she hear Meghan's name than she turns tail and runs."

I looked the trailer over. We'd parked the car facing the door where we'd just had our encounter with Dulcie. To the right of that door was a window and to the left of it, another window. I had once lived in a trailer with a family who'd taken in four foster kids and I knew that window to my left was probably the main living area where there would be a bench built into the wall, a table, and no doubt, that TV that still blared the sounds of applause and cheers and now and again, a commercial for cars or hearing aids or dishwasher soap.

"The bedroom windows are probably at the side," I mumbled, and before Declan could ask why I cared, I took off in that direction.

Just as I expected, there were two windows that faced the side of the trailer next door. They were surrounded with a rhododendron big enough to swallow the entire side of the trailer. I waded my way into the heart of it.

Or at least I would have if Declan hadn't grabbed on to my sleeve.

"What are you doing?" His voice was a harsh whisper.

I shook off his hold. "I just want to look, that's all. Maybe from here I can see what she's doing."

Why I thought it would make a difference, I can't say, but I knew I wasn't ready to just give up on Dulcie Thoroughgood, not when she reacted the way she did when I mentioned Meghan's name.

I slipped behind the rhododendron and closer to the window.

Here, the voices from the TV were louder than ever, and it was just as well because I tripped over a discarded beer bottle and mumbled a curse.

To remind myself not to do it again, I clapped a hand over my mouth, stood on tiptoe, and peeked into Dulcie's bedroom.

There was a twin-size mattress on the floor in one corner, the blankets thrown back and the sheets rumpled. Nearby were three pairs of shoes, a pair of jeans, and a pair of fuzzy bunny slippers.

I kept scanning the room, from the dresser strewn with earrings and necklaces and various pieces of filmy lingerie to the picture on the wall across from where I stood.

Meghan.

She was wearing the fabulous purple velvet gown with a plunging neckline and a narrow skirt that I remembered her having made for the Oscars one year. Her hair was swept up, her smile wide and bright. The picture had been torn from a magazine, full page and in living color.

There was a kitchen knife stuck into the center of it.

Right into Meghan's heart.

Chapter 10

"We need to talk to Dulcie Thoroughgood."

It went without saying, but I said it anyway, just as Declan and I got back to the Terminal.

"She knows something."

"Something she doesn't want us to know." He held the door for me and I slipped inside the restaurant just in time to see that the waiting area was filled with hungry patrons and Sophie wasn't paying attention to any of them. How could she when she was standing behind the cash register clutching a tabloid newspaper, her nose red and her eyes swollen?

By now Declan knew enough about how the Terminal operated, so when I gave him a look, he knew exactly what to do. While I went behind the counter to wind my arm through Sophie's and get her out of there, he grabbed a handful of menus and ushered the first waiting party to a table.

"What's going on?" I asked Sophie even before we were all the way to the office. "What's wrong?"

"It's . . . it's . . ."

Luckily, we got into the office and I closed the door behind us right before she burst into tears.

I put both my hands on Sophie's shoulders, settled her into the chair in front of the desk, and reached over to where we kept a case of bottled water.

"Drink," I told her, uncapping the bottle and handing it to her. "And tell me what's going on."

Sophie took a glug, coughed, sniffled, took another drink. "I know I'm being silly." She wiped her eyes. "I just can't help myself. I love the Terminal. You know that, Laurel. This place is my life."

I pulled up a chair and sat knee to knee with her. "There's nothing silly about how you feel about the Terminal, and nothing's going to change that. Or the Terminal, either."

"Well, I don't know. What if . . ." The waterworks started all over again, and I waited—not very patiently, I'll admit—for her to get it out of her system. When she finally did, she took another drink, blinked back tears, and handed me the newspaper that had been clenched in her hand.

I had to smooth it out to see the main story on the front page, and when I did—

"Oh!" Feeling as if I'd been sucker punched, I plumped back in my chair and stared, my mouth open and my heart beating double time, at the picture on the front page of the tabloid.

The big picture in the center of the page.

The one in living color.

The one that showed the door of the freezer where I'd found Meghan's body and had a bold, blaring headline printed over it.

Death Trap!

It took me exactly two seconds to recover and in that time, my surprise morphed into total and complete outrage.

By way of showing Sophie exactly what I thought of the photograph and the sentiment, I wadded up the tabloid and tossed it in the trash can.

"It's not your fault," I told her. "Not what happened to Meghan and not how people are trying to profit from it and sensationalize it."

She sniffed. "I know. It's not anyone's fault. Not anyone but the horrible person who killed Meghan. But if people see that picture . . . if they think the Terminal is shady or, worse, if they think it's dangerous, it's going to hurt our business. What if it . . ." Her face paled, her breath caught. "What if we're forced to close?"

"That's not going to happen." I was so sure of it, my words rang with confidence. "I won't let it happen, and there's no reason for it to happen. That picture doesn't mean anything. Neither does that stupid headline. It's just some smarmy reporter's attempt at selling more papers. Nobody believes the Terminal is a death trap, and if they do . . ." The very thought made my blood boil. "Well, they're wrong, aren't they? All they have to do is ask the people who've been coming here for years. The people who bring their kids and their grandkids here. And if I see any more of this nonsense in the media, I'm going to sic Declan on them. Let's see how they like hearing from our attorney!"

A watery smile brightened Sophie's expression. She patted my hand. "You have a good heart."

"I don't know about that, but I do know I'm not going to let anyone take advantage of you. And besides—"

A thought struck and my words dissolved.

"What is it?" Sophie asked.

I retrieved the newspaper from the garbage and smoothed it out on my lap so I could poke one finger into the center of the photograph. "How did they get in the kitchen to take pictures?" I asked, but I didn't give Sophie a chance to answer. Before she could, I'd already popped out of my chair, bumped out of the office door, and made a beeline through the restaurant, waving Inez and Dolly into the kitchen.

When the kitchen door swung shut behind them, I waved the offending tabloid like a flag.

"We've got to be more careful," I told them, and George, too, since he was standing over at the grill cooking the day's special, grilled Italian sausage with peppers and onions. "I don't want reporters peeking into the window in the kitchen door and I sure don't want them coming into the kitchen. I don't care what kind of questions they ask or what excuses they give you. I don't care what they say they want to see or what they're trying to find out. One of them could slip and get hurt in here, and then we'd be in real trouble and our insurance rates would skyrocket. Besides, they have no business in here. Dolly!"

When I called her name, Dolly flinched.

"Get some paper out of that drawer over there." I

pointed. "And tape it to the inside of the window on the kitchen door. No way I'm going to give them an opportunity to take any more photographs."

Dolly scuttled by and got to work, and watching her tape the paper in place, Inez shook her head. "It's going to be harder," she said. "You know, to see who's coming and going. To know if we're going to bump into anyone."

"Well, then, we're all just going to have to take it slow and be more careful." I said this nice and loud so that both Dolly over by the door and George at the sizzling grill could hear me. "I don't want to sacrifice safety, that's for sure, but I'm not going to take the chance of providing those jackals with more fodder for the tabloids."

Dolly scurried away from the door and when she passed by, I took the tape dispenser from her hands. "That's it, folks. Thanks! I just want you all to remember to be careful and to keep your mouths shut. We can't take the chance of damaging the reputation of the Terminal. That hurts business and more importantly, it hurts Sophie."

Inez and Dolly both went back into the dining room. George flipped the sausages.

"What?" I asked him.

He glanced over his shoulder at me. "What what? I didn't say anything."

"You're thinking something."

"Thinking and saying are two different things." He grabbed a roll and split it, loaded it with sausage, peppers, and onions, and handed it to me. "You don't eat enough."

I eat plenty. But that didn't stop me from wolfing down the sausage. It was browned just right, and the peppers and onions were perfection, and I told George so.

I was actually thinking about asking for seconds—and digging just a little deeper so I could understand that cagey look he gave me as I finished up our impromptu staff meeting—when the kitchen door swung open.

Inez poked her head in. "Just so you know, there's one of those nosy reporters out here now," she told me. "She's asking all kinds of questions about Meghan and about you, too. And she wants to know if any of us have seen that What's-His-Name, that race car driver."

That's all I needed to hear; I marched out into the dining room. With a tip of her head, Inez indicated a blonde seated alone near the back windows, and I grabbed a pitcher of water and strolled to her table.

The woman was young and pretty, or I should say her lips were well shaped and she had a perfect nose. Not too long. Not too short. Turned up just a tad at the very tip.

I can't really say much for the rest of her face because she was wearing big sunglasses with yellow frames.

I filled her glass. "We appreciate your business," I said, and I meant it. "But I don't appreciate you pestering the staff. We're not answering questions. Not from you or any other reporters."

"I didn't . . ." The woman swallowed whatever else she might have said and curled her hands on the table in front of her. "It's only natural to be curious," she said, her voice low and with the slight trace of an accent that might have been British. "I asked only about Benito Gallo."

"And there's not a thing we can tell you about him."

"He's been here?"

I slanted her a look. "Like I said, there's not a thing we can tell you."

Her lips were plump and red and she stuck out her lower lip in a perfect pout. "It's just a simple question."

"Today's special is Italian sausage," I told her. "I'll send Inez over to take your order."

Believe me, I've worked in the service industry for enough years to know to be gracious, but I committed the cardinal sin—I turned around and walked away just as she was going to say something, then signaled to Inez.

"The nerve of some people." Declan had just escorted another group of diners to their table and I met him just as we both stepped into the waiting area. There was no one around, but I made sure to keep my voice low.

He glanced over to where Inez stood, order pad in hand, at the table where the blonde was seated. "Hey, if they didn't have nerve, they wouldn't be reporters. It's their job to try and wheedle information out of people."

"And it's our job not to give it." I told Declan about my meeting with the staff in the kitchen. "We can't get sucked into the drama. It's bad enough what happened to Meghan here. I don't want to compound it by becoming part of the story."

Declan made a face. "It's already too late for that."

"I know, but—"

"No. What I mean is, it's really too late for that."

It was my turn to make a face.

And his turn to explain.

"I just took a call." He tipped his head in the direction of the phone behind the counter. "From Bartholomew Presky."

The name was vaguely familiar, but I could be excused for not placing it right away. What with striking out on our visit to Dulcie Thoroughgood and coming back to the Terminal to find Sophie upset about the tabloid story, it was no wonder my head was a little fuzzy.

"He's Meghan's attorney," Declan explained.

Of course. Though I'd never had any interaction with Bart Presky, I'd seen him come and go at Meghan's a number of times. He was a man nearing retirement age with a shock of silvery hair, a wardrobe of expensive suits, a Rolls and a driver, and a reputation for building impenetrable brick walls around his clients, their finances, and their business dealings. In other words, when it came to Hollywood attorneys he was number one at the top of the list of every mover and shaker.

"Why would Bart call here?" I asked Declan.

"Because he's coming."

"Here? Why?"

"Well, for one thing, I figured you wouldn't want me to turn down the business, so I agreed to let him rent out the Terminal for this evening."

"Because . . . ?"

"Because, don't ask me how, but he knows that everyone who was close to Meghan is somewhere close by. He's called Corrine and Ben Gallo and Wilma and Spencer, and he wants you to be here, too."

I hated to repeat myself, but . . .

"Because?"

"Because . . ." Declan looped his arm through mine. "He's going to show up here at seven tonight to read Meghan's will."

WE MADE SURE our patrons and all the paparazzi and the legitimate reporters who'd been hanging around all day were gone by six, took in the Italian flag that had been hanging from the pole out front, put out our CLOSED sign, and waited for our guests to arrive.

Since we knew there was bound to be a feeding frenzy if the media caught wind of what was scheduled to happen at the Terminal that night, we had our guests park behind the Irish store, then Declan ferried them over in his car, parked behind the Terminal, and we let them in the back door that led into the kitchen.

Wilma and Spencer were the first to arrive. They were followed by Ben Gallo, who said nothing more to his son than a brief hello, then plunked down in a chair and checked his text messages. Corrine burst through the door just as the clock was about to hit seven.

"The others are in the dining room," I told her, and I don't think it was my imagination that she wasn't listening. Corrine's face was a thundercloud. Her cheeks flamed, her eyes were squinched, her breaths came hard and fast.

"Problem?" I asked when she stomped by.

Corrine didn't answer.

"Don't look at me!" When she pounded through the door and into the dining room, Declan grabbed one of the chocolate and almond biscotti I was just putting out on a serving plate along with cannoli stuffed with creamy ricotta filling, and anise-flavored pizzelles. He chomped through the biscotti and crumbs sprinkled down on his green sweater. "She was acting like that when she got over to the Irish store. I didn't do a thing to offend her."

"Somebody sure did." I glanced over to where the kitchen door still swung back and forth thanks to the hefty push Corrine had given it, then handed Declan the platter of cookies and he took it over to a nearby counter. Because one of her kids was sick, Inez couldn't stick around for the evening, but that wasn't a problem. Dolly had volunteered to help serve coffee and cookies, and she and George were getting everything organized on serving trays.

"Give us fifteen minutes," I told Dolly. "By then, everyone should be settled and you can bring the cookies in."

I took a deep breath and, with Declan at my side, walked into the dining room.

It had been a challenge to engineer this meeting so that prying reporters couldn't peek in or eavesdrop, but between me and Sophie, we had managed. We'd cleaned out the room upstairs that we used to store extra paper products and clean linens, and I scrambled by the tall piles of boxes of linens we'd ferried down to the waiting area and (not coincidentally) put in front of the windows so that no one could get a look inside.

Which didn't mean someone couldn't try to take a peek outside.

We found Corrine wedged between a pile of boxes

that contained takeaway containers and another, taller stack of boxes where we kept the white tablecloths we used only for very special occasions. She had her nose pressed to the front window.

"Not a good idea." I put a hand on her shoulder and she jumped. "You know what Bart told you when he called you," I reminded her. "He told all of us. He'd like to keep this meeting as hush-hush as he can. Otherwise, the media is going to be a nuisance. It's better if no one sees you and knows you're here."

She turned away from the window, but she didn't say a thing. Her eyes narrowed, she merely joined our other guests where they waited in the dining room.

"Sorry for the secrecy," I told them all. "But like I just reminded Corrine, Bart has asked us all to be careful and quiet about this meeting. If you'll follow me . . ." I waved toward the waiting area and beyond it to the stairway that led up to the second floor. "We've got a room set up and we'll be sure to have privacy upstairs."

I will admit, it was not the most conducive of settings, not for the reading of the will of one of the most high-powered women in the country. But Sophie and I had applied more than a little elbow grease that afternoon, and the storage room was clean. We'd topped the table in the center of the room with one of our special-occasion cloths and put a bouquet of fresh flowers in the center of it, lit a candle on a sideboard on the far side of the room, and turned down the light on the overhead ceiling fan so that it was bright enough to allow Bart to be able to read and dim enough to be soothing and lend just the right atmosphere to the somber gathering.

Bonus—there were no windows in the room so no chance of being spied on by reporters.

"This is madness." Ben's top lip curled. "This is where we will talk about dear Meghan?"

"Dear!" Corrine nudged her way around him and faced him from the other side of the table. "Since when is she your dear Meghan?" she asked him. "You haven't had a nice thing to say about her in fifteen years."

Wilma cleared her throat and stood next to Corrine. "You're forgetting that Spencer is here," she said, even though I think we were all pretty sure that Corrine wasn't forgetting that for one moment. "Why don't we all take a seat and relax for a moment so we're ready when Mr. Presky arrives."

Wilma led the way, hesitating only for one moment when Spencer chose the seat not next to hers, but next to his father's.

Ben checked his text messages.

Corrine sucked on her bottom lip.

Spencer tried for a conversation with his father and when that didn't work, he sat back and pulled the brim of his baseball cap over his eyes.

Wilma gave me a small smile. "Can I help in any way?" she asked.

"We've got everything under control."

"Somebody want to explain why we're participating in this ridiculous charade?" Ben plunked his phone on the table and clutched his hands together on top of it. "This is crazy."

"This is the way Meghan wanted it."

The voice came from the hallway and belonged to Bart Presky, who, with a nod, thanked Declan for showing him the way, walked into the room, and closed the door behind him.

"I'm simply following the instructions Meghan left for me," he informed us all.

"She wanted us to meet in some dumpy restaurant?" I shot Ben a look.

He didn't apologize.

"She wanted . . ." Bart set his crocodile attaché on the table and slipped out of his Burberry trench coat. When he saw there was no place to hang it, he draped it over the back of the metal chair in front of him and sat down.

"Meghan was very specific," he said, glancing all around. "She left instructions that if anything were ever to happen to her, she wanted all of you to be present at the reading of her will. I admit, I was surprised it was so easy to get you all together. Especially since Meghan insisted the reading be done as soon after her death as possible. Since we're all present and some of us are paying attention . . ." He shot Spencer a look that the kid couldn't possibly have seen since his hat was over his eyes.

Ben whipped the hat off and tossed it aside and Spencer sat up and took us all in with a glare that reminded me of the way his mother had once looked at me when she thought the tomato bisque I served (which, just for the record, was perfection itself) didn't have enough basil in it.

"As I was saying . . ." Bart cleared his throat. "We can get started if—"

Dolly timed her entrance to the minute. She showed up with the cookies, put the platter on the table, then went back out in the hallway for the coffee tray I had no doubt George had brought up for her. She poured, passed cups, and left, and Wilma took a few cookies and put them on a plate for Spencer. Ben took a pizzelle.

Bart glanced my way and for a second, a smile cracked his somber expression. "I remember what a good cook you are, Laurel. I don't want to eat now, but if you could pack up a few cookies for me to take back to my hotel, I'd appreciate it."

I assured him I would, and with that settled and the moment upon us, the energy in the room changed.

Ben stopped messing with his phone. Corrine fidgeted in her chair, her expression not as thunderous as it was eager. Spencer sat up and I swear, I could see the dollar signs in the kid's eyes. Wilma clutched her hands together on the table, closed her eyes, and held her breath.

I stayed near the tray with the coffee carafe on it just in case someone needed more, still wondering as I had been since I heard about this meeting, why I was part of it.

When Bart clicked open his attaché, we all flinched.

He withdrew a sheaf of papers. "You've heard it all before," he said, glancing at the papers, then at the people assembled. "You know all the preliminary wording, but according to what Meghan and I agreed upon, I'm going to read it, anyway. So here goes."

He cleared his throat.

"'I, Meghan Cohan, being of sound mind and body, do hereby declare that this document is my last will and testament. In executing such document, I hereby declare that:

"'I revoke all wills and codicils that I have previously made, that I am currently unmarried and have one son, Spencer, now living . . .'"

Spencer brightened noticeably.

"'And I instruct my executor to distribute my estate the following way.'"

Bart looked toward the tray Dolly had left and the water pitcher on it, and I filled a glass and handed it to him and, I swear, every last person in that room held their breath while he took a drink.

"'To my former chef, Laurel Inwood . . .'"

It was the last name I expected to hear, and I gasped and sent up a silent prayer. *Not me, no! Please don't leave anything to me!* Meghan had fired me and I'd walked away and begun a new life. I didn't want any reason to feel beholden.

"'I leave my sincerest apologies. I know you weren't the one who talked to the press, but by the time I found out, it was too late.'"

I smiled. "She did have a heart!"

Bart held up a hand. "Not so fast." He went back to reading. "'But just so you know, I wasn't planning to keep you around, anyway. Too many of my lovers spent too much of their time looking at you instead of me. Good luck, Laurel. It was real.'"

I should have been outraged. I knew that was the reaction Meghan expected.

Maybe that explains why I puffed out a laugh.

I put a hand over my mouth when Bart started to read again.

"'To my former husband, Ben . . .'"

The handsome race car driver sat up and pulled back his shoulders.

"'to my devoted housekeeper, Wilma . . .'" She squeezed her eyes shut and lowered her head.

"'to my son, Spencer . . .'" My guess is he would have crowed if Bart had given him the time.

"'And of course to dear Corrine . . .'" She was so excited, she twitched.

"'I want you all to know that the whole of my estate, my homes, my financial interests in my production company, my movie royalties, and all monies earned and accumulated from such will be given in their entirety to the Palangka Raya Orangutan Rescue in Borneo.'"

Chapter 11

The old saying goes, hell hath no fury like a woman scorned.

But a woman scorned has nothing on a room full of people (well, except for me because, like I said, I really didn't care) who thought they were about to inherit a fortune and instead would be lucky if they got a Christmas card from the folks over in Borneo.

Ben, who was, after all, an ex and really shouldn't have expected anything in the first place, stomped out of the room mumbling Italian words I was grateful I couldn't understand.

Spencer bounded out of his chair, then just for good measure, took a swing at the wall. Predictably, that accomplished little more than causing him a whole lot of pain and what looked to be a couple of broken fingers. The last I saw him, Wilma was hurrying him down to the kitchen so she could get him an ice pack and she was talking to Declan about directions to the nearest emergency room.

Bart Presky, I could only imagine, didn't really care a fig about any of this and it was obvious why. He had quickly read the rest of the will and we'd learned that he was serving as executor and as such, got a chunk of Meghan's fortune. He slipped into his Burberry and wished us all a good night.

That left Corrine and me in the upstairs storage room.

And like I said, I didn't really count. The halfhearted apology I'd gotten from Meghan was more than enough to satisfy me, and it went a long way toward reminding me that though no one should have to die the way she did, she was not the paragon being praised in the press. Whoever murdered Meghan, I would bet a week's (pretty small) Terminal paycheck that it was someone who had a beef with her. I'd even go so far as to say the beef was justified.

"So . . ." I was cleaning up the last of the coffee cups and cookie plates and I loaded them onto the tray and looked to where Corrine sat as she'd been sitting since Bart had spoken those ill-fated words, "Palangka Raya Orangutan Rescue in Borneo." She was as still as a statue. As white as a sheet. And quiet as a . . .

Well, bad similes aside, I'll just say that Corrine was not one happy camper.

"Declan's probably waiting downstairs to get you back to your car."

"I . . . I have something I need to do. I don't need a ride to my car." Corrine pushed away from the table and took off for the door.

Before I could even ask where she was headed, I heard her footsteps pounding down the stairway.

"Who lit her shoes on fire?" George asked me when I got back to the kitchen.

"She always was a little weird," I confided, unloading the tray. "Dolly gone?"

"Cleared out of here in a hurry just a little bit ago," he told me.

"Well, you can go, too. I'll clean and lock up."

George unlooped the white apron from around his neck. "And that Mr. Fury, he says to tell you he was going to drive that lady and the kid to the ER in Youngstown. You know, so the kid can get his hand looked at." George grabbed his jacket. "Mr. Fury, he said to tell you that if you want, you can wait here and he'll see you in a little while."

If I wanted?

After a day like I'd had, knowing Declan would be back to get me in just a little while was the best news ever.

With that thought in mind and anticipation whirring through my bloodstream, I made quick work of the cups and dishes, put away the cookies our guests hadn't eaten and Bart Presky hadn't taken with him, and switched off the lights in the kitchen. While I waited for Declan, I'd catch up on some paperwork. I'd already started for the office when I saw a glow from out in the direction of the waiting area and realized I hadn't turned off the lights upstairs. A quick trip up, a quick trip down, and I was ready to get down to business.

I would have, too, if the oddest thing hadn't happened.

I was just sidling my way past the stacks of boxes packed with linens when the room tipped.

Well, at least that's what I thought happened in that split second before I figured out there was more going on here than I realized.

But by that time, it was too late.

The stack of heavy linen boxes rocked, swayed, and crashed over on top of me.

"LAUREL! LAUREL!"

The voice came from a million miles away, not soft and blurred like I would expect of a voice out of the blue, but loud and persistent. My eyes fluttered open, but I couldn't see. The world was dark, closed in. It was hard for me to breathe, and yet I could hear the muffled, desperate syllables of the voice out of the blackness. They were punctuated by words that didn't make any sense.

"Emergency . . . ambulance . . . right away."

This did not seem to concern me, and as if to prove it to myself, I let my eyes drift shut again.

A second later—or was it longer?—a sound scraped close to my ear and light washed over me.

I blinked. "Declan?"

It was impossible. Somewhere in the back of my mind, I remembered that he'd left the Terminal to take Spencer to the emergency room in Youngstown. No way he could be back so soon.

He lifted another box off me and knelt at my side. "Don't talk. Don't move. There's a squad on the way."

"Don't need . . ." I looked from Declan to the ceiling

of the waiting area and realized that I was on the floor on my back. "I'm fine," I whispered.

"Well, that's not a medical opinion, and I'm not a doctor. We're going to make sure." He wound his fingers through mine. "I called you. A bunch of times. And when you didn't answer . . ." I must have been dazed by the impact of that stack of boxes coming down on me; I swore I saw Declan's eyes mist. He gave my hand a squeeze. "Then when I walked in and realized the back door was open—"

"Didn't have a chance to lock up." I remembered that clearly enough.

"And the mess in the kitchen."

My heart stuttered, then stopped. I might not be thinking straight, but I was awake enough to know he was talking nonsense. "Washed the dishes," I told him. "Put away the cookies. Kitchen is—"

"Don't worry about it." When the sounds of a pulsing siren split the night, he lifted his head. "Help is here. You just relax. I'll take care of everything."

"You'll take care of . . . everything." My skull felt as if it had been split in two. My right arm was twisted under me at a funny angle. My left leg was bent and pinned by one of the boxes and had a serious cramp in it.

But Declan was going to take care of everything.

I sighed.

And smiled.

And fell back into unconsciousness.

I'M NOT SURE it counts as dreaming when you're unconscious.

Maybe it's more like hallucinating.

Or imagining.

Whatever it's called, the pictures that flitted through my brain were pleasant ones. Declan kneeling at my side. Declan smiling down at me.

"Declan." I whispered the name, grinned, and opened my eyes.

"Oh!"

"Well, that's a fine way to be greeted." Gus Oberlin glowered at me, popped the last bite of a glazed donut into his mouth, and chomped it down. "I've been here waiting for you to wake up for . . ." He checked his watch. "Two hours. I've been here with you for two hours and all I get is 'Oh!'"

"Sorry." I didn't know if I was, I knew only it was cruel to be so blunt with a man with donut crumbs in the corners of his mouth and bits of glimmering sugar glaze on his tie. "I thought Declan—"

"I practically had to threaten to arrest him to get him out of here. He left a few minutes ago to get a cup of coffee."

"Where am—"

"Hospital." Gus had a cup of coffee with him and he swallowed down the last of it in one monumental chug. "It's Tuesday afternoon."

It took a moment for me to process this news. "I've been—"

"Knocked out cold. And I can tell you, we were worried." I guess Gus didn't want me to notice when the tips of his ears got red because he hurried right on. "Well, Declan was worried, but you know how the Irish are. Way too emotional. And then there's Sophie, of course. She's been pacing this room like a crazy person. There's probably a path worn in the linoleum."

"That's Sophie." I smiled and was glad when I realized it didn't hurt. Well, at least not too much. "What happened?"

"I was hoping you could tell me." Gus plunked into the seat next to my bed and the old plastic and vinyl chair creaked in protest. "Fury says when he found you, you were underneath a pile of boxes."

Yes, I remembered that.

"They tipped," I told Gus.

"Or did someone push them over on you?"

I stared at him. Probably for a long time, because Gus shifted, the chair groaned, and he leaned nearer.

"Did you see anyone?" he asked. "Did you hear anything?"

I sifted through the cloud bank that was my brain. "I forgot to turn off the light upstairs and I went and did it and then . . ." I grumbled my frustration. "That's all I remember."

"It's all right." Far be it from Gus to ever show any actual compassion. He patted the bed instead of my hand, and I decided that was good enough. "We'll figure out what happened and who did this to you."

The words were tight in my throat. "You mean it wasn't . . . it wasn't an accident?"

Gus opened his mouth to answer, but he never had a chance. That's because Sophie tumbled into the room, took one look at me awake and talking, and burst into tears.

Declan was right behind her. He gave her a quick hug and hurried over to my bed.

"How's your head?" he asked.

"Now that you mention it, it feels like there's a herd of elephants in there doing jumping jacks."

His smile was soft. "I'll call the nurse."

No sooner did he move away to do that than Sophie took his place. Her cheeks were streaked with tears, her eyes were red and swollen. Her hair stood up around her head, a spiked halo. "You had us so worried!" She sniffled and smiled and laughed, all at the same time. "We thought you might never wake up."

"We never thought that. Not for one minute." Declan came to stand beside her, his hand on her shoulder. "We knew you'd be fine. Otherwise . . ." He had a coffee cup in his hand, and he waggled it in my direction. "I wouldn't have gone for coffee."

"Coffee!" I might have been flat on my back in a hospital bed with every muscle in my body aching like the dickens, but it smelled heavenly. "If I could get some . . ."

"We'll see what the doc says," Declan told me. "For now—"

I knew what he was going to say. He was going to tell me to close my eyes and get some rest. He was going to tell me to relax. That's why I didn't give him a chance to say anything.

"Gus says it wasn't an accident," I said.

Declan gave the cop the briefest of harsh looks. "Gus should know better than to make an injured woman worry."

"Except she'd worry less if she knew what was going on," I insisted.

When Declan had the nerve to actually think about

it, I pushed myself up on my elbows. "If you don't tell me what's going on, I'm going to find out myself. I'll just check myself out of here and—"

"Okay. All right."

He relented, and I was glad I didn't have to follow through with my threat. Just that little bit of movement made my head spin. Rather than let any of them know it, I pretended to settle back and compose myself when what I was really doing was giving the room time to stop twirling.

Declan hit the button that made the head of the bed rise so that I could see everyone better, and once I could, I also saw that my right arm was bandaged. I wiggled my fingers and gave my wrist a try. All okay there. "All right," I said. "Tell me what's going on."

"It's the kitchen. At the Terminal," Declan told me. "If it hadn't been ransacked—"

"Again?" I was convinced I hadn't heard him right back when he told me this at the Terminal so it was no wonder I sounded so skeptical. "You're kidding me, right?"

Before he had time to tell me he was or he wasn't, the nurse showed up, shooed everyone out into the hallway, and did things like check my vital signs, the size of my pupils, and my reflexes. Before she left, she said she'd make sure the kitchen sent up a tray of hospital food.

I wasn't sure if that was a promise or a threat.

One by one, my visitors straggled back in and arranged themselves around my bed and I pinned Declan with a look.

"You were saying?"

He let out a sigh. "I mentioned it to you last night. You probably don't remember and it really doesn't matter, anyway. I got back from taking Spencer to the ER—"

I'd forgotten. "Is he all right?" I asked.

"Nothing time and a whole lot of ice bags won't cure," Declan assured me. "But I was gone longer than I expected to be, and I called to tell you, and you didn't answer your phone. I tried the restaurant phone and got no answer there, either. I figured something was up."

"He should have called me so I could have gone over to the Terminal to see what was up." Sophie's voice rang with so much conviction, I didn't have the heart to tell her it was the last thing she should have done. If she had, she might have been in danger, too.

"And the kitchen?" I asked.

"First thing I saw when I walked in the back door, of course," Declan said. "A mess. Just like it was the night Meghan went through the place. Cookbooks everywhere."

"Cookbooks." Then, like now, I thought this was significant. Now, unlike then, I couldn't think my way through the problem, not with the way my head was pounding.

"Somebody's looking for something." Gus stated the obvious.

"Except we checked and we didn't find anything. It doesn't make any sense!" I pounded a fist against the mattress. "Meghan was looking for something and now Meghan's dead and someone else is looking for something. Do you think they found it?"

It was not especially encouraging to see all three of them shrug at the same time.

I passed a hand over my eyes. "Maybe it all comes down to what we learned last night. Only, Gus . . ." When I looked his way I made sure not to turn my head too quickly. "You don't know, do you? About the orangutans?"

He threw his hands in the air and let them land against his thighs with a slap. "As if this whole thing wasn't complicated enough, now we've got orangutans to worry about?"

I tried to hide my smile. "Not exactly. But everyone else does. I mean Ben and Corrine and Wilma and Spencer. You see, the orangutans, that's who's getting all of Meghan's money."

"Orangu—" Gus let out a long, low whistle. "That changes things."

"Well, it does if any of the people at last night's meeting knew about the terms of the will." This seemed obvious, even to a woman with a thumping head, but just to be sure, I looked from one of them to the other. "If any of our suspects knew that Meghan was leaving her money to the animal rescue then, yeah, it would only make sense for that person to be angry and maybe decide to get their revenge. We're talking lots and lots of money."

"But if they didn't know . . ." Considering the possibilities, Gus squeezed his eyes into slits.

"What do you think, Laurel?" Declan perched himself on the edge of my bed. "You were there at the meeting. Did any of the others there seem not to be surprised by the news?"

"Well, certainly not Spencer," I said. "The kid was so mad, he punched a wall, and I don't think anyone makes up that kind of surprise if they're trying to fool the other people in the room."

I forced myself to envision the looks of the people around the table when Bart Presky read Meghan's will. "Ben was angry. Wilma was . . ." I thought about it. Or at least I tried. A wave of exhaustion washed over me, I yawned, then put a hand on Declan's arm when I saw he was going to use that as an excuse to stop discussing our case. "Wilma wasn't exactly nervous the whole time. It was more like she was waiting for something. Like she . . ." I was hardly in any shape to come up with some good comparison so I said the only thing I could think of, the only thing that struck me as odd. "Like she was underwater and holding her breath and waiting to get rescued. Then once Spencer reacted the way he did, well, Wilma didn't have time for anything but worrying about him. She jumped right up and went to find ice and Declan."

"And what about Corrine Kellogg?" Gus asked.

"She took off. Said she had something to do. Was her car gone from behind the Irish store when you got back from the hospital?" I asked Declan.

He made a face. "I never checked. I was so worried when you didn't answer the phone, I raced back to Hubbard, parked right at the Terminal, and went inside. I forgot all about Corrine."

"It might not matter, anyway. None of it. If none of these people knew Meghan had cut them out of her will, then none of them had a motive."

"If." The single word from Gus fell flat against the green linoleum.

"And if not . . ." For a few moments, I let them consider the implications, my words floating in the air, much like my brain was doing. "If not, then maybe someone killed her because they figured once she was dead, they were going to inherit. And if not that, then there's another reason someone wanted Meghan dead. And our job is to find out what it is."

Chapter 12

"It's not a good idea."

Really, Declan didn't need to repeat himself. He'd already said the same thing twice. Did he think the third time would be the charm?

To prove it wasn't, I slipped on my jacket. Carefully. My right arm wasn't broken, thank goodness, but it was scraped, sprained, and tender. In addition to making an appointment to see the doctor again later in the week, when I'd left the hospital Tuesday evening, I'd promised to take it easy.

"Going to the Terminal is taking it easy." I put words to what I was thinking.

Declan didn't look convinced.

He didn't look like he was going to back off, either.

Behind me in the kitchen at Pacifique, he tugged a sweatshirt over his head. "I'm coming with you."

"I can see that."

I waited for him to walk outside before I locked the door.

"You can drop me at the Terminal before you go over to the Irish store," I told him.

"You don't get it, I'm coming with you."

We were already in the car—his car since he'd refused to let me drive home from the hospital—and I slanted him a look. "You mean you're coming to work with me?"

"I mean I'm coming with you to work."

I didn't argue. Not at that moment, anyway, because at that moment, I thought it was just a figure of speech.

Oh, how wrong I was!

Declan did, indeed, come with me to work.

He hung around the kitchen while I made coffee and George got the grill going.

He hung around the waiting area while I organized the menus and wiped down the front counter.

He hung around some more when the breakfast crowd showed (a number of them reporters) and I helped out as much as I was able, one-handed, with the crostata (an Italian breakfast tart with a buttery crust) and the eggs and the small bowls of fresh fruit we served with the pancakes and the oatmeal.

By lunchtime, he was still hanging around.

As nice as it was to have him there to help, I was a little perplexed.

I'd just seated a party of eight over at the back of the restaurant where they could see the trains rumble by on the tracks outside and I ran into Declan—literally—when I turned around to head to the front waiting area.

I had to tilt my head up so I could look into his eyes. "Don't you have an Irish shop to run?" I asked him.

"What?" He dared to give me one of those smiles that make my toes curl. "You don't like having me around?"

"Of course I like having you around." A customer at a nearby table asked for a refill on water and I got a pitcher from a nearby tray and took care of it, then went back to Declan's side. "But you're around."

"Having a person around means they're around," he told me, ever the philosopher.

I didn't have time to debate it. There were other parties waiting to be seated and frankly, I didn't care if they were there just because of the publicity we'd gotten from Meghan's murder or that the word had gotten out about our terrific food. A full house meant full coffers, and that thrilled me no end.

In fact, I was so busy acting as the day's hostess, I didn't have a chance to think about Declan's strange behavior.

That is, until after lunch when I pushed into the kitchen (carefully, since the window in the door that led from the kitchen to the restaurant was still covered with paper so reporters couldn't snoop) and nearly slammed right into him.

"Did the Irish store go out of business?" I asked him.

"Of course not. Everyone loves the Irish store."

"Then why aren't you there working in it?"

"Mom's watching the store today."

I set down the empty iced tea pitcher I'd been carrying. "Because . . . ?"

"Because she wanted to."

"She never wanted to before."

"She always wanted to. I just never let her."

"But now you let her."

"That's right."

I bit back a screech. "Why?"

"I wanted to spend more time with you."

This was, in fact, a lovely sentiment, and I would have taken it at face value and enjoyed the warm and fuzzy feelings it stirred inside me if a thought didn't hit like the proverbial bolt out of the blue.

I pointed an accusatory finger at Declan. "You're keeping an eye on me!"

He grinned. "I always keep an eye on you. You're beautiful and I love you."

I wagged that finger for emphasis. "Oh no! That's not why you're keeping an eye on me. Not today. You're keeping an eye on me because you're afraid something's going to happen to me."

"Something already happened to you."

He didn't need to remind me. After a lunchtime of helping out—even carefully—my right arm ached and my head pounded.

As if I was going to admit it!

When I rolled my eyes, I made sure to add a special dollop of *Oh please!*

"That doesn't mean anything's going to happen again," I reminded him.

"That doesn't mean I'm going to take any chances. And you shouldn't, either. Somebody tried to kill you, Laurel."

"They did not!" I was sure of this. After all, if someone wanted me permanently out of the picture, there

were more efficient ways of doing it than dropping a
stack of boxes on top of me. Still . . .

In spite of the fact that we were in the kitchen and
no one was around but me and Declan and George, my
pulse suddenly raced and my stomach went cold. I shot
a look around the room.

Declan took this as the sign of weakness it was.
"See? There! You're worried, too."

"Don't be silly." To prove it, I steadied my shoulders
and marched over to the sink so I could deposit the
pitcher in the sudsy water George had waiting there.
"I'm perfectly safe here at the Terminal."

"You were at the Terminal when those boxes came
down on you. You weren't safe then."

"Amen," George mumbled.

At least until I silenced him with a laser look.

"Whoever pushed those boxes over on me . . ." I
grumbled my frustration. While I'd been in the hospital, Inez and Dolly had taken care of not only getting
all those boxes of linens back in the storage room upstairs, but straightening the kitchen again, too. There
was nothing to wave toward, but I waved, anyway, in
the direction where I imagined the mess had been.
"They were looking for something. Just like Meghan
was looking for something. That's why the kitchen was
all torn apart again. I was in the way. That's the only
reason I got knocked out."

"And if they're still looking for that something?"

As much as I hate to admit it, Declan's question
stayed with me the rest of that Wednesday afternoon.
I'm not a nervous person. I'm not high-strung, and I

have never considered myself a wimp. If I was, I'd never have been able to get through my growing-up years.

And yet something about Declan's warning tapped at my insides when I worked with George to show him how to make a proper Bolognese. He did fine browning the ground beef chuck. I did not-so-fine showing him how to grate whole nutmeg with a Microplane. But then, doing things left-handed was taking some getting used to.

The thought of everything I'd gone through on Monday night—and everything that might happen if my attacker returned—continued to niggle at me as we set up for dinner. When Inez dropped a glass and it shattered on the kitchen floor, I flinched. When it was particularly quiet and the phone rang, I jumped. When Dolly dumped a tray of just-washed silverware, I sucked in a breath and slapped a hand to my heart.

Declan had the good sense not to make a big deal out of any of this, but I knew he was watching. He dogged my steps all day and that, in addition to the games my imagination was playing with me, made me feel like I was going to jump out of my skin.

I reminded myself it was crazy, and I went through the motions, my chin high and my shoulders back, just to prove to the world—and to myself—that I wasn't going to let my fears get the best of me.

It actually might have worked if I hadn't just seated a group of six and stepped back behind the register to catch my breath. While I was at it, I glanced through the day's receipts.

When someone tapped me on the shoulder, I jumped a mile high.

"Oh, it's you!" I stared across the front counter at Spencer. The kid had the good sense to hide from the media underneath a ball cap pulled down low over his head with the hood of a sweatshirt pulled up over it. His right hand was in a cast.

"Looks like we're twins, huh?" To prove it, I lifted my own bandaged right arm. "Except you did it up bigger than I did."

"Whatever." He barely spared his broken hand a look. "That's not what I came to see you about."

These were more words than I had ever head Spencer string together in all the years I had known him, so it was no wonder I was interested.

I glanced around. "You want to talk?"

He looked where I'd looked. "Not here."

I called Dolly over, told her I was going to be out for a few minutes, waved Declan off when he stepped forward, and escorted Spencer out the front door and through the sea of TV video trucks that had set up permanent shop outside the Terminal.

"This way." I gave the kid a nudge in the right direction and together we walked over to Caf-Fiends, the neighborhood coffee shop.

As usual, the two front windows that flanked the door were decked out in cheery decorations—a passel of stuffed dogs and cats cavorting in a garden of paper flowers and teapots on my left, and a miniature hot-air balloon over on the right, its basket piled with one-pound bags of Caf-Fiends' special blend of beans.

We walked inside and I waved to Barb, one of the owners, who was behind the cash register, then led Spencer to a two-seat table in a quiet, private corner.

Now that push came to shove, Spencer fidgeted with the aquamarine napkin on the table that almost (but not quite) matched the color of the walls.

I dipped my head, the better to try and get a look at his face below the shadow of the brim of his ball cap. "So what's up?"

He opened his mouth, but before he had a chance to say a word, Myra, the waitress, came over.

"Oh, it's you." Her top lip curled.

I knew better than to let her get to me. Myra, see, has this thing for Declan. This very unrequited thing. She's been jealous of me since the first time she saw me with him, and she wasn't very good about hiding it.

Which is why I made sure my smile was a mile wide when I said, "Hi, Myra. How are you today?"

Myra's hair was chestnut brown and she wore it in a ponytail that twitched over her shoulder when she tossed her head. "What can I get for you and your . . ." Her gaze slid to Spencer. "You and your date?"

I inched up my smile just a bit. "This one's a little young for me. I like my men older and more mature. You know, like Declan Fury."

Her lips puckered. "Whaddya want?"

I ordered iced green tea and told Spencer that Caf-Fiends had the best key lime pie in town, so he ordered a slice.

Once Myra was gone, he leaned nearer. "I need to talk to you," he said.

He sounded so serious, so mature, I had to keep myself from grinning. "About what?"

"My mom, for one thing."

I put my hands on the table, but I didn't dare reach

across it and give his fingers a squeeze. He was seventeen, after all, and a man. At least in his own eyes. I couldn't afford to scare him off by being too friendly or too patronizing.

"Is this about the will?" I asked him.

His lips puckered. "That was one cheap trick she pulled."

"Are you surprised?"

He actually had to think about it for a minute. "Not surprised, exactly. More like pissed. That's a lot of money going to monkeys."

"And none going to the people who your mom should have cared about most."

"You mean, like Wilma."

"I mean, like first and foremost, you. Then, yeah, people like Wilma and Corrine." If there was a code of ethics for amateur sleuths, I had no doubt one of the first rules was not to take advantage of anyone under the age of eighteen. I was about to break that rule. Sure, I felt guilty. A little. But I also knew this might be my only chance to get Spencer's perspective on the crime. He was young. He was a screwup. And I'd bet anything he knew more than anyone about what made his mother tick.

"Did Wilma or Corrine know about the will? I mean, before yesterday when Mr. Presky showed up."

"I dunno. What difference would it make, anyway? Oh!" I knew Spencer wasn't dumb. Which was exactly why he caught on so quickly. "You're thinking if one of them knew Mom was going to leave them high and dry, they might have gotten mad and killed her."

"I'm not saying it's likely, I'm just saying it's possible."

He swallowed hard. "Even with all that about the money, she didn't deserve to die."

"No. You're right. She didn't."

"But someone . . ." Another gulp and it was a good thing my green tea arrived. When I offered it to Spencer, he took a long drink to wash away the emotion that muffled his voice. When he was done—after Myra brought his pie and I asked for another glass of green tea—his gaze flickered to mine.

"Do you know who did it?" he asked.

"I wish I did. I'd tell the police. Then they could arrest that person."

"Except Wilma, she says—"

"What?"

He scooped up a forkful of the pie and stuffed it in his mouth and if I didn't know better and know how cool and worldly and devil-may-care he was trying to be—just like I'd always tried to be at his age—I would have commented when he closed his eyes and sighed with real pleasure.

I waited until he chewed and swallowed. "What did Wilma say?" I asked him.

He took another bite of pie before he answered. "She says she always knew you were smart. And she says she thinks you're trying to figure out who killed my mom. You know, like a detective."

"Well, I'm not a detective. I work in a restaurant." Sometimes I had to remind even myself. "But I have been asking some questions, talking to some people."

"You talked to my dad."

"I saw your dad at the coroner's office where we

went to . . ." I reminded myself I was talking to a kid. "Where your mother's body is. He didn't have much to say."

"He got married." Spencer must have known that anybody in the world who listened to the news or read the papers or stood in line at the grocery store and saw those celebrity magazines near the checkout would be well aware of this, but I didn't point it out. He was a kid, after all, and I could see this kid was hurting.

"Your mom was married a few times."

He trailed the tip of his fork through the whipped cream on top of what was left of his pie. "That's different. Mom was . . ." I let him find the words on his own. "She was needy like that. You know, when it came to men."

Big points for a kid so young being so insightful.

"And your dad?" I asked him.

"It's not like he hasn't had a string of lovers." They were so blunt, out of any other teenager's mouth, the words would have seemed odd, but Spencer had grown up in the Hollywood limelight and it was just another fact of life for him. "They're always lookers, and some of them were gold diggers. You know, just hanging around because Dad is rich and famous."

"Do you think his new wife is different?"

He finished off the last of the pie while he thought about it. "I only met her once," he admitted. "They made me go to the wedding and Wilma came along, too. You know, on account of how my mom figured I wasn't old enough to travel that far by myself."

"A wedding in Italy must have been very exciting."

"I guess." His shoulders rose and fell. "There were a lot of photographers there and some of the reporters wanted to interview me."

"Did your dad let them?"

"My dad had a car waiting. As soon as the wedding service was over and we took a few pictures, he put me and Wilma into it and sent us back to the airport. I guess . . ." Another shrug. This one made Spencer look like the little kid he was. "I guess once the photographers left, he didn't need me around anymore."

"I'm sorry." I was, so I wasn't embarrassed about saying it. "Sometimes a family can be a tough thing to have."

"You never had one. How would you know?"

"I can tell. From listening to people like you talk."

"Yeah. Well . . ." There was only a smidgen of whipped cream left, and Spencer laid his fork on its side and ran it all around the plate, making sure to get every last little bit of it. "Like I was saying, if you're investigating . . . well . . ." He shoved his plate away and sat back. "I want to help."

For a few seconds, I was too stunned to think of the best way to respond. I guess I decided on a half-truth because I couldn't think of anything else to say. "What I'm doing isn't exactly investigating."

"But I could help." He propped his elbows on the table. "Nobody ever pays any attention to me. That means I hear things. All the time. Sometimes it's stuff I shouldn't hear, you know?"

"Have you heard anything you shouldn't have heard in regard to your mother's murder?" I asked him.

He slumped in his seat. "Not yet. But that doesn't

mean it's not going to happen. I could listen, you know, when nobody thinks I'm paying any attention, when they don't know I'm around. I can listen and I can remember what they talked about. I'm really good at remembering."

"I'm sure you are, but—"

"But nothing." Spencer pushed his chair back and jumped to his feet. "You don't want me to help because you think I'm just a kid and I'm not good for anything. But I'm going to show you, Laurel. I'm going to show everybody. I'm going to figure out who killed my mom. Then you'll see."

"Spencer—" There was no use arguing because he had already walked away and pushed through the front door.

By the time I paid our bill and got outside, Spencer was long gone.

Declan, however, was waiting for me out on the sidewalk.

"Did you see which way he went?"

He knew exactly what I was talking about. "Over to the bookstore. That should keep him busy for a while. Wilma's over at the Terminal. I'll tell her where he is and she can keep an eye on him."

"And I can get across the street by myself," I reminded him.

"Of course you can." He fell into step beside me, weaving in and out of the media vans, stepping over wires, sidestepping reporters, just like I did. "What did the kid want?"

"Validation that there's somebody in the world who cares about him."

We walked back into the Terminal just in time for
the early dinner rush and I immediately got to work. As
frustrating as it had been to try and talk to Spencer, to
try and get him to listen and understand that murder
was not something that should involve a seventeen-
year-old, my time with him had accomplished one
thing—at least when I was talking to Spencer, I wasn't
thinking about the crash of that stack of linen boxes and
wondering if my attacker would have another go at me.

I should have known better than to even consider it.
The familiar rat-a-tat of nerves started up inside my rib
cage again. Declan was there. Declan was watching. I
reminded myself of the fact over and over.

Still, the blond reporter with the big sunglasses who'd
been asking questions about Ben was back and when I
took a pitcher of water over to her table, I couldn't help
but glance around. On a normal Wednesday night, the
Terminal would be full of patrons, friends. Tonight, like
every night lately, it was packed with strangers, and I
wondered which of them might come at me.

Is it my fault a car drove by at that very moment and
backfired?

I jumped a foot. The pitcher slipped out of my hand.
Water poured all over the reporter.

She jumped up and yelled something that sounded
like, "Key a Volvo," but what that had to do with the
drenching she got, I wasn't sure.

Inez hurried over with plenty of dry napkins. Dolly
showed up out of nowhere with apologies falling from
her lips. Sophie took over like the Terminal general she
was, soothing the reporter, offering a free meal, prom-
ising it would never happen again.

And me?

Well, I didn't stick around long. That's because Declan's arms went around my waist and he dragged me from the restaurant.

"What are you doing?" Once we were outside, I fought against his hold, but there was no chance I was going to break it. I kicked and squirmed, anyway.

"Where are you taking me?" I demanded.

"Away from here," he told me. "You need a couple days of rest and relaxation. And I'm going to make sure you get them!"

Chapter 13

With my background, I can't afford to be a snob. Sure, I'd traveled with Meghan to the snazziest places in the world and though I was working while I was there, I still had some time to take advantage of pristine beaches, glorious vistas, and accommodations that weren't just luxurious, they were decadent.

But, believe me, I never forgot where I came from.

Which would explain why I didn't turn up my nose at Erie, Pennsylvania.

Even if I was dragged there kicking and screaming.

"I don't need witness protection," I told Declan when we checked into the Sheraton on the Lake Erie waterfront.

"You do need to relax," was his response.

Though I would never admit it, I think the fact that I walked into the hotel room and immediately collapsed on the bed and slept for an hour might have proved his point.

"Hey, sleepyhead!"

His smiling face was the first thing I saw when I opened my eyes. He held up a cup. "I made coffee."

"Coffee!" I realized it was the delectable aroma that had roused me from my nap. "That sounds heavenly."

"Dinner sounds heavenly." He got the coffee for me and I sat up in bed and cradled the cup in my hands. "It's nearly eight."

"Is it?" I yawned and stretched. "I'm sorry I made you wait."

There was a magazine on the desk, the kind that features articles on local attractions and is found in every hotel all over the world. Declan picked it up and waved it at me. "I've been doing my homework. I thought we could go to the casino."

I didn't mean to turn up my nose—the reaction was automatic. "You're not a gambler, are you?"

"I am not," he assured me. "In fact, I can't think of anything more boring. But I hear there are a few restaurants to choose from there and that the food's pretty decent. What do you say?"

It didn't take me more than a few minutes to get ready, and a few minutes after that, we found ourselves at the town's only casino. It was typical of such places—plenty of neon, plenty of noise, plenty of computer-generated sounds playing jolly little tunes intended to entice folks to play the slots or sit down at the card tables.

Like Declan, I wasn't a gambler, but I did like the energy and excitement of places like that.

Well, except when my head was still a little achy.

"Can we find a restaurant where there isn't too much noise?" I asked.

What we found was a bar with plenty of wood, plenty of metal, and a ridiculous number of big-screen TVs. Fortunately there was a table way in the corner that fit the bill for quiet, and we settled down, me facing the bar and Declan with his back to it.

Our waiter came over with a wine list, and Declan handed it back without even looking at it. "You remember what the doctor said." He was obviously talking to me, not the waiter. "Alcohol does not mix well with concussions. And if you can't drink wine, I won't, either."

We both ordered coffee then looked over the menu and placed our orders. I sighed and sat back.

"See? I was right." Since Declan grinned when he said this, I didn't take it personally. At least not too personally. "You did need to get away. You're finally starting to relax."

I was, and I admitted it. "I didn't even realize how tense I'd been. Now that I'm away from the Terminal . . ." I looked around at the people who sat at the nearby tables, people I didn't have to worry about knocking over a stack of boxes on top of me. "I do feel better. Thank you."

Declan lifted his coffee cup in a toast. "I talked to Sophie while you were sleeping. She said you don't need to get back to the Terminal until Friday. That gives us almost forty-eight hours, and in forty-eight hours—"

Since I leapt out of my chair, Declan never had a chance to finish what he was saying. "Where are you going?" he asked when I took off.

"The bar!"

When he turned in his seat, he saw exactly why.

A bartender had just come on duty, a skinny woman with bleached-blond hair, tiny eyes, and skin as pale as the half-and-half she was just pouring into a glass to make a White Russian.

I slid onto the barstool closest to where she worked. "Hello, Dulcie!"

I would have said she paled when she saw me, but she was already so anemic-looking, I don't think that would be possible. Instead, Dulcie sucked in her lower lip, handed the drink over to the customer who was waiting for it, and said, "What can I get you?"

"I'll have scotch," I said, though I had no intention of drinking it. "The most expensive stuff on the shelf."

She raised her eyebrows and got to work and when Declan joined me, I asked for the same for him.

I paid the exorbitant price of the scotch in cash and added just as much for a tip.

That got Dulcie's attention. I kept my hand on top of the pile of bills, and her gaze slid from the money to my face.

"How did you find me?" she asked.

I swirled the liquor in my glass and lied like a pro. "It wasn't hard. I don't give up easily, not when it's important for me to talk to someone."

"You're a private investigator."

I didn't confirm or deny.

"I don't know nothing," she assured me.

Declan had taken the seat next to mine. He leaned his elbows on the bar. "You mean about Meghan Cohan's murder."

"Ain't seen her in years."

A tingle that bordered on excitement zinged through my insides. Declan and I exchanged looks.

"Any chance we could talk in private?" I asked Dulcie.

She glanced down to where I drummed my fingers against that stack of money. "I get a break in an hour."

"Perfect." I slid the money her way, left the scotch, and headed back to our table. "That will give us a chance to eat dinner. And it will give me . . ." I sat down, still facing the bar. "It will give me," I told Declan, "the perfect place to sit so I can keep my eye on her."

Dinner was good and since we'd passed on wine, Declan said we were owed the calories and insisted on dessert. I make a better fudge brownie than the one our waiter brought from the kitchen, but I wasn't complaining. There is something about chocolate that soothes the soul. In my case, I'd hit my own special investigative Triple Crown—someone tried to kill me, I'd spent a night in the hospital, and now I was hoping to interview a woman who was outright hostile when I recently knocked at her trailer door.

Yes, I needed chocolate.

I kept a careful eye on the time and when an hour was up, I caught Dulcie's eye.

Now? I mouthed the word.

She stuck a hand in the pocket of the black pants she wore with a white shirt, no doubt reminding herself of the whopping tip I'd left her.

And she nodded.

"We're on," I told Declan, and when Dulcie walked around to the front of the bar, then headed to a door marked EMPLOYEES ONLY, we followed right along. We found ourselves in a nondescript corridor with a door at the end of it. Dulcie pushed through it, we did, too, and we were in a back parking lot.

Before she said a word, she lit a cigarette.

"You knew her," I said, and the heck with edging into the conversation. I jumped in with both feet. "You said you hadn't seen Meghan in years. Which means you had seen her years ago. You knew Meghan Cohan."

Since the only light out there was from the security light above the door, it was hard to read the expression on Dulcie's face. If I had to give it a name, it would have been *sarcastic*.

She proved it when she laughed. "I never knew Meghan Cohan. No, sirree. But I knew Tina Moretti, that's for sure."

Declan and I can be excused for exchanging quizzical looks. Just like we could be excused when we both said, "Who?"

Dulcie's laugh deepened to a good old-fashioned guffaw. She laughed until there were tears in her eyes, until she had to press a hand to her stomach, and she coughed, deep and nasty and for what seemed like forever.

When she finally caught her breath, she finished the last puff of her cigarette, dropped the butt on the ground, and ground it under the sole of her black shoe.

She eyed me up and down. "Some private investigator you are. You don't know much of nothing."

"If I knew everything I needed to know, I wouldn't be here talking to you." Notice how smoothly I sidestepped the whole private-investigator subject. "What do you know, Dulcie? And who's Tina?"

"Me and Tina, we went to acting school together."

All right, this at least was starting to make sense. If Dulcie and Tina went to acting school, maybe Meghan was a friend of Tina's. Maybe that's how Dulcie and Meghan knew each other?

"Are you doing any acting these days?" I asked, more because I was trying to be polite than because I cared.

Dulcie's top lip curled over those stained, straight teeth of hers. "The only acting I do these days is acting like I'm interested in the crap people tell me when they sit at the bar and drink. And, you know what? I'm just about as not interested in what they have to say as I am in what you have to say."

She would have pushed right past us and gone back inside if I didn't slap a hand to my shoulder bag.

"I'll pay you," I said, and I ignored the look Declan gave me, the one that clearly reminded me that if I paid Dulcie any more now, she'd only drag out this conversation for as long as she could and for as much as she could.

"I don't have deep pockets." I told her the truth. "But I've got some cash with me." To prove it, I got out my wallet and counted the bills inside it. "One hundred dollars," I said, and looked at Declan.

It took him a second to catch on and reach for his wallet. "I've got one hundred and twenty." He handed the money over to me.

Just to make myself perfectly clear, I clutched the money when I said, "Not one penny more. But you've got to tell me what you know about Meghan, and who this Tina person is and why she matters."

She glanced down at my wallet. "Two hundred and twenty?"

Just so she could see, I counted out all the bills, but I didn't hand them over.

"Two hundred and twenty." I waved the money in her direction. "Start talking."

She ran her tongue over her lips. "And if I do and you end up thinking I killed Miss Meghan Cohan, what then?"

"Did you kill her?" Declan asked the question before I could.

Dulcie lit another cigarette and leaned her back against the building. "Like I said, I ain't seen her in years. So if I ain't seen her, I can't be the one who killed her."

"Then whatever you tell us, it won't be more than background." I didn't want to look as eager as I felt so I took a careful step toward Dulcie. "Give us a break here, Dulcie. You said you saw Meghan years ago, but then you said you didn't know Meghan but you knew someone named—"

Blame it on the concussion. When what felt like a cherry bomb exploded in my brain, I winced and my mouth fell open.

"So you're not as dumb as you look," Dulcie purred.

I reviewed the thought pounding through my head one last time before I dared to put it into words. "Are you telling me Meghan's real name was Tina Moretti?"

Her smile was sly. "Kept that out of the newspapers and all those fan magazines, didn't she? Tina Moretti, a nothing from nowhere. What's it they call it, the wrong side of the tracks? That was Tina's part of town, all right."

"And you two went to acting school together?" I could excuse the twist of disbelief in Declan's voice because I knew exactly how he was feeling. Dulcie did not seem like the type who could read, much less act.

"You ever seen her website?" Dulcie asked. "It says *Miss Meghan Cohan studied at a prestigious acting school.*"

That was exactly what it said.

Dulcie laughed again. "Jack Kolinsky's School of Drama. That's the place. And not even in New York. Girls like me and Tina, we couldn't afford no acting schools in New York. Kolinsky's, in Hoboken, that was more our kind of place. The prestigious school . . ." She put on a hoity-toity accent. "In back of a butcher's shop. Ha! Them tabloids. Wouldn't they love the real story!"

I remembered our trip to Dulcie's trailer and the picture of Meghan on her bedroom wall. "You and Meghan . . . er . . . Tina, you knew each other in acting school, but you didn't like each other, am I right?"

"Are you kidding me? We were best friends! All the time we were getting fleeced by Kolinsky and his stupid school and his stupid acting methods, and after we graduated, too. Then . . . well, we figured our next stop was the silver screen." As if picturing her name in lights, Dulcie threw her head back and spread her arms wide. "We shared an apartment for a while, and I'll tell you what, nobody coulda been closer than me and Tina."

"What was she like?" I couldn't help but ask it. "Before she was Meghan, back when she was just Tina, what was she like?"

One corner of Dulcie's mouth twisted. "Not the prettiest girl, not at first, anyway. Not until she got a lot of work done."

I shouldn't have been surprised, yet somehow, since I'd always known Meghan as the embodiment of ideal feminine beauty, I never imagined her as anything but. "Was that when you were in acting school?" I asked her.

Dulcie nodded. "Tina, I don't think she ever thought anything but that she was the hottest thing in the whole, wide world. But then Kolinsky, he had a way of pointing out people's faults. He's the one who said something about Tina's big nose."

That explained Spencer's schnoz!

"Once she got that worked on, then he'd mention other things bit by bit. You know, her chin or the lines around her eyes. All that sort of stuff. I think he knew, see, the more she got worked on, the prettier she'd be. He knew if she was pretty enough, talent, it didn't matter. Not that he cared. All he wanted to do was wait until Tina was a star, then say that he was the one who taught her everything she knew."

"Only he didn't, did he?" It struck me as odd. "Otherwise the press would have caught wind of Meghan's background and her true identity."

"Paid him off." Dulcie spat out the words. "Just like she did—" When she realized she'd said too much, she gulped.

It didn't take a genius to fill in the blanks. "She paid you, too. The trailer?"

Her nod was barely perceptible.

"Was she still paying you? All these years? Were you still getting money from Meghan?"

"Like clockwork," Dulcie admitted. "Though I was thinking lately that maybe I should ask for a little more. You know, like a cost-of-living raise." Dulcie's grin was sly. "So you see, I couldn't have killed Tina. Why would I? If I did, I'd lose the check I got every month."

So Meghan was subsidizing Dulcie's income. Call me crazy, but that told me Dulcie should have loved the woman, or at least felt less angry than a person who stabbed a knife through the heart of Meghan's picture.

"You were a better actress." I played the jealousy angle, dangling the suggestion in front of Dulcie like a fat worm on a fishing line.

"Damn straight." She dropped her cigarette butt and stomped it out, but when she made a move toward the door, I signaled to Declan. While he stepped up behind her to stymie her exit, I ruffled my fingers through the bills in my hand.

Dulcie ignored Declan and looked at the money.

"So how did Tina turn into the star and you didn't?" I asked her.

"Well, her looks, for one thing, thanks to all that cosmetic surgery. I couldn't afford it, but then, I wasn't sleeping with every rich guy I happened to meet."

"You were working hard, working at your art."

"You bet I was. Paid my dues, too, in every crappy neighborhood drama group, and every crappy summer stock theater, and in a couple productions so off-Broadway you'd need a map to even find the Great White Way from there."

"Did Tina?" Declan wanted to know.

She nodded begrudgingly. "She took a couple small parts here, a couple small parts there. But Tina, she always said she shouldn't have had to bother with walk-ons. She said she was destined for bigger things. Oh, she was destined, all right, wasn't she? Destined to get smashed over the head and left in some freezer. Tina the Snowman!" Dulcie thought this was pretty funny. That would explain why she laughed.

"But you were still friends all the time you two were working to get noticed? You were still roommates?" I asked.

"Oh yeah. I mean, in the great scheme of things, sure, she had more rich boyfriends than me, but I ended up getting more roles." A slow smile brightened Dulcie's face. "That really ate at her. Me, getting the calls from the casting directors." As quickly as it came, her smile faded. "That's what finally got to her. That's why she did it. Okay, so I wasn't going to be the next Marilyn Monroe, but I did a couple commercials, and I got a couple nibbles. I had a part on *Law & Order*, you know. I mean, I didn't have any lines 'cause I played the dead hooker they found in an alley behind a bar, but it was a break. It was a big break. And it bugged the heck out of Tina!"

"But you have a picture of her on your bedroom wall with a knife stabbed through her heart, and I can't say for sure because I was just her chef, after all, and I didn't have any reason to go through Meghan's private rooms, but my guess is she sure didn't have a picture of you anywhere in her house, not with or without a knife through your heart."

Dulcie chewed her lower lip. "If it wasn't for me, Tina never woulda got that part in *None Are Waiting*."

"The picture that made her a star?" Declan's curiosity was only natural.

Dulcie nodded. "Bet when she gave interviews, she never mentioned how it really happened. Bet when she was on TV, she never told the story, not the real story. Bet she smiled and simpered and batted those eyelashes of hers and pulled back her shoulders to show off her bought-and-paid-for breasts and she never once told the truth about how she landed that role."

"But you know the truth?" I could feel it in my bones and in the aura of resentment and anger around Dulcie. "What really happened, Dulcie? Do you remember?"

She barked out a laugh. "July 22, 2001. You bet I remember. Like it was yesterday. That was the day Tina showed up for the screen test for *None Are Waiting*. She knocked the socks off the casting director, the producer, the director, her costars. They said she was made to play Sheila and they offered her the role on the spot. And yeah, that film, that made her career. She knew it was gonna, too, that's why she changed her name."

"That is the story Meghan tells, but it's not the truth?"

"By that time, she was married. To that What's-His-Name, that Italian with the big ego and the big mouth. They was living in an apartment over in Brooklyn, and to read about their marriage now, you'd think it was all a bed of roses. But it wasn't. They weren't married that long and Tina already had a kid and she was miserable. She came over one day to moan and complain about her husband, and her bawling baby, and how her career was going nowhere fast. And me . . ." Even now, Dulcie couldn't believe the whims of fate. She shook her head. "I stepped out of my apartment long enough to go answer the door when the Chinese we ordered showed up. My phone rang, and when I got back inside, Tina, she tells me it was a wrong number. Only it wasn't. I didn't find out until years later. It was no wrong number. It was the casting director inviting me to try out for the part of Sheila in *None Are Waiting.*"

I sucked in a breath. "She didn't tell you? She—"

"Went in my place. Showed up there on July 22, 2001. You want to know why I have that picture of Tina on my wall with the knife in it?" Dulcie plucked the money out of my hand and whirled to go back inside. "Because Tina, she sweet-talked her way into the screen test that should have been mine, and she became a star because of it. Am I glad she's dead?" Dulcie's smile was positively creepy. "You bet I am. But why should I kill the golden goose? Besides, I couldn't have. I was working here the night Tina was killed."

Chapter 14

"It's all very interesting, but it's not exactly helpful. And it's not really surprising, is it?"

The next morning across the breakfast table at a greasy spoon that served better-than-average coffee and worse-than-average pancakes, Declan looked up from his bacon and eggs.

"You mean about Meghan? About her taking advantage of Dulcie?" he asked.

"'Taking advantage' is putting it mildly, don't you think? What she did to Dulcie was downright . . ." The thought sat uneasily with me, and I shook my shoulders. "What a rotten thing to do!" I swirled my spoon through the fresh cup of coffee our waitress had just brought over. Yes, it was my third of the morning. Like I said, it was really good coffee. "I always knew Meghan had an ego a mile wide, but lying to cheat Dulcie out of the role of a lifetime? That's as low as low can get. No wonder Dulcie hated Meghan."

"Too bad about her alibi, huh? She'd be the perfect suspect."

Too bad, indeed.

The night before, after Dulcie went back to work behind the bar, Declan and I found her supervisor and talked to him. Dulcie had, indeed, been on duty the night Meghan was killed. All night, in fact, because a pipe had burst in the kitchen and Dulcie had worked until the next morning helping with the cleanup. Just for the record (not that I'm paranoid or anything) I'd also asked about the night Meghan's will was read and I was attacked. Yep, Dulcie had been at the casino that night, too.

"Maybe she paid a hit man," I said, and took it back almost immediately. "I know, she hardly looks like she could afford one."

"Unless she's been banking the money Meghan sent her every month."

"To pay for Meghan's murder." Okay, it wasn't funny. I mean, murder never is. But there was a certain irony in the situation that made me smile.

At least until I thought about what it all meant.

"We're nowhere," I grumbled.

"We're somewhere," Declan countered. "We've eliminated a suspect."

"Great." I pushed aside the dish where my half-eaten pancakes sat looking as flat and mushy as I felt. "We need a breakthrough, a super-duper clue, a—"

My phone rang.

"Maybe that's it," Declan suggested.

As much as I doubted it, I answered.

"We gotta talk." The voice on the other end of the phone bumped to the staccato rhythm of excitement. Or maybe it was nervousness. "Now."

"But, Spencer, I'm in—"

"I'm at the restaurant. You're not here. We gotta talk. Where are you, Laurel?"

"Where am I?" I signaled to our waitress for our check. "I'm on my way, that's where I am."

TWO AND A half hours later, I pushed through the front door of the Terminal and had a quick look around.

No Spencer.

My shoulders sagged, and the adrenaline that had fueled the world's quickest pack-up-and-get-back-home trip ever didn't just drain out of me, it washed away completely and left me feeling limp.

Not unlike my breakfast pancakes.

"You're not supposed to be back here yet." When Dolly zipped by I couldn't tell if she was relieved to see me or if she was disappointed I'd shown up again so soon after I claimed I was taking time off. She bobbled the tray she was carrying, righted it, recovered. "I thought you were out of town resting."

I leaned over to have another look into the overflow seating area outside the office and the kitchen. No Spencer. "Has anyone been here looking for me?"

"You mean the kid?" Dolly, of course, knew exactly who *the kid* was, but I gave her credit for playing it cool. There were people around, and some of them were reporters.

She tipped her head toward the office. "Waiting for you," she said. "And eating us out of house and home."

As soon as I opened the office door, Spencer looked up from the pizza he was halfway through finishing. He glanced over my shoulder. "You alone?"

"If you're talking about Declan, he's parking the car."

"Good." Spencer took a glug of Coke. "I don't want anybody to know this. Anybody but you."

On the phone, I had sensed the nervous tension in his voice, but seeing Spencer really brought his jitters home. He lifted a piece of pizza to his mouth, decided he didn't want it, dropped it on the plate. He squirmed in the chair in front of the desk, crossed his legs, uncrossed them.

"What's wrong?" I asked him.

Again, he looked toward the door.

"Nobody's going to disturb us," I assured him. "Nobody's going to eavesdrop."

When he lowered his chin, raised his eyebrows, and looked at me as if to challenge me with *Really?* he looked so much like his mother (in spite of his big nose), I caught my breath.

"I might be a kid, but even I'm not that dumb." There was a tabloid newspaper on Sophie's desk, and he handed it to me.

Reading the headline, my heart thumped. "The will? They have the story about the will? Somebody knows about—"

"The monkeys, yeah." Spencer plucked the tabloid out of my hands and tossed it on the floor. "So I get to go back to school and have every kid there know that all the money that should have been mine is going to monkeys in some place I can't even pronounce."

"They're apes, actually." I slipped into the guest chair. "And the money probably doesn't matter, anyway. You won't be broke. You'll never be broke. Your dad has plenty of money."

"Yeah, well, a mother who liked animals more than she liked me still makes me look like a loser." He pouted the way only a seventeen-year-old can.

"And it makes me wonder . . ." I retrieved the newspaper and glanced over it again. "How did the story become public so quickly?"

The question wasn't worth a two-shoulder shrug, so Spencer used just one. "Nobody said we couldn't talk about it."

"Did you talk to anyone about it?"

"Who am I going to talk to in this dumpy town?" Spencer dismissed my question altogether. "Besides, that's not what I need to talk to you about." He leaned forward, his elbows on his knees. He sat back, wriggled, cleared his throat.

"You should know, it doesn't mean anything," he said.

I could be excused for not catching on fast enough. "It . . . what's the *it* that doesn't mean anything?"

"What I'm going to tell you." He threw his left hand in the air and let it slap back down on his lap next to his hand with the cast on it. "I wouldn't even be telling you at all except that we should share information, seeing as how we're both investigating."

"Like I told you, I'm not investigating," I told him. "And you shouldn't be, either."

"Yeah, well, I have been." He picked up a slice of pizza, then slapped it back down on the plate. "If I was smart, I'd just keep my mouth shut. But . . ."

"But . . . ?"

"My mom . . ." When his voice broke, Spencer cleared his throat. "My mom didn't always pay a whole lot of attention to me. Not that I blame her," he added quickly in case I got the idea that he cared. "She was busy. And important. She had a lot of stuff to do."

"And a lot of people who depended on her, what with her production company and the movies she directed, and the charities she worked so hard to raise money for."

"Yeah, like I said, she was busy. So, I mean, it's not like in the movies where some kid doesn't know what to do and some adult takes an interest and says something stupid and kind like *Believe in yourself* or *Follow your heart*. Because in real life, adults, they don't say stuff like that."

"Some of them do," I assured him. "Not always to kids like you, and not always to kids like the kid I was. But there are good adults out there."

"Are you one of them?"

His question caused a tight ball of emotion to form in my throat. "I try to be," I assured him. "It doesn't always work."

One corner of his mouth pulled tight. "I know what you mean. But you . . . when that stupid story about me being a junkie showed up in the tabloids, my mom said you were the one behind it, but I know that wasn't true."

"You're right. It wasn't. But how do you—"

"I did it." He sat up and pulled back his shoulders. "I'm the one who tipped off that reporter."

It took a moment to process what he was saying. "You're the one who broke the news about your drug addiction?"

There was no way in the world I could be any dumber than I was.

At least that's what the look Spencer gave me said.

He shook his head. "Don't you get it? It wasn't true. I made the whole thing up."

"Because . . . ?"

"Because I wanted to see what my mom would do about it. And what she did . . ." His shoulders sagged. "Sorry she fired you. I was just trying to get her to notice me."

After what I'd learned from Dulcie, I felt a little funny defending Meghan. "Well, she did notice. Of course she noticed. Didn't she put you in a rehab program?"

"That was Wilma," Spencer told me. "I stayed exactly two days. That was enough for me. I told my counselor the truth. I told Wilma the truth. My mom . . ." His lips puckered. "I didn't set her straight. Why bother?"

Honestly, I would have pulled the kid into a hug if I knew I could get away with it and not embarrass him to death.

Instead, I cleared away the tremor in my voice. "Is that what you wanted to talk to me about?"

"No. I mean, not exactly. See, I was thinking about how things are like that in movies. You know, like I said, when a kid needs advice and some smart adult gives it to him. And I was thinking that even if I didn't want to tell you something, I should tell you because, you know . . ." He looked away. "I need to follow my heart."

My voice clogged all over again. "That's very brave."

"It isn't, not really. Because it's just you and me talk-ing and, like I said, what I'm going to tell you, it doesn't really mean anything. But I found out yesterday, see, and last night, I figured I just wouldn't tell anyone on account of how bad it was going to look if I did. And the funny thing is, I couldn't sleep. Not all night long."

He wrinkled his nose, thinking his way through this baffling turn of events.

"Is that what they call conscience?" he asked.

I dared to lean nearer. "It is. And when you're ma-ture enough to listen to your conscience, that's what they call growing up."

"It's not much fun."

"It can be," I assured him. "But not all the time. Sometimes, it's all about doing what's right. What's the right thing you know you have to do, Spencer?"

"Like I told you, I was investigating." He looked at me, then quickly looked away, obviously gauging my reaction. "And before you get all bent out of shape and start talking about how dangerous something like that is, let me tell you that it's not like I was out poking around anyplace I shouldn't be or anything. I was back at the hotel where me and Wilma are staying. It's kind of like a suite, you know? I have a bedroom and Wilma has a bedroom and there's a door in between that we can open. My mom . . ." Just thinking about it made him shake his head in wonder. "I bet she never dreamed she'd ever stay in a place like that."

I thought back to what we'd learned about Tina Moretti from Dulcie and wondered if that was true.

"So you were at the hotel." I got Spencer back on track. "And what happened?"

"It was Wilma. She was on the phone and—" Spencer popped out of his chair. "It doesn't mean anything," he said, his voice high and tight. "I shouldn't have bothered you. I was just messing around, that's all, pretending to be a detective and listening to her on the phone, and what I heard, it doesn't matter because it doesn't mean anything."

From the note of despair in his voice, I knew I was going to lose Spencer, and whatever information he might have. I had to move slowly, cautiously. I forced myself to sit back and I can't say if I looked casual or not. I can say only that I sure tried.

"You know, I've solved a couple of murders," I told Spencer.

He didn't want to be interested, but he couldn't help himself. His eyes lit up. "You said you weren't a detective."

"Well, I'm not. Not really. But that doesn't mean I can't watch people. And listen. And pay attention to what's happening around me. That's what detectives do, right?"

"In the movies, they have car chases and gun battles."

"But you know the movies aren't real. In real life, solving crimes isn't about chases and shooting, it's all about thinking, all about using your head." I should have known better than to knock my index finger against my skull so soon after having a head injury, but it seemed like the perfect way to demonstrate and at least it didn't hurt. Well, not too much.

"What I do is look at a situation and evaluate it. I use logic and reasoning. You learned about that in school, right?"

He made a face. "I don't always pay attention in school."

I laughed. "I never did, either. And you know what, I'm sorry now that I didn't listen better. Everything I've learned about being a detective, I've had to learn on my own. It hasn't been easy."

"But they don't teach you how to be a detective in school."

"No, but they teach you how to think. And what detectives do is think. Like you were thinking yesterday back when you were at the hotel and you heard Wilma on the phone. Now, as a detective, what you need to do is step back and think about that incident. You need to consider what you saw and what you heard. You need to spend time thinking about what it is that kept you awake all night. You remember everything you saw and heard, right?"

He nodded.

"Well, the next step is to evaluate it all. Then you make decisions based on what you found out. Only when you're just starting out as a detective, you can't always do all that on your own. You need a sidekick."

"You mean like"—he ran his tongue over his lips—"you?"

"Well, I'd be happy to be your sidekick if you'll have me. But only if you'll be mine."

"Really?" He sat on the edge of his chair. "You'd do that? For me? You'll let me join in on the investigation?

Wow! We have a lot we need to talk about. Like code words, you know?"

I didn't, and I admitted it.

It was obvious that in Spencer's eyes, I was really old, or really lame. Or both.

His sigh pretty much communicated that loud and clear.

"When we talk to each other, you know, on the phone," he said. "We should have a way of letting each other know if the coast is clear, or if there's a problem."

"You mean like if the coast is clear, we should say the coast is clear."

This time I earned an eye roll for my efforts.

"I think we need to be more subtle than that." The kid sure had a flare for the dramatic. But then, his mother was no slouch in that department. "So let's say . . ." Thinking, he squinched his eyes shut. "If everything's okay, we'll say *Rabbit*. Or we'll put it in a text. Can you remember that?"

I felt a little weird getting directions from a seventeen-year-old, but I knew I had to play along.

"Rabbit." I nodded. "Got it."

"And if there's a problem . . . if somebody's got their eye on us, or if somebody's following us or something, then we'll say . . ."

"Ostrich," I suggested.

"That's good." When Spencer grinned, I realized it was one of the few times I'd seen the kid smile. That made the whole James Bond, secret-code thing worth it. "Since neither one of us would probably say *rabbit* or *ostrich* just talking everyday talk, it's perfect. So that's it. We're partners. So . . . now . . ." He pulled his phone out of his pocket. "Now we can keep track of each other and we'll know where we are in our investigation."

"You mean, like I'll call you and you'll call me?"

Spencer shook his head. I was, apparently, just not with it.

"Like with this app." He brought it up on his phone. "Place My Pals. It will let me see where you are, and you can see where I am, too. Go ahead." He motioned for me to get out my phone. "Add it to your apps."

I can't say I was convinced of the benefits, but I did as I was instructed.

"There." For Spencer, that's all it took to make the whole thing official. "We're partners, you have to tell me everything." With a wave of his left hand, Spencer urged me to spill the beans. "What do you know so far?"

"Not very much. I do know there's an old friend of your mother's in the area, a woman named Dulcie Thoroughgood. Do you remember your mom ever talking about her?"

He shook his head, and I wasn't surprised. Other than having some nameless accountant write that check to Dulcie every month, I was sure Meghan never spared her a thought. I was also sure, though, that doling out this little tidbit of information would make me look like I was willing to share. Just like I hoped Spencer would be.

"Did Dulcie kill my mom?" he asked.

"I don't think so. Which is why I'm still collecting information. If you have any, I'd love to hear it."

"Even if it doesn't mean anything?" His expression was pained.

"Even if it doesn't mean anything."

He drew in a long breath and let it out slowly. "So here's the thing. We were at the hotel, me and Wilma. And she said I needed to relax and she made me some hot chocolate. What's with her? She always thinks that hot chocolate, or soup, or cookies . . . she always thinks something like that will make me feel better."

"She cares about you."

"Yeah, well, maybe." He swallowed hard. "But last night, what she cared about after I was in my room and she thought I was asleep was that money she thought she was getting from the will, the money she didn't get because none of us got any."

I sat up. "Really? What did she say?"

"She wasn't talking to me. She was on the phone. I don't know who she called, but she was plenty steamed."

"About the money."

He nodded.

"She told the person on the phone that she was sure she was going to inherit a bundle. She said Mom owed it to her and she couldn't believe the—" The tips of Spencer's ears got red. "I'm not a kid and I know what the word means, but I'm not going to repeat it, not when I'm talking about my own mother."

"You don't have to," I told him.

"She said something about a movie and an . . . an investment. Yeah, that's what she called it. And I couldn't hear everything really clear, so I got out of bed and I opened my door just a crack. You know, like a detective would. And Wilma, she was telling the person on the other end of the phone that a couple years ago, she invested all the money she had into *Guinevere*, you know, that big epic movie Mom was all set to make, the one that flopped because that actor who was going to play King Arthur ended up in jail for tax fraud right when they were set to start filming and Mom's production company lost a ton of money because of it."

"A ton of money that came from investors like Wilma," I said.

Spencer nodded. "That's right. That's what Wilma told the person on the phone. Wilma, she said she thought that movie was a sure thing, and that she lost five hundred thousand dollars in the deal and that it was all the money she had saved up for her retirement."

"Was she angry?" I asked.

One corner of Spencer's mouth pulled into a cynical sneer. "What do you think?"

"Did she say she was angry at your mom before your mom . . ." Call me a wimp, I just couldn't look the kid in the eye and say the words *before your mom was murdered.* "Before your mom came to Hubbard?"

"She said she was more than angry. She said . . . well, that's what I need you to understand, Laurel. Because, see, Wilma was mad, first because she lost all that money and then, because once Mom was dead, she figured she'd get it back. You know, that Mom would make sure something was left to her in the will. So you can't blame her for being pissed all over again, like it just happened yesterday. But she said . . ." Spencer pulled in a breath and let it out with a whoosh. "She said that Mom getting murdered, it was the best thing that ever happened, that my mom deserved it. But honest, Laurel, I don't think she could have meant anything. I mean, anything other than that she was mad and she was getting her feelings out in the open. That's what my therapist tells me I need to do if I'm ever feeling mad. She says I should express myself, I shouldn't hold anything in. So that's why I'm telling you all this, so I can express myself. But you've got to understand, Laurel, you know her. You know Wilma wouldn't kill anybody."

Chapter 15

"You don't really think she did it, do you?"

It was a logical question so I gave Declan the logical answer. "Of course not. But don't you get it? That's exactly why I need to talk to Wilma. I've got to prove she didn't do it. Before Gus somehow gets wind of all this and thinks he's found his killer."

"How well do you know her?"

We were standing in the kitchen at the Terminal, Declan over by the sink and me at the grill because George was taking a break and had gone outside to get some air that wasn't heavy with the scents of the basil and fennel we'd be using in the shrimp and lemon pasta we were featuring that evening. Unlike George, who would wear fried-onion aftershave if there were such a thing, I happen to love the scent of fennel, and I drew in a deep breath and flipped the two burgers sizzling in front of me. "We worked side by side for six years."

"And . . . ?"

"And you learn a lot about a person, working with them."

"But you didn't know she lost all her money in a lousy investment and blamed Meghan for it."

"No." My voice sank along with my spirits. "I didn't know anything about that."

"It's a strong motive. If Wilma was angry . . ."

I remembered what Spencer had told me. "She was, and who can blame her?"

"Then she might have decided revenge was the only possible solution to an impossible problem. Sure, it wasn't Meghan's fault the film never got made, but it was her production company behind it. Or let's look at it another way. Maybe now that all her money's gone, Wilma figured that once Meghan was dead, she was sure to inherit. Wilma might have seen murder as the only way to get back her life savings."

"It makes sense."

"But?"

I gave the burgers another flip before I scooped them off the grill and put them on thick kaiser rolls. Not exactly an Italian dish, but burgers were always popular so we kept them on the menu, no matter what ethnic cuisine we were featuring. Done plating, I went to the front of the kitchen and rang the bell that alerted the waitstaff to the fact that an order was ready for pickup.

Once Inez had come to the kitchen and left with the burgers, I crossed my arms over my chest and leaned back against the stainless counter. "But I don't know,"

I admitted. "But I'm going to find out. I have to. I've got to clear Wilma's name. She's all Spencer has and if she goes down for this crime, it will break the kid's heart. As soon as George gets back—"

He picked that moment to walk in through the back door, and I unlooped the white apron from around my neck and handed it to Declan.

"I'm heading out to see Wilma," I told him.

"Sure you are. And I'm coming with you."

A SHORT WHILE later we were in Austintown. I convinced Declan I might have better luck tackling Wilma alone so he waited in the car while I went to Wilma's room. I can't say if she was surprised to see me. I know Spencer wasn't.

"Rabbit," he said, barely controlling a conspiratorial smile when he stepped around me and went through the adjoining door and into his room.

Wilma carefully folded a gray cardigan and set it on top of the suitcase open on the couch.

"You're leaving?"

She sailed back to the bed and brought over a pile of clothing. "There doesn't seem to be any reason for us to stay. Spencer wanted to follow his mother. He did, and . . ." She sighed and pressed the clothes close to her chest. "Well, nothing good has come of it, has it? The poor boy will live the rest of his life with the memory of his mother's murder."

"It wouldn't be any different if he was back in California."

She set the clothes in the suitcase. "Maybe not."

"And it wouldn't have changed the reading of Meghan's will. Or the terms of it."

At her sides, Wilma's hands curled into fists. "No. We would have been obliged to be present for that, wouldn't we? No matter where the will was read. Poor Spencer, subject to such humiliation!"

"I guess he's not the only one. Especially now that the story has gone public and the world knows what Meghan wants done with all her money."

Wilma stooped to retrieve a pair of powder blue slippers. She tucked them into her bag. "I'll get over it," she assured me, and slid a look at Spencer's door, which, I noted, was closed—but not all the way. "I'm not so sure about him. A child does not easily forget a parent's cruelty."

"Just like an adult doesn't forget when they lose a whole lot of money on a movie that never got made."

Wilma froze. But only for a heartbeat. Then her shoulders rose and fell. "How did you find out?"

"Does it matter?"

"No. Just like the money no longer matters. I thought once Meghan was dead, my troubles would be over and my retirement fund would be infused with my inheritance. I was wrong."

"And angry."

"About the movie? Or about the money I didn't inherit?"

"Both, I imagine."

Wilma's smile was tight. "Like I said, I'll get over it."

"It's a nice thought, but it doesn't help much when it comes to motive."

She winced as if I'd slapped her. "You don't think—"

"Honestly, Wilma, I don't know what to think. But I do know that if someone caused me to lose all the money I'd saved for my retirement, I'd be pretty unhappy about it. Motive number one: revenge. Motive number two? If I figured I could kill that person and get all my money back as a result of the terms of the will—"

"No, no, no!" Two spots of high color rose in Wilma's pale cheeks. "That is not possible. You know me, Laurel, you know I could never do such a thing."

"But I do know that desperate people do desperate things."

"Desperate? Yes." As if all the air had gone out of her, Wilma sank into the nearest chair and put her head in her hands. "I have always been frugal. I never needed to spend my money. Oh yes, when I first went to work for Ms. Cohan, I did spend most of my salary. But then, I had an elderly aunt who needed my help and much of my paycheck went to her care. Once she died . . . well, what did I need the money for besides personal items? I lived in Ms. Cohan's homes, I ate her food. I didn't need to pay for my travel or my health care. She was a generous employer."

"She was."

"So all that money . . ." As if she was picturing fat stacks of dollar bills, Wilma sighed. "I put aside all that money."

"And then along came *Guinevere*."

"Yes. Ms. Cohan was so excited about the picture. She was going to star, of course, as well as produce and direct. Such a talented woman. One day, she told me all about it. Such a picture she painted!" Wilma's smile was fleeting. "But you know how Hollywood is, Laurel.

Fickle. Difficult. Ms. Cohan, she confessed that her production company was having trouble raising the funds for the film. Costume dramas are not the big draw they once were."

"So she asked you for help."

"Not in so many words. She said she was raising money from a number of sources, and I told her I would be honored to be part of such a project. I am not naive," Wilma pointed out. "I am hardly the type to have stars in my eyes. But I knew that, like every other film Ms. Cohan was associated with, *Guinevere* should have been a blockbuster. I expected a very good return on my investment."

"Except that the leading man was busted."

"And his contract . . . well, there was some mumbo jumbo in it that said he was the only one who could play the lead role, no matter what. The film went down the tubes because of it." Tears streaked Wilma's cheeks. "At first when I heard the news, I couldn't believe it. Ms. Cohan's projects, they were always a sure thing. I spoke to her about it, of course. I asked what I could do. I explained it was all my money in the world and Ms. Cohan, she . . ." As if she still couldn't believe it, Wilma shook her head in wonder. "She said, 'That's showbiz!' And she went on with her life. And I looked into the future and wondered what would happen to me." She sat up and straightened her shoulders.

"I suppose it was a valuable lesson to learn. Unfortunately, I learned it too late in life. All my money, it is gone."

"And you were angry."

"Yes. Very angry."

"Angry enough to kill Meghan?"

Wilma rose on shaking legs. "Yes. Of course I was. Who wouldn't be? But I didn't kill Ms. Cohan. I couldn't have. I was right here that night. I couldn't leave Spencer alone."

"Can anyone verify that?"

Wilma's lips folded in on themselves. "You are telling me I need an alibi."

"You were in town that night."

"Yes."

"You had plenty of good reasons to kill Meghan, about five hundred thousand of them, from what I've heard."

"Yes."

"So can anyone verify you were here? How about Spencer?"

"No!" As if she thought I was going to go into his room and grill him right then and there, Wilma stepped to her left, blocking my path to Spencer's door. "It is not right to involve him further," she said. "He was tired from our trip and went to bed right after we checked in to the hotel. There's nothing he can tell you."

"Then no one can vouch for you that night?"

As if making up her mind about something, she closed her eyes. "Corrine," she said. The decision made, Wilma opened her eyes and gave me a steady look. "Corrine called."

"She knew you were in town?"

"No, she called my cell. She thought I was still in Malibu. We talked, and I told her I was here."

"Why?"

Wilma did a turn around the small room, stopping

long enough to look out the window near the couch. Like Corrine's room, this one faced the parking lot. She pushed aside the vertical blinds and stared at the black-top so long, I wondered if she forgot I was there. Finally, she turned to face me.

"When Corrine called, she was extremely upset."

"Did she say what that was all about?"

"I asked, of course, but she was crying so hard, it was difficult to get much out of her that made any sense. She said she needed to talk to someone. That's why she called. She said . . ." Wilma swallowed hard. "She said she had done a terrible thing."

My heart slammed into my ribs. "A terrible thing like rolling through a stop sign? Or a terrible thing like murder?"

She shook her head. "Corrine didn't say. She couldn't say. She was distraught, nearly unintelligible." Wilma glanced at me from beneath her snowy eyelashes. "I have never been a fan."

I asked even though I didn't need to. "Of Corrine, you mean?"

As if the very thought was too much to consider standing still, she threw her hands in the air and paced to the door and back. "She's disorganized. She's disrespectful. She could never get phone messages straight. The woman is a disaster, start to finish."

"And yet Meghan kept her on."

"Yes."

"And Corrine told you she did something terrible." I let the words settle in the air between us. "Do you think she murdered Meghan?"

Another shake of her head. "This, I cannot say. I do know that the woman was so overwrought I couldn't stand it. That's when I told her we were here in Ohio, staying at the same hotel she and Meghan were. I told her I would meet her in the lobby so we could talk face-to-face."

"And did you?"

Wilma ran her tongue across her lips. "No. After all that, she did not want to meet. She said she'd be fine. But don't you see, Laurel, I talked to her the night of the murder, and I was right here when I did it. Isn't that enough to prove I had nothing to do with Meghan's death?"

I felt a weight lift off my shoulders. I know, I know . . . it was hardly the reaction a detective who claimed to be objective and unbiased should have, but I couldn't help it. Spencer had been through enough in his young life. I didn't want to add Wilma going to the slammer to the list.

I looked at her suitcase. "The cops, they're all right with you leaving?"

"I will check, of course," she assured me. "But I don't know why they would care. They can find us if they need us. And if you need us, Laurel . . ." Her silvery brows dropped low over her eyes. "I will call and leave you the information." Wilma sucked in a breath. "Ms. Cohan's houses, they will all be sold, won't they? Honestly, I don't know where I'll be going or what I'll do when I get there."

"If I can help . . ."

She stepped forward and put a hand on my arm.

"Thank you, Laurel. You were always a good friend to me. Someday, perhaps I will take you up on your offer. For now, I need time to sit quietly and think. What you can do to help . . ." Color touched her cheeks and she tightened the hold on my arm. "Find out who killed Spencer's mother. Bring that person to justice. It is all he has now."

"He has his father."

Wilma patted my arm. "It is all Spencer has now."

I was still considering her words when I stepped out of the room and saw Corrine walking down the corridor.

I called out to her. She hesitated, then kept walking.

Like I was going to let that stop me?

"Corrine!" This time, I closed in on her when I yelled, "You're just the person I want to talk to."

I heard her gulp before she turned to face me. "I am? Why?"

I wondered if my smile looked as strained as it felt. "Why not? We're old friends, aren't we?"

As if she expected some secret camera was hidden someplace, recording our every move, she looked around. "Are we?" she asked.

Rather than lie, I scooted around her, effectively blocking off the door to her hotel room. "Why don't we go sit in the lobby?" Before I even suggested it, I got ahold of her arm and was moving that way.

Corrine might not be the brightest bulb in the box, but she knew when she was outmaneuvered. A minute later we were seated on the not-so-comfortable couches on either side of a massive coffee table piled with magazines and adorned with a fake flower arrangement in shades of mauve, navy, and white.

I moved to my right, the better to see Corrine beyond the silk foliage.

She moved to her left.

I moved to my left.

She scooted to her right.

"So . . ." Leaning over, I grabbed the arrangement and moved it from the table to the floor. "What have you been up to?"

"Up? To?" She folded her hands together on her lap. "Nothing, of course. What makes you think I've been up to anything?"

"Just wondering how you're passing the time."

"I'm . . ." She glanced away.

"Thinking about all the money you didn't inherit?" I suggested.

Corrine played it cool. Or at least she tried. The little twitch at the corner of her mouth told me she wasn't as unflappable as she pretended to be.

"It's no wonder you're upset," I said. "Who wouldn't be?"

She made a little clicking noise with her tongue. "Meghan dissed you in her will."

"She did. But she flat-out eviscerated you in it."

"Not exactly," Corrine countered. "What she did was—"

"Insult the heck out of you and everyone else who thought she cared for them."

Her shoulders slumped. But only for a second. In a heartbeat, Corrine was back to playing the brave little soldier. Chin up, shoulders back, she tipped her head and studied me. "Is this what we came all the way down here to talk about?" she asked.

Since "all the way down here" was maybe thirty steps down the hallway, I ignored that part of her question. "Actually, I wanted to talk to you about the night of the murder."

"I didn't do it!"

I think the denial—as abrupt and passionate as it was—surprised even Corrine. She swallowed hard and did her best to fold herself into the navy and white upholstery. When that didn't work, she blinked and stared and waited for me to make the next move.

I let her sweat for a couple of minutes.

"Actually," I finally said at just about the time Corrine looked like she was going to jump out of her skin, "I wanted to ask you about the phone call you made to Wilma that night."

If Wilma's story was a lie, I expected Corrine to jump in with both feet and ask, *Phone call? What phone call?*

When she didn't, I knew I was onto something.

"What were you upset about?" I asked her.

She tried a little too hard to look like it didn't matter. "It was nothing. Really. I just . . . well, I just got a little carried away about something. Something personal."

"Something terrible."

Like a robin sighting a worm, she leaned forward. "Terrible? Is that what Wilma told you? I don't recall saying anything like that."

"Wilma remembers it very well."

She blew a puff out of one side of her mouth. "Wilma's old."

"But not stupid."

"She's confused."

"She asked if you wanted to meet to talk about whatever was bothering you. Why didn't you?"

As if I'd slapped her, Corrine reared up. "What do you mean, why didn't I? I told her I would."

"Here in the lobby."

"No." She shook her head so hard, that too-red hair of hers twitched over her shoulders. "Not here. Wilma suggested we meet here, but I didn't . . ." As if she might still be there, watching, Corrine looked down the hallway. "I didn't want Meghan to show up and see us together talking."

"Why not?"

"Like I said, it was personal."

So was the way I'd been thinking about the alibi Wilma had flung my way. Had I been so worried about Spencer that I was willing to believe whatever Wilma told me about how she hadn't left the hotel room that night?

Before I jumped to (any more) conclusions, I reminded myself to get a grip.

"So where did you meet?" I asked Corrine.

"Well, that's the funny thing," she said. "It's not like either one of us is familiar with the area. So I looked in one of those magazines, you know, the kind in the room that list restaurants and activities in the area. And I found a Denny's that's open twenty-four hours. That's where we agreed to meet."

Denny's.

Away from the hotel.

Away from Spencer.

And far from the alibi Wilma had given me.

I reined in the tingle that told me I might be onto something.

"And . . . ?" I gave Corrine the kind of look that told her I needed more to go on.

She shrugged. "And nothing. Wilma never showed."

Chapter 16

"Never showed because she had second thoughts and decided she didn't want to leave Spencer alone? Or never showed because she was here in Hubbard clubbing Meghan on the head and dragging her into the freezer?"

"Your guess is as good as mine."

I'd just finished tearing fresh spinach leaves and putting them into a colander so they could be used as the finishing touch in our Friday lunch special, penne pasta with bacon, tomatoes, and spinach. I took the colander over to the sink so George could drain the pasta over it. The boiling water would provide all the cooking the tender baby spinach would need before we mixed the dish together.

Back at the counter, I cleaned up the bits and pieces of spinach stem that I'd discarded.

"What do you think?" I asked Declan.

"What do you think?" he asked me in return.

"I think . . ." I finished with the cleanup and plunked down on the high stool next to the counter. "I think I don't know. And I think I hate not knowing. And I think . . ." I screeched my frustration. Quietly, of course, since it was lunchtime and the Terminal was hopping and I didn't want to scare our customers.

"I think I'm tired of wasting brain cells on what's becoming more confusing by the moment," I confessed. "I'm supposed to be the Terminal's chef, not its personal detective. You know what I think?" My mind made up, I gave the stainless counter a slap just to prove how determined I was. "I think I'm going to spend the rest of the day thinking about food instead of murder. Starting right now."

I kept my word, throwing myself into cooking and cleaning and menu planning with so much zeal, Declan was forced to take cover back at the Irish store, and George learned—fast—to stay out of my way. I chopped mushrooms. I made sauce for the pizzas we'd feature on the evening menu. I called Luigi Lasagna and each and every one of his *amici* to make sure they'd be at the Terminal at six sharp to provide the music that evening. While I was at it, I even requested they play a couple of songs, one of which just happened to be the sort-of-Italian-sounding "Que Sera, Sera" just to remind myself that when it came to the investigation, what would be, would be.

Ready to face what was sure to be a busy Friday evening, I poured a cup of coffee and thought about the next week's specials.

We'd keep pizza on the menu because it was popular, easy to make, and, according to our customers, the best-tasting pizza in town.

We'd get rid of the shrimp and lemon with fennel and basil because as much as I hated to admit it, George was right: our customers weren't crazy about the taste of fennel.

We'd add . . .

I was holding a pencil, and I tapped it against the counter where I was seated, thinking about the Italian dishes I'd made throughout the years, the ones I'd loved, the ones I'd hated, the ones that were too complicated or too expensive for a place like the Terminal, the ones that were simple enough to prepare and always made an impression.

"Fra diavolo!" I announced. Probably too loudly since over where George was washing a sink full of pans, he jumped. "It's a pasta sauce," I explained just as loudly so he couldn't fail to hear me.

George grumbled.

This did not deter me. Filled with fresh enthusiasm for the job that was supposed to be my job when I wasn't working on a job that wasn't and getting no-where doing it, I pulled out a pad and wrote down the ingredients we'd need for the simple, spicy sauce.

Tomato puree.

Garlic.

Basil, mint, parsley.

I had these fresh herbs growing in pots back on the kitchen windowsill of Pacifique, and I wrote a note to myself so I wouldn't forget to bring them to the Terminal.

Red pepper flakes.

Again, I tapped my pencil as I thought, wondering what I could substitute for so common an ingredient to add a little more pizzazz, a little more something for our customers to talk about, a little more (forgive the pun) spice.

I decided on chile de arbol peppers, those small, long, and skinny peppers that are often used on wreaths because they don't lose their color after they're dehydrated. The peppers have about as much kick as red pepper flakes, but they are a little more exotic, a little more flavorful, and I liked the thought of putting my own spin on an old tried-and-true recipe. Chile de arbol are just spicy enough. They would be the perfect way to add the right kick to a dish that literally translates to "devil monk."

"Fra diavolo," I said, this time to myself because for some reason I couldn't explain, the words tapped around inside my mind like a Morse code message.

If only I could think what it wanted to tell me!

"Diavolo!"

The answer hit and I shoved off the stool so fast, it tipped and fell and the noise made George jump a foot.

"I'll pick it up!" I assured him. "As soon as I get back!"

And I headed out into the restaurant.

A quick scan of the patrons at the tables, and I found exactly what I was looking for.

Or, I should say more precisely, exactly *who* I was looking for.

"Good afternoon!" The blond reporter with the big yellow sunglasses was at her usual table near the back windows and I approached with a smile and this time, without a pitcher of water. "I hope you're enjoying your lunch."

She poked her fork through the penne on her dish, her voice muffled and low. "It is . . . acceptable."

Though I hadn't been invited, I slipped into the chair across from hers. "I didn't really come over here to talk to you about the food. I was just thinking about the last time I saw you."

She obviously hadn't forgotten, either. One corner of her mouth pulled tight. "It is best not to remind me of such an incident."

"Exactly." I rested my chin in my hand, waiting for her to catch on. I'm not sure she ever did, so I explained. "You didn't like getting water spilled on you, and who can blame you. And you say the food is acceptable, so that tells me you're not crazy about it. But still, you keep coming back." I held up one hand to stop what I was sure was going to be some half-baked protest about how she was a reporter and had to sacrifice herself—and her taste buds—for the sake of a story.

"It was what happened last time you were here that got me thinking," I told her.

As if she could still feel the cold water on her back, she shivered. "Unprofessional."

"I absolutely agree. But then, you pretending to be a reporter isn't exactly on the up-and-up, either."

She reared back and that phony-sounding British accent disappeared like a dish of gelato left in the Tuscan sun. Her voice dripped Italian ire. "How dare you question me? How can you think that I am not what I say I am?!"

"Only if you say you're the countess Adalina Crocetti."

Just like that, all that bluster was gone. Her mouth fell open and she plumped back in her chair. "How did you . . . ?"

"It shouldn't have taken me as long as it did," I admitted. "You gave yourself away that day I dumped the water on you. When it happened, I thought you said 'Key a Volvo'! But let's face it, that doesn't make a whole lot of sense. I should have known you were speaking Italian. You said '*Che diavolo*,' which is pretty much the Italian equivalent of 'What the hell!' Between that and all the questions you've been asking about Ben—"

"Ben?" Her voice didn't just drip sarcasm, it pretty much gushed. "You must know him well to use his name so freely. Are you the reason he is here in this silly little place? Has he fallen in love with you?"

It was probably the wrong time to laugh, but I couldn't help myself. When I was done, I wiped away tears and looked at her hard. "He's here because Meghan Cohan got murdered. If you don't know that, you're the only one on the planet who missed the story."

"Meghan, Meghan. Yes. Of course." She steadied herself, straightening and restraightening the silverware next to her plate. "But he did not love her. He loves me. He married me."

"And you showed up here in disguise to ask questions about your husband. Why?"

She puckered. In a high-class sort of way, of course. "It is not wrong to be curious."

"It's not wrong to wonder about the guy you're married to, either, but I'd think if you had questions, you'd ask Ben directly. Except . . ." I scooted forward in my seat. "He doesn't know you're here, does he?"

She clicked her tongue. "Of course he knows."

"Then why are you hanging around waiting for him to show up here?"

"It is because . . ."

Maybe I looked too eager, like the paparazzi she was used to following in her wake.

Maybe I looked too common and not worth confiding in.

Whatever the reason, she gathered her patrician wits and pushed back her chair. "You are nervy. You have no business asking these questions."

"You're right. Sort of. If I was just being nosy . . . well, that would be one thing. But, you see, I'm working with the police, looking into the murder." Okay, so it wasn't absolutely true, but it was sort of true. For now, I was willing to live with *sort of.* "And as far as I can tell, you have absolutely no reason to be in Hubbard. Unless it has something to do with Meghan's murder."

Her shoulders went rigid. "Absolutely not!"

"Then why are you here?"

"My husband . . . my Ben, he is racing nearby and—"

"And you thought you'd surprise him."

A slow smile lifted the corners of her mouth, revealing teeth that were so pearly, they glistened. "Yes, that is it. I thought I would surprise him."

"Only you've had plenty of time. And yet, here you still are in that silly disguise." As if sharing a confidence, I leaned nearer. "The wig's got to go. But then . . ." As if I'd just thought of it, I allowed myself a moment of pretend surprise and looked all around the restaurant. "There are dozens of reporters around here all the time. Wouldn't they love to interview you? You probably know more about what went on in Ben and Meghan's marriage than just about anyone. He has talked to you about it, hasn't he?"

"We keep no secrets from each other."

"Except the fact that you followed him all the way to . . . what did you call it? . . . this silly little town. Except that you followed him all the way here and you're lying low, watching and waiting. For what?"

Her top lip curled. "My check."

"No worries." When she rose to her feet, I did, too. "Lunch is on me."

She didn't thank me. But then, she'd hardly touched her penne, so she probably didn't know how really delicious it was. Instead, the countess, still hiding behind those big sunglasses, sailed out of the Terminal like an elegant Venetian gondola.

"You didn't dump water on her again, did you?"

I could hardly blame Sophie for coming over and asking. We both watched the countess—her Italian pique like an aura around her—push out the front door and disappear down the street.

"I don't think she'll be back," I said.

But that didn't keep me from wondering what an Italian countess was doing in our town in the first place.

The answer, of course, did not come that Friday, and it was just as well.

Between Luigi, his *amici*, legions of patrons, and the Meghan fans who showed up outside to mark the one-week anniversary of her passing with bouquets of flowers, candles, and a prayer vigil, I was a tad busy.

So busy, in fact, I never had a chance to tell Declan what I'd discovered until the last of the *amici* had put away his concertina and gone home.

"It's strange, don't you think, the countess being here?"

Declan might have agreed with me. Then again, since he was in the midst of shoving an entire slice of pepperoni pizza in his mouth when he mumbled an answer, maybe he didn't.

"Why is she wearing a disguise? What is she looking for? Do you think Ben even knows she's here?"

These were obviously legitimate questions and just as obviously, I knew Declan wouldn't know the answers, but I asked them, anyway, by way of emphasizing what I saw as the strangeness of the whole thing. "Why would the countess kill Meghan?"

Declan swallowed and grabbed a paper napkin from the counter to wipe pizza sauce off his chin. "Who says she did?"

"Not me. But I wonder if she has motive. What else would she be doing here?"

"Spying on her husband?"

My lips puckered. "Do you think wives need to spy on their husbands?"

"Did I say that?"

He didn't, but I wasn't going to let him off so easily. "If wives and husbands have secrets from each other, if they can't trust each other, they shouldn't be married in the first place."

"You won't get an argument from me about that. And, by the way, you know you can trust me. Always."

Since I was sure he was grinning at me when he said this, and since his grin had a way of heating my insides and making me crazy in the head, I didn't bother to glance his way. "I bet Ben has no idea she's here."

"Maybe she wants to surprise him. And what's he been up to, anyway? Why would a guy like that hang around a place like this?"

"Like you don't love Hubbard."

"Of course I do." He came up behind me and wrapped his arms around my waist. "I love Hubbard and I love you. Only if I had to choose, you would come first." He brushed a kiss against my neck. "Only I'm pretty sure Ben doesn't love Hubbard, and I know he doesn't love you, although how anyone who knows you couldn't love you is a mystery to me."

"Plenty of people know me and don't love me." I scooted out of his arms. It was that or lose myself in the prickles of awareness that danced up and down my spine anytime Declan was near. "They were already divorced by the time I met Ben."

"You mean Ben and Meghan."

"Well, I guess I really mean Ben and Tina Moretti. Because, remember what Dulcie Thoroughgood told us. Meghan was Tina back in those days. She only changed her name when she was set to star in *None Are Waiting*. So Tina, the kid from nowhere, married the daring young race car driver. And they both later became stars. That in itself sounds like something out of a movie." I sighed. But then, thinking about it all made me feel . . . well, not hopeless, exactly. More like there was something out there that I should know, something I should have noticed, that just wasn't making sense yet.

"Hey, don't get discouraged." Declan looped an arm around my shoulders. "You'll figure it out. You always do. For now, we'll lock up and get home and—"

"I've got penne for dinner." I went to the fridge and pulled out the to-go dinners I'd packed for us. "And there's some salad at home and—"

"Oh no. Not tonight."

We stepped out of the kitchen and I flicked off the lights.

"Tonight," Declan informed me, "we're going to switch things up a bit. You said it yourself this afternoon. You said you had to stop spending so much time thinking about the murder. And eating Italian food is bound to get you thinking about the murder."

"So what are we having for dinner?" I asked him.

He grabbed a shopping bag from the front counter, where he'd obviously left it when he came in. "Corned beef sandwiches." He joggled the bag at me. "Big, fat pickles. Sides of potato salad. Nothing Italian in this bag, I promise you."

It was a sweet gesture and when I pulled the front door closed and locked it behind me, I was smiling.

At least until I heard a voice behind me.

"Laurel!"

I flinched, but not to worry. As promised, Declan was right at my side, his fists clenched, his feet apart, and that bag of sandwiches at his feet just in case the person standing in the shadows posed a threat.

He eased up—at least a little—when Wilma stepped out from around the side of the building.

"I thought you went back to California," I told her.

She pressed her lips together. "You were right. That detective Oberlin, he was not pleased with the idea of me being so far away. He asked us to stay on a few more days."

"And that's what you came here to tell me?"

In the faint light of the streetlamps, her smile looked like a slash across her chin.

"No, no," Wilma said. "You see, I spoke to Corrine. This afternoon. We ran into each other in the hotel lobby. She told me you asked her about the night of the murder. About me, about my . . ." As if it tasted bad, she swallowed around the word. "About my alibi."

"And she told me you didn't have one. Not like you said you did."

"Well, she is wrong." When Wilma reached into her purse, Declan tensed again, but only until she pulled out a piece of paper. She held it up for me to see. "This will prove I am telling the truth."

Actually, all it proved was that it's impossible to read the printing on a piece of paper in lousy light.

I grabbed my phone and turned on the flashlight app.

"It's a receipt," I said. "From—"

"From the all-night Denny's, the place I agreed to meet Corrine on the night of the murder. You'll see by the time stamp"—she pointed it out—"that I was there late into the night. Just like I said I was."

"But Corrine said—"

"Corrine said she was there and I was not. She's a foolish woman. She always has been. She should have known how easily I could prove her wrong. You see, I was there. But Corrine . . . Corrine was not."

Chapter 17

"Thought you'd want to know."

Honest, those were the first words I heard when I answered my phone. I didn't hold this lack of chitchat against the caller. After all, he wasn't the *good morning, how are you doing?* type, and I knew it. Which is exactly why I couldn't help but tease, just a little.

"Good morning to you, Gus. And how are you this fine Saturday morning?"

Why did I have the feeling he'd never been asked the question before?

That would explain Gus's hesitation.

"I'm feeling a little . . ." He actually sounded like he was on the verge of being friendly, then snorted. "I'm working, that's how I am. And I'm going to keep working until I can make sense of this mess we're in. But I thought you'd want to know."

It was early and I was already at the Terminal. Since the Irish store didn't open for another couple of hours, and since Declan still didn't like the idea of me being alone in the restaurant, he was out by the register. The night before at Pacifique, he'd printed up the Today's Specials menus on paper with wide bands of green, white, and red on it, the perfect mirror to the Italian flag that flapped from the flagpole out front. He was paper-clipping one sheet of our specials to each of our regular menus. (Just for the record, that day's specials were pizza, vegetable lasagna, and Italian sausage and zuc-chini served over campanelle pasta, those two-inch-long noodles that look like ruffly edged bellflowers.)

My phone to my ear, I took a cup of coffee out to Declan. He raised his eyebrows, the universal sign— *Who are you talking to? What are you talking about?*— that all phone-talkers recognize.

I gave him the universal countersign, one index finger raised to say, *Give me a sec and I'll tell you when I'm done.*

"What is it you want me to know?" I asked Gus.

He, apparently, had a cup of coffee, too. He slurped. "The coroner's releasing the body. Ms. Cohan's going to be shipped back to California on Tuesday."

By now, I was used to the thought of Meghan being dead. I wasn't used to hearing her referred to as cargo.

Before the heebie-jeebies had a chance to overwhelm me, Gus sailed right on. "They've got some big to-do funeral planned out in Hollywood next weekend."

"Who's in charge?"

"Of the funeral?" I heard the sound of shuffling pa-pers. "Looks like that assistant, that Corrine Kellogg.

And the ex-husband. He's in Pittsburgh, you know. In some big race later today. I drove over there yesterday and talked to him again. Just routine, of course, and he's the one who told me he's involved in planning the funeral. Told me he owes it to their son to make sure his mother gets the kind of send-off a star like her deserves."

I had no doubt the funeral would be a production worthy of DeMille and surprisingly, I realized Ben was right—it was exactly what Meghan deserved. There was no one who loved more pomp and ceremony—not to mention the limelight—than Meghan. And this was her last chance to shine.

"What does all this mean in terms of our . . ." I realized what I'd said and swallowed down my mortification. "In terms of your investigation?" I asked Gus.

If he caught the gaffe, he didn't point it out. Which was remarkably civilized—and thus, unexpected—on Gus's part.

"It means I'm going to be telling everyone from out of town that they can return to their homes."

A block of ice formed in my stomach. "All our . . ." Another hard swallow. If he missed it last time, he sure wouldn't this time. "All your suspects?"

"That's right, all our suspects."

He might have been using the *our* to refer to the police department. But I didn't think so. The realization did nothing to thaw the iceberg in my tummy, but it did make me bold enough to ask, "What are we going to do?"

"Well, remember, there's no statute of limitations on murder."

"Sure. Yes. Of course. I'm sure you'll keep the case open, and if anything comes of it, you can always go out to California, or Italy, or wherever everyone's gone off to, and talk to them. But it sure would be easier to solve this thing before everyone leaves town."

On the other end of the phone, I heard what I thought was paper being crumpled. It took me a moment to realize it was actually Gus laughing.

"Yeah, we need to solve this before anyone leaves town." He coughed to clear his throat. "So get to work."

"Before everyone leaves town." Gus had already ended the call so when I looked at my phone and said this, I guess I was talking to myself.

Only Declan was right there listening.

"So what do we do?"

"You mean after you finish with the Today's Specials menus?"

He got the not-so-subtle hint and went right back to work, and so did I while I thought about everything Gus had told me. By the time George arrived, I'd already browned the sausage for the campanelle pasta dish, and I'd chopped carrots and celery, too.

"You know, you could hire somebody to do all that prep work for you," George grumbled on his way by with an armload of boxes of lasagna noodles.

"Yeah, I'll do that. As soon as we win the lottery."

He set down the boxes of pasta. "Don't need to wait that long. If you're smart. You could do what that fellow's doing on the Internet. You know, about Meghan Cohan."

I could be excused for being a tad confused. I'd been so busy talking to Gus and thinking about what he said and what our options were regarding the case, I hadn't had one sip of coffee. Now I poured a cup, took a glug, and gave George a level look. "What are you talking about?"

"Saw some things on the Internet last night," he said. "I was messing around. You know, on account of all the commotion around here. I wondered what everyone was saying about the Terminal."

"And what are they saying about the Terminal?" I asked.

His lips puckered with the effort of remembering. "Good food. Nice service. A little crowded."

"Because of the murder."

"Because of the murder." He nodded and pulled a piece of paper out of his pocket and unfolded it. "Then I looked a little more, and I found this."

Since he didn't hand it over, I had no choice but to ask, "What is it?"

"A listing on one of those auction sites. They got all sorts of Meghan Cohan stuff up there for sale, movie posters, and photographs, and autographs. You know how it is with these things, somebody dies and all of a sudden, everything they've ever touched or been part of is more valuable than it used to be. But then I saw this." He turned the paper around and waved it in my direction. I could make out a picture and some text, but since I was still too far away to see what it was all about, I stepped closer.

I squinted, stared, backed up.

"Silverware?"

"Not just any silverware." George flapped the paper to smooth out the folds and read the description printed under the picture.

"'For sale, the place setting of silverware from the

restaurant where Meghan Cohan spent her last night upon this earth, from the restaurant where she was killed.'"

My stomach swooped. "It actually says that?"

"You wanna know the asking price?"

I held up a hand because really, I didn't. "How could anybody be that dishonest? And how could any buyer be that gullible? Why would anyone fall for a hoax like that?"

"Only, Laurel . . ."

I didn't like the way George said that.

Like I hadn't been listening.

Like it mattered.

A lot.

This time, he was the one who closed in on me, the better to show me the picture of the knife, fork, and spoon again.

He poked a finger at the picture. "Take a look. It's our silverware, all right. Heck, I wash enough of it every day. I'd recognize the pattern anywhere."

He was right, and this time, my stomach didn't just swoop, it slid and dove and bounced back up again. When I took the paper from him, my hands were shaking.

"Who . . . ? How . . . ?"

George crossed burly arms over burly chest. "You're a smart woman. Least I always thought you were."

So did I. Which is why I was disappointed I had to think for a while before I blurted out, "Dolly!"

"Took you long enough." George turned to the grill.

I raced over and angled myself between him and the order of sizzling pancakes he'd already put on for the breakfast regulars he knew would be stopping by at any minute. "You knew?"

"What is it you would say, Laurel? I suspected. She is the one who had a picture of Meghan Cohan's car."

"And she must be the one who took the picture of the freezer and gave it to the tabloids."

George dipped his chin, the better to give me an eagle-eyed stare.

"She sold it to the tabloids." I caught on soon enough and George lightened up that look. "And she took the silverware from the table where Meghan sat that night, and now she's selling that, too. After I told everyone here not to talk to the press—"

"She's not exactly talking to them," George pointed out.

"But she is profiting from a terrible murder." I wrapped my arms around myself, the better to control the shiver that snaked up my spine.

"What are you gonna do?" George asked.

"I'm going to . . ." Because I didn't know what I was going to do, I stalked out into the restaurant.

As fate would have it, the first person I saw was Dolly, who'd just come in the front door.

I froze, and stared, the words right there on my lips. *You're fired!*

"What's up, Laurel?"

Her greeting snapped me out of my thoughts. "Not a thing," I assured her, and eyes wide in yet another easily recognized expression—*Wait until I tell you!*—I turned my back on her and went over to where Declan was just finishing up with the menus.

Yeah, it was sort of a weaselly way out of the situation, but I had a perfectly good excuse.

I was too busy thinking to do anything in the way of interacting.

Thinking about Dolly, the starstruck fan who seemed to know every detail about Meghan's career.

About Dolly profiting from Meghan's murder.

About the fact that suddenly, it looked like I might have another suspect on my hands.

SATURDAYS ARE ALWAYS busy, and that one was no exception. It wasn't until after the breakfast crowd was gone and lunch was over that I had a chance to catch up with Dolly, and as it worked out, that was just fine. All those meals served and all that time, it gave me a chance to think.

Dolly and I were in the kitchen and with a tiny tip of my head, I suggested that George go outside and get a breath of fresh air.

He's an obliging sort. One look at me, another at Dolly, and he knew exactly what was up. He skedaddled.

"They're going to have Meghan's funeral next weekend," I said, as oh so casual as I could be.

She'd been rolling sets of silverware—yeah, just like the one she was selling online—in napkins, and she sucked in a breath and stopped working. She pressed both her hands to her heart.

"Are you going?" she asked me.

I hadn't even considered it, but now that she mentioned it, I knew my answer. "No. A funeral should be for people who are near and dear to the departed. I'm an outsider. I always was in Meghan's world. I have no business there."

"There will be thousands of fans." As if just thinking about it conjured images of how weeping crowds would line the roads surrounding Meghan's mansion, Dolly's cheeks shot through with color and her eyes welled. "Oh, how I wish I could be there! Not that I'd ever think to ask for the time off," she added quickly. "I know I just started here and it wouldn't be fair to take vacation days so soon."

She paused for an appropriate amount of time here, waiting for me to tell her that of course she could take the time.

When I didn't, Dolly hung her head. "It would be awfully expensive to get there."

It was the most perfect opening I could imagine, but I wasn't ready yet to ask about selling out Meghan and the Terminal to the paparazzi. Excuse the cooking pun, but I had other fish to fry.

"I know how disappointed you must be, but there will be plenty of press coverage. Besides, you've got something none of those fans who'll be watching the funeral out in Hollywood will ever have. You have your memories of Meghan being right here on the last day of her life," I reminded her. "You talked to her."

Dolly sniffled. "I remember every minute of it."

When she put a hand in her pocket, I cringed, expecting her to bring out the word-for-word account of her encounter with Meghan. Instead, she pulled out a tissue and dabbed it to her nose. She tucked the tissue away, went to the sink to wash her hands, then went back to rolling silverware. But only for a moment. She

stopped again, her head cocked, her eyes glassy with a
faraway look. "I just wish I knew that night. I just wish
I knew it was her."

"So thinking about that night . . ." I leaned against
the counter and grabbed some silverware, too, and
started rolling. If there's one thing I'd learned from a
lifetime in the food industry, it's that help is always appreciated. If there's one thing I'd learned from being an
amateur detective, it's that appreciative people are more
likely to talk. "What did you do? I mean, after work
that night? I know what I did. That was the night I got
home and found out my house had been broken into. I
stayed up until the wee hours while the police searched
the place and we did all the paperwork we needed to
file a report. How about you? What did you do that night?
What did you do the next night, the night Meghan was
killed?"

"Oh, I don't know!" Dolly jiggled her shoulders, the
gesture all too awkward to be totally convincing.
"Nothing much, I suppose."

"Come on, Dolly. You met Meghan Cohan! Sure, you
didn't know it at the time, but you found out soon enough.
If I was as big a fan as you are, and I found that out, I
would have memorized every moment of that night,
maybe written it down like you wrote down the conversation you had with Meghan. Just so I'd never forget."

"It's not important." She wasn't finished with the
silverware, but she stepped away from the counter and
checked the order window. There were no plates of
food waiting to be taken out into the restaurant so she
went the long way around the kitchen and got a bottle
of water out of the fridge. She didn't crack it open; she

juggled it from hand to hand. "What I do when I leave here at night, none of that is very important."

"If you did leave here that night."

Aside from the fact that she tends to be a little too talkative, Dolly is a good waitress. Though she's not especially efficient, she makes up for it with enthusiasm. What she's not is especially quick on the uptake.

She stared at me staring at her.

"What are you talking about?" she asked.

Whatever wise person once said *A picture is worth a thousand words* really knew what he—or she—was talking about. I grabbed the computer printout George had conveniently left nearby for me and waved it at Dolly.

"You're making money off Meghan's death," I told her.

Her face turned as white as the apron on a hook near where we stood, and Dolly sucked in a breath. Her green beaded earrings seemed to lose their twinkle. "How did you . . . ? How could you . . . ?"

"Am I wrong?"

The way her bottom lip quivered told me I wasn't.

Yeah, I know, a detective is supposed to be objective. Hard-hearted. Quick enough to make deductions and steely enough so that those conclusions aren't influenced by emotion. But heck, I couldn't just stand there and watch her whimper.

I grabbed the water bottle from Dolly, opened it, and handed it back to her. "Drink," I commanded.

She did, but even the icy water wasn't enough to keep her voice from quavering when she asked, "Are you . . . are you going to fire me?"

"That all depends. Are you just selling pictures and information to the press? Or did you kill Meghan Cohan?"

She slapped a hand to her heart, and it was a good thing there was a high stool nearby, because Dolly collapsed against it.

"Spill the beans," I ordered. "And do it fast before the dinner crowd shows up. That way I'll know if I'm going to be down one waitress and I'll have to work the floor myself tonight."

She wrung her hands. A dramatic motion, I know, and I wasn't sure I'd ever seen it used before to such striking effect. This should have made me more cynical, more suspicious. Instead, it only made me want to shake some sense into her.

I refrained, but even I couldn't guarantee my patience would last. "Dolly!"

When I barked her name, she winced.

"What is going on?" I asked her.

A tear slipped down her cheek. "You're right. About how I've been meeting with reporters and giving them pictures and telling them what's been going on around here. I wasn't doing it to make money." She brushed tears from her cheeks. "Not at first, anyway. At first, it was just a way for me to be part of the story. Imagine!" She managed a watery smile. "Imagine that when those reporters were writing their stories about Meghan, they were thinking about me, too. They had to be, because I was the one who gave them the information. It was a way . . ." She dragged out that tissue again and pressed it to her eyes. "It was a way for my essence and Meghan's to be linked for all time."

I wasn't so sure about this essence business, but I did know profit when I saw it.

I reminded Dolly of this.

"Yes, yes." She nodded. "You're right about that. One of the reporters, see, offered me five hundred dollars for my picture of Meghan's rental car. Five hundred dollars! And then another reporter, he asked about the freezer, and somebody else said I'd probably be around when the will was read and if I could just stand outside the door and listen . . ."

"And the silverware?" I asked. "You can't possibly know it was the actual place setting she used."

"But it might be, and if there was even the slightest chance it was hers, I would keep it forever and ever if I could."

"But you can't."

"I can't. I want to, but . . ."

But what, I didn't find out. Not right then, anyway.

That's because Dolly burst into tears and ran out of the kitchen.

"Great." It wasn't, so I grumbled the word. Not only did I wonder if Dolly was the murderer, but now I also wondered if I'd be waiting tables that night.

Chapter 18

I waited tables that night.

Not because I fired Dolly, but because by the time I scrambled after her into the restaurant, I was just in time to see her hightail it out the front door. She didn't come back that evening. I wondered if she ever would.

I also wondered what secrets she'd taken with her.

"The folks at table eleven are waiting for their pizza." Inez whizzed by, a pitcher of iced tea in one hand and a tray of food in the other, and thank goodness she's professional enough to keep her voice down. I would have hated if the customers seated nearby thought we were falling down on the job.

Inez tipped her head closer to mine. "They asked why their waitress isn't faster."

"Their waitress isn't faster because their waitress isn't a waitress," I mumbled, but didn't waste any time.

I picked up the order and delivered it along with my apologies, then scurried back to the kitchen where I belonged. In all my years in the food service industry, I'd waited tables only once. The very first day I did, I found out how grueling serving work is and decided to become a chef.

Behind the closed kitchen door, I rubbed a hand to the small of my back. "I'm not meant to wait tables."

"Tough work," George acknowledged. "Especially when you have two orders sitting there waiting for you."

I did.

I took George's not-so-subtle hint and grabbed the campanelle pasta and the pizza and headed back into the restaurant.

From behind the front counter, Sophie gave me the thumbs-up when I zipped by. It was enough to remind me that not only was she depending on me, but that I was a member of the team, and as such, I had to do what I could to make the best of a bad situation.

"Pizza." I set it down in front of the man at table number eight who'd requested extra mushrooms (check), no olives (for sure), and not too much sauce (never!). "And pasta." I gave that order to the man seated across from him. "Enjoy."

"Where's that other one?" The guy who'd ordered the campanelle looked past me to scan the restaurant. He was middle-aged, with a receding hairline and puffy cheeks, and he had an iPad open on the table in front of him that wasn't there when he placed his order. There was a notepad there, too, the pages covered with writing that was pretty much illegible.

I'd been so busy taking their orders, I hadn't paid a

whole lot of attention to them earlier, but now, my Spi-
dey sense sent a tingle like an electrical charge down
my back.

I thanked my lucky stars that in all the years I'd
worked for Meghan, I'd been careful to avoid the media
as much as possible. Oh sure, my picture had been in
the tabloids a couple of times. But apparently, not the
one this guy wrote for. And not any one he read. He had
no idea who I was, and that was just fine with me.

"If you're looking for Dolly," I told him, "she had an
emergency and had to leave. Is there something I can
help you with?"

"Maybe. How long have you worked here?"

"Awhile," I told him, playing it cool.

"But I haven't seen you before and I've been here
plenty this last week. Lucky thing the food is good.
Remember that place in Taos?" He looked at his com-
panion and made a face. "Ate chile rellenos two weeks
running and, I'll tell you what, it wasn't pretty."

Rather than address that particular issue, I smiled.
"I mostly work in the kitchen."

"Yeah? Well, I was just wondering if maybe that
Dolly, when she had to leave, maybe she said something to you about me stopping in? Maybe she left
something with you? She was supposed to give it to me
tonight."

I propped the tray I was carrying against my hip,
stalling while I tried to figure out my options. As far as
I could see, I didn't have many so I went with my first
instinct: lie like an expert and don't back down.

"She did say something." I tried to make it look like
I was thinking hard. "Something about a piece of paper

or some information or . . ." Remembering Dolly's history, I took a chance. "A picture?"

"A photo. That's right." I was grateful he'd risen to the bait, but I didn't dare show it, especially when he leaned a little nearer and I hoped for more information.

"She told you about it, right?" The reporter chuckled. "That Dolly, she looks about as harmless as one of them . . . You know . . ."

"Puppies." His friend supplied the word.

"Yeah, yeah. As harmless as a cute little baby golden retriever. But she's got some tricks up her sleeve, eh? Must be something to work with a woman like that."

"Oh, it's something, all right," I assured him, though at that point, if I was working with Dolly—or if she'd just made the cut and been officially taken off our employee list—was something of a question.

One I wasn't going to consider right then and there.

Instead, I took a step toward the kitchen. "I can check and see if she left something in the back for you. A photograph, right? It might help if I knew what it was a photograph of."

"What else? Meghan Cohan!"

Silently, I prayed Dolly hadn't somehow gotten near enough to take a picture of the body before it was removed from our freezer. I told myself it wasn't possible. I told myself not to worry.

Tell that to the spurt of sourness in my stomach.

I swallowed it down. "You mean the photograph of Meghan's car?"

The reporter waved away the very idea. "Got that one from ol' Dolly, and paid a pretty penny for it, too. No, no. This is something new. Something different.

Something Dolly said will give me a scoop nobody else has got. Dolly, she told me she found it when she was doing a little undercover work for me." He gave me a wink designed to make me believe we were in this together.

Yes, I was shameless. I went right along with him.

"Dolly was thrilled she was able to help you out. I mean, the whole thing was like something out of a James Bond movie, you know, with Dolly poking around in there and nobody . . ." It was my turn to lean closer and lower my voice. "And nobody figuring out what she was up to. She's really good at stuff like that."

"And, believe you me, she's going to get paid. You will, too," he added, almost as an afterthought. "I mean, I'd cut you in. You know, if Dolly left the photo and you'd just go get it for me."

Oh, I was going to look for the photo, all right, and I told the reporter as much.

Only he didn't know that meant as soon as I left the table, I zipped into the office, looked up Dolly's home address, and made a quick phone call.

"Just closing up for the night." On the other end of the phone, I heard the sounds of Declan's computer shutting down. "My mom and dad said they're coming by for dinner. I thought I'd eat with them."

"That's terrific, but I need something more in the way of a waiter," I told him.

He considered it, but only for a second, and when he arrived, I gave him last-minute instructions and sent him out onto the floor and once he was busy, I took off out the back door, headed out on a little James Bond mission of my own.

*   *   *

DOLLY LIVED AS far east of Hubbard as it was possible
to get and still be in the great state of Ohio. There on
the border with Pennsylvania, I pulled up in front of a
small frame house with a chain-link fence surrounding
it and pansies planted outside the gate, though since it
was late and already dark, I couldn't tell if the flowers
were white or yellow.

I couldn't quite see the sign that hung on the gate,
either, and I leaned forward and squinted, and when
that didn't work, I got out of the car.

Though there was activity next door—the off-key
sounds of a garage band that needed oh so much more
in the way of rehearsals—there were no lights on inside
Dolly's house. The curtains were closed and there was
no car parked out front.

I pulled out my phone and hit my flashlight app,
aiming it at the sign.

It was red, maybe eighteen-inches square, and the
entire left side of the sign was taken up by the cartoon
image of a grinning orange cat with big green eyes. The
rest of the sign was printed in gold letters.

JUST KITTEN

CAT RESCUE

I had never pegged Dolly as the kitty cat type, but I
checked the address again and, sure I was in the right
place, I went up the front walk and rang the doorbell.

The curtains on the window to my left twitched and
encouraged, I rang the bell again.

Another twitch and this time, the curtains parted to
reveal a tabby cat the size of a raccoon. A big raccoon.

Over its shoulder, I saw another cat appear, this one smaller and Siamese-looking. A black cat joined them to stare at me.

I tried the bell a third time.

From the other side of the door, I heard a chorus of meows and the scramble of claws against the floor, and from the window on my right, three more cats appeared.

Cats, yes.

But no Dolly.

Just to be sure, I circled the house and aimed my flashlight into the back window and what turned out to be the kitchen.

More cats—five . . . six . . . seven of them—but no sign of the Terminal waitress who might be the former Terminal waitress before the night was over.

Sure, I was discouraged, but I would not be deterred. I promised myself another trip over in the morning and headed back to the restaurant. By the time I got there, the dinner hour was just winding down.

Declan happened to be in the kitchen when I walked in the back door and he slanted me a look. "You were out."

"And returned safe and sound." I dropped my purse and keys on the nearest counter. "Any sign of Dolly?"

"Sophie said Dolly walked out. She said that's why you needed my help."

He had a smudge of pasta sauce across the white apron he wore over a navy golf shirt, a splotch of olive oil on his jeans, and what looked like pizza crust crumbs stuck to his arm.

I leaned closer and plucked away the crumbs.

"How's it going?" I asked.

"The bar exam was easier than waiting tables. And I've still got three people out there waiting for—"

George rang the little bell that signaled the staff that an order was ready. "Your pasta's up!" he called out to Declan.

With a sigh, he grabbed the order and took it out front.

"And how about you?" George glanced over to where I leaned against the prep counter. "You eat tonight?"

"I'm not all that hungry."

"Which doesn't answer my question."

I can't say how he came by it so quickly or why it wasn't destined for one of the patrons still waiting out front, but all of a sudden, there was a pepperoni and red pepper pizza on a dish in front of me.

"Mangia." George chuckled. "That's what they say, right? The Italians? It means 'Eat up.'"

It did. I did, grateful to have the chance to sit and think for a while.

"So, George . . ." He was just finishing cleaning the grill and he didn't turn around, but I knew he was listening. George is always listening. "Have you ever noticed Dolly doing anything . . . anything odd?"

"You mean other than obsessing about that Meghan Cohan?"

"I mean here in the restaurant. Yeah, I know she took the pictures of Meghan's car and the freezer door. And I know she's been talking to reporters on the sly. But did you ever find her looking around, maybe someplace she wasn't supposed to be?"

"Except when you work here, where aren't you supposed to be?"

It was a valid question. Like I've mentioned before, we're a team, and as a team, each of us pitched in to do what needed to be done. Sometimes that meant Inez and Dolly helped with seating customers. Sometimes it meant I rolled silverware or swept the floor. We tried to spare Sophie any of the hard work, but sometimes (more than sometimes), she was only too eager to help, too, cleaning, toting, lifting, moving, chopping, washing, cooking.

"But Dolly never helps with the cooking. Not that I've ever seen." I said this more to myself than to George, but he acknowledged the statement with a grunt. "So if she was messing around in here . . ." I raised my voice when I said this because now, I did want his input. "You would have noticed, right? If she was doing something other than the something she was supposed to be doing?"

"You mean like looking through your cookbooks?"

The words sent a tingle of what I can only call electricity cascading through me.

Cookbooks!

Like the cookbooks Declan and I had meticulously searched when we tried to figure out what Meghan was looking for here at the Terminal the night she died!

Because there was no room for error, I raced over to stand in front of George, the better to look him in the eye.

"When?" I asked.

He considered the question. "A few days ago."

"Why?"

"I asked." He pursed his lips and nodded. "Wondered why she'd want to mess with your cookbooks, only I didn't exactly say it like that on account of you know how sensitive Dolly is. Just asked if I could help, you know. Just asked what she was looking for."

Exactly like Dolly had the time Declan and I were looking through the cookbooks and she walked into the kitchen and asked how she could help.

"Which cookbooks?" I asked George.

This time, he took a little longer to consider. But then, as I've already mentioned, I have quite a few cookbooks there at the Terminal. Fists on hips, I went to stand in front of the shelves where they were arrayed, looking from book to book.

"Not those." George wiped his hands on a towel and stalked closer. "She didn't much care about those. As a matter of fact, she wasn't even looking for them. She was really looking for a ponytail holder."

Yes, I was confused.

George knew it. Since he never exactly smiled, I'd say the look he gave me was more of a grimace. "She came in here looking for a ponytail holder. Said something about her hair being messy. And she was looking through the drawers, and that's when she found the cookbook."

"The cookbook!" I knew exactly which one George was talking about. I raced over to the drawer where I'd tucked the cookbook that contained the recipe for ta-gliatelle with asparagus and marjoram. I'd tucked it away because I knew I'd use the recipe again during our Italian food extravaganza.

So Dolly had been rooting around in the drawer for a hair band.

I wondered, what else had she found?

I didn't exactly have a chance to think through the question.

That's because the smoke alarm out in the restaurant started blaring.

WE'D ONCE HAD a small fire in the Terminal. Luckily, there were no customers around at the time. Now, I knew we had patrons out in the restaurant, just like I knew that no matter how tempting it was to find out what Dolly was up to, those people were more important than any photograph of Meghan Cohan.

George knew the drill, too. While I called 911, he hit the gas valve shutoff on the stove and made sure the back door was unlocked in case the fire department needed to get in that way. Like we'd practiced the times we'd staged fire drills for the staff, his next job was to head out the back door and circle around to the front of the restaurant to help with the evacuation.

My job was twofold and I handled the first stage of it the minute I was back out front. Sophie was behind the cash register, her eyes wide with a combination of terror and worry, and because I knew there would be no way to stop her from trying to help in any way she could and that in helping in any way she could, she would slow the rest of us down, I latched on to her arm and pulled her out the front door.

She locked her knees and dragged her feet. "But, Laurel!"

"But nothing." I handed Sophie off to George, who was already on the front sidewalk, and I darted back inside.

Declan had never participated in one of our drills, but as I may have mentioned a time or two (or three) before, he is as smart as he is handsome. Calmly and carefully, he went from table to table, rounding up the patrons who sat there wondering what was going on and escorting them out to the waiting area. From there, I took over. I propped open the front door and ushered them all outside.

"Got everybody?" He yelled the question above the clamoring of the smoke alarm and the sounds of sirens closing the distance between the local fire station and the Terminal.

I did a quick turn around the restaurant, checking every corner and every table and every booth. There was a sheen of smoke in the air, but it wasn't enough— at least not yet—to stick in my throat or sting my eyes.

"I'll check the restrooms," I called out to Declan.

"And I'll look upstairs. Just in case."

We met back at the front door and, satisfied that the Terminal was empty, we joined our patrons outside.

Declan's parents, Ellen and Malachi, were in the crowd and as soon as she saw me, his mother's eyes filled with tears.

"Oh, honey, are you all right?" She wrapped an arm around my shoulders.

Before I answered, I looked around, checking to be sure Sophie wasn't trying to play the hero and had gone back inside.

"I'm fine," I told Ellen. "I just can't imagine where a fire could have started. It wasn't in the kitchen."

"Not out in the restaurant, either," Declan assured me. There was an elderly couple standing hand in hand watching as the hook and ladder truck swung down the street, and carefully, Declan walked them to stand in front of the building next door so they wouldn't be in the way.

"The smoke wasn't coming from the basement," I said, sure I would have seen it curling under the door that led from the kitchen to the basement stairs.

"How about upstairs?" Malachi pointed to the window above the front entrance.

Declan was back in time to hear his dad's question, and when he shook his head, a curl of inky hair dipped over his forehead. "I didn't see a thing up there, either."

It seemed very odd to me, and considering it, I thought through the problem out loud.

"It's as if someone lit a piece of paper and held it up to one of the smoke alarms to—"

The words might have frozen right there on my lips, but that didn't keep my body from springing into action. Just as the first firefighters stepped up to the Terminal, axes and hoses ready, I pushed past them and into the restaurant. I heard Declan call out my name. I knew he was right behind me. But that didn't stop me.

Nothing could.

At least until I put on the brakes just inside the kitchen door.

But then, that was when I found Dolly standing at the prep counter, my Italian cookbook in hand.

I'd bet a dime to a donut she wasn't looking for the recipe for tagliatelle with asparagus and marjoram.

Chapter 19

There is something about a tall, hulking firefighter in helmet, boots, coveralls, and jacket reading the riot act to a woman and reminding her that arson is against the law that tends to turn said woman into a quivering mass.

Quiver, Dolly did.

She also cried, moaned, and got so pale and breathless, that same firefighter slapped an oxygen mask on her.

While Dolly breathed in deeply, he turned to me. "I'm going to need to report this to the police."

This, I did not argue with. Aside from the fact that Dolly had panicked our customers, ruined any number of meals, and made poor Sophie's blood pressure shoot through the roof (she was out front sucking oxygen, too), Dolly had betrayed the Terminal in the worst possible way.

Still, her hapless attempt at espionage had provided me with what I was looking for.

Or at least the place to look for it.

"If you could give me just a couple minutes to talk to her, I'd really appreciate it," I told the firefighter, then added, "You guys have time for pizza?"

I didn't have to ask twice. While he went to collect his fellow firefighters and get them seated in the restaurant, I told George to get the ovens going again.

Then I closed in on Dolly.

For a minute, I watched her breathe in, then out. When one of those breaths finally staggered, it was time for me to make my move.

I crossed my arms over my chest. "That was incredibly stupid. What did you do, light a piece of paper on fire and hold it up to the smoke alarm in the ladies' room?"

She nodded, inhaled, coughed, before she unlooped the oxygen mask from around her neck and hung her head. "That's exactly what I did, then I ran outside and hid in the back parking lot. I didn't know how else I could get back here to find what I needed. I didn't want anyone to see me. I didn't want anyone to know. I'm sorry."

"You think 'sorry' covers it? We had customers in here, Dolly." As if she didn't know where the restaurant was, I swung an arm toward the kitchen door. "If it wasn't for Inez and Declan handling the situation like pros and getting everyone outside quickly and efficiently, somebody might have panicked. Somebody could have gotten hurt."

"I never . . ." A single tear slipped down her doughy cheek. "I never thought of that."

"I guess you were too busy thinking about how much money you were going to make from that balding reporter."

This time when she sucked in a breath, it had nothing to do with needing air. "How do you—"

"Does it matter? I know. I know you told him you'd get a very interesting picture for him. I know he told you he'd pay you for it."

She nodded.

"You want to give that picture to me instead?"

Her hands shaking, she reached for the cookbook she'd been holding when I burst into the kitchen. "I . . ." Her voice quivered. She cleared her throat. "I found the photo when I was looking for—"

"A ponytail holder. Yeah, I know that, too."

"It's . . ." Dolly flipped open the cookbook to a page near the back and slipped out a photograph. "It was just sitting there and I figured no one even knew about it and no one would miss it, and—"

"And so you decided to steal it."

Why did I have the feeling she'd never thought of it that way?

That would explain why Dolly's cheeks went back to being as pale as they were pre-oxygen. "Only I didn't steal it, did I? Because here it still is." This particular bit of logic was supposed to soften my heart.

It didn't work.

When she handed over the picture, Dolly's bottom lip trembled.

I stepped back and took a close look at the photograph with a single, smiling woman in it.

From the looks of the clothing—

I turned the picture in my hands, the better to get rid of the glare and take a better gander.

The picture was taken from maybe ten feet away, but there was no mistaking Meghan Cohan. From the little hints provided by the clothes she was wearing—hoop earrings, a fedora, and a pair of tight pants with a logo on the butt—I'd say the photo was taken maybe sixteen or seventeen years earlier.

Back when Meghan Cohan didn't exist, and Tina Moretti was a kid from nowhere with an almost-pretty face and dreams as big as the whole, wide world.

"It's not exactly exciting. Or interesting. Meghan, standing near a park bench." I squinted and looked more closely at the buildings in the background. "In some big city."

Dolly shrugged. "I didn't think it was anything earthshaking, either, but when I told that reporter about it, when I told him it looked old and that I was pretty sure it was a picture of Meghan before she got really famous, well, that's when he said he was interested. See . . ." She leaned over and pointed at Meghan's smiling face. "It must have been before she had her lips done. And her chin. See her chin? By the time she made *None Are Waiting*, Meghan's chin was more sculpted and her lips were plumper."

"And that reporter thought this picture was news?"

"Everything about Meghan is news." Nothing would

ever convince Dolly otherwise. "He was willing to pay me a thousand dollars for the photo. A thousand dollars! But then this morning you told me you knew about the picture of the car and the picture of the freezer door, and I got upset, and I walked out, and . . ."

"And you figured the only way you could get back in here to get the picture was to start a bit of a fire, wait for everyone to leave the building, then sneak inside and grab the photograph."

As if she couldn't have put it better herself, she nodded and reminded me, "A thousand dollars is a lot of money!"

"Is it worth a thousand dollars to sell out your employer and the people who thought you were a friend?"

Her eyes glistened with tears. "I wouldn't have done it if I didn't have to."

Inez picked that moment to scurry into the kitchen with the pizza orders for the firefighters. I pointed to the nearest stool, told Dolly to stay put, and helped chop mushrooms and peppers and search for a can of pineapple, because one of the firefighters had requested that on his pizza. Another of the men wanted tuna on his. I may be opinionated, but I am not judgmental, so I kept my mouth shut about that particular culinary request. I opened the can of tuna, handed it off to George, and once the pizzas were popped in the oven, I got back to the matter at hand.

I fully expected to ask Dolly why she was so desperate for money, but as it turned out, I didn't need to.

"Tuna!" The idea hit, and I slapped the counter, then pointed a finger at Dolly. "You did it for the tuna!"

She had no idea what I was talking about, and hey, who could blame her?

"Just Kitten," I said, watching her face as I spoke the words and knowing I hit a nerve.

Color washed over Dolly's cheeks and blotched her chin. As if she were the one with whiskers, her nose twitched. Her eyes cascaded tears.

"Do you have any idea how expensive it is to provide a good home to cats?" she wailed.

"I have an idea that if you had fewer cats, it would be easier and less expensive to take care of them."

"Yes. Yes. Of course." She nodded like a bobble-head. "That's how it started. That's how it always starts. With just a few. I started with Mittens and Buffy. Then Tabitha came along, and Grant, and Lester and . . ." Her chest heaved. "There are so many poor kitties that need homes, and I took them in and I meant to find them places to live and send them on. But I love them, Laurel. I love all of them so much I could never get rid of any of them! And every time I see another one, or I hear there are more somewhere with no one to love them and care for them, I pick them up, and I take them in. That's what I was doing the night Meghan was murdered. There was a call that went out to rescue groups about a litter that was found under a bridge. I didn't think . . . If I told you, I didn't think you'd understand."

"So that's why you sold the pictures to the paparazzi. And why you're trying to sell Terminal silverware on the Internet. You need money to keep the rescue going. Not that it's much of a rescue since you're keeping all the cats yourself."

"Those poor kitties." Dolly sobbed. "Those poor, poor kitties."

Since there wasn't much I could say, it was a good

thing Declan and Inez showed up to pick up the pizza orders. While they were at it, they put in orders—all gratis, of course—for everyone who'd been in the restaurant when the smoke alarms went off and had decided to come back in. Just as I'd hoped, seeing the firefighters in there enjoying dinner erased their worries about any more emergencies.

"Can't have too many hands helping out." Declan's mom, Ellen, sailed into the kitchen and grabbed a pizza, too. On her way by, she managed to give me a one-armed hug. "You did great during the crisis. You all did great."

We had, and if nothing else, I suppose that was one thing the evening proved. The staff at the Terminal—minus Dolly, of course, and plus Declan, since he wasn't officially staff—worked like a well-oiled machine.

After all the angst of the evening, the thought caused a curl of warmth inside me. The next time Declan hurried by, I gave him a smile.

"What?" He smiled back.

"Just feeling grateful." I glanced at Dolly, who was still weeping quietly, then grabbed the cookbook where she'd tucked the old photo. "This is what the whole thing was all about," I told him. "Dolly trying to get this old picture of Meghan so she could sell it. It's crazy."

His eyes narrowed, he stepped back. "You don't suppose that photograph was what Meghan was looking for when she came to the Terminal, do you?"

I'd been so busy with the emergency and its aftermath, I hadn't had a chance to think about it.

Now I did, and I knew the answer. "No way. Why

would she go through all that trouble to find an old picture of herself? Unless . . ."

As if we'd choreographed it, Declan and I both slid a look at the cookbook at the exact same time.

"That book wasn't with the other books," I told him. "I put it away in a drawer. The day I made the tagliatelle. So when Meghan was here—"

"She couldn't have looked in that book."

"Which is why she never found the photograph."

"Except you're right, why would she want it, anyway?" Even Declan's keen lawyer mind couldn't make sense of it.

That made two of us.

Which didn't keep me from trying.

I tapped a finger to the cover of the cookbook, where the photo had been tucked. "I had this cookbook in California," I said.

"So it's one of the books Meghan knew you had."

"And one of the books she knew, or at least could have figured, that I'd taken with me when I walked out of her house that night."

Careful to stay far away from Dolly, who I was convinced could snoop even through a cascade of tears, I propped the cookbook under my arm and headed for my office. Once Declan and I were seated in there and the door was closed behind us, we began our search.

Page by page, we went through the cookbook.

"No more photographs," Declan commented when we were about halfway through.

"No anything," I grumbled.

At least until I turned to a page that featured a recipe

for spaghetti and strawberries. Not that I don't love both, but, let's face it, the sound of the combination is chill-inducing.

A single piece of folded paper fluttered out of the book and floated to the floor.

"What is it?" My question bumped out between the furious beats of my heart, and when Declan unfolded the paper and didn't answer, I stood up and went to stand behind him so I could peer over his shoulder.

"It's paperwork on a divorce from the great state of Texas," he said. "The two parties are Benito Gallo and Tina Moretti."

Not that I didn't believe him, but I took the paper out of Declan's hands for a better look.

"Why would Meghan be so desperate to get the papers for a divorce that everyone in the world knows about?" I asked no one in particular.

Neither Declan nor I had the chance to answer.

My phone rang, and when I saw Spencer's number come up on the screen, I answered.

"What's up?" I asked him, and because it felt so weird to talk to the kid while I was holding the paper that dissolved his parents' marriage, I set the paper down on the desk. "What are you up to?"

"Up to finding out answers, that's what I'm up to." Spencer's voice was tight with excitement. "I got a lot to tell you, Laurel. You know, detective to detective."

I was afraid to ask. "Can it wait until morning?"

"I don't think so, it's pretty important. I just found out—"

Spencer grumbled a word he shouldn't have used.

"Somebody's at the door." From the way his voice bounced along, I could tell he was already walking to answer it. "Just hold on a minute."

I can't say why an alarm every bit as demanding and discordant as the Terminal's smoke alarm went off inside my head. I know only that the next thing I knew, I was yelling into my phone.

"Let Wilma answer the door!"

"Wilma went out to get us some snacks. Hold on."

The sound was suddenly muffled; Spencer had taken the phone away from his ear, maybe tucked it in his pocket.

Still, I heard him say, "Oh, it's you," like it was the most natural thing in the world. At least until the panic kicked in and he yelled, "Hey, stop that! Let me go!"

"Spencer! Spencer!"

I didn't get an answer.

In fact, the only thing I could hear was the kid's voice coming from what sounded like far away when he screamed, "Ostrich! Ostrich!"

Chapter 20

"Kidnapped? What do you mean, kidnapped?"

To me, there didn't seem all that many ways to explain it, but I tried. "Kidnapped, Gus. As in, taken against his free will. I was talking to Spencer on the phone and someone came to the door of the hotel room and the next thing I knew, he was in trouble."

"And you could tell this, how?"

"Because he yelled 'Ostrich!'" I screeched my frustration and even though Declan was driving and he knew perfectly well how to get to Austintown, I pointed at the next turn to indicate the way. "Never mind why it matters, Gus. Trust me, it does. *Ostrich* is a kind of code word. It's what Spencer told me he was going to say if he ever got in trouble."

"And you think he's in trouble."

"I think someone came to the door of that hotel

room and either took Spencer, or . . ." I had to swallow before I could even say it. "Or did something to him."

"I'll get a car right over there," Gus told me, his voice more animated than I'd ever heard it. "And I'll be there in a couple minutes. Are you—"

"Almost there." We barreled into the parking lot of the Holiday Inn, or at least we barreled as much as the wise and careful attorney driving the car knew he could get away with. Even before Declan had the car in park, I punched open the door and headed inside.

I had just turned into the hallway where Wilma and Spencer's rooms were located when I saw her walk up to the door, a bag of groceries in each hand.

"Don't touch anything!" I don't know why I thought this was important. Maybe it came from too many hours of watching cop shows in front of the TV.

Wilma had always been unflappable, even in the face of Meghan's sometimes over-the-top household demands. This time was no exception. She juggled the bags to get her swipe key out of her purse.

"What are you doing here, Laurel?" she asked.

"Don't touch anything!" I couldn't be any clearer, but just in case, I closed in on her and snatched the key from her hand. "The cops are on their way."

Awareness washed over her like a wave, so strong and so cold, I could see the effects it left in its wake.

First one, then the other, of the grocery bags dropped to the floor.

So did Wilma's purse.

Her cheeks got chalky.

"Please! Don't tell me. Not . . . not Spencer!"

"I don't know. Not for sure. But the cops are almost here. I think we need to let them take a look at things before we go into the room and touch anything."

We didn't have to wait long.

No sooner did Declan come into the hotel, than a couple of Hubbard cops joined us. They were followed by two of Austintown's finest, and finally, by Gus, who had the hotel manager with him. Gus was wearing bright red shorts and a T-shirt (a little snug over the tummy) with a picture of Tweety Bird on it.

I had never thought of him as the Tweety Bird type.

"Someone, please tell me." We backed out of the way so the cops could get the room open, and Wilma slumped against the wall, her hands clutched at her waist and her mouth twisted. "Tell me, please, what is going on?"

"We're going to know really soon," I promised her. I put one hand on her shoulder and held my breath when the cops walked into the room.

"Clear," I heard one of them call out, and let go of the breath I was holding.

Spencer wasn't there. Spencer wasn't lying there hurt.

By now, people up and down the hallway were outside their rooms, and Gus stepped into the hallway. "It's fine! Nothing to worry about," he assured them. "We'd like all of you to stay in your rooms. Unless somebody can tell me something about the kid who was staying here?"

"You mean that noisy kid playing some kind of game? Calling out 'Ostrich! Ostrich!'?"

"Did you see him leave?" Gus asked.

The guy shook his head. "By the time I came out in the hallway to tell the manager to get things under control, there was no sign of anybody."

One by one, the room doors shut. Gus put a hand on my elbow. "We're going to process the room. You know, check for fingerprints and such."

"No sign of Spencer?" I asked him.

"No. The manager said you three can wait in the lobby." He walked me that way. "I'll have an officer stay with you and that way if any of you gets a call from Spencer or thinks of anything or—"

"Wait!" I stopped so fast that behind me, Declan slammed into me. I would have hit the floor if he didn't loop an arm around my waist. Once I was back on my feet, I closed in on Gus, my phone in my hands.

"I know where he is," I said.

"Spencer? You know—"

"Well, not exactly. Not yet. But I know how to find him."

IT WAS SO easy, it was almost funny. Or at least it would have been funny if I wasn't so worried about Spencer.

What did he know that had made him a target?

Who thought he was a liability?

And would we find the kid there when we followed the Place My Pals app?

Or had the kidnapper come to his (or her) senses, gotten rid of Spencer's phone, and taken the kid to parts unknown?

In the back of the squad car with its lights flashing

and its siren blaring, I reached over and grabbed Declan's hand.

"We've got this," he told me. "Don't worry."

"But what if—"

"Spencer's lucky you're looking out for him."

"And I'm lucky . . ." The words wedged behind the ball of emotion in my throat. "Thanks for helping."

"You mean with waiting tables?"

"I mean with everything. With waiting tables and figuring out mysteries and even with the dead tomatoes."

He slid me a look. "I ordered more."

"Tomato plants?" I realized it was something I'd been meaning to do and never had the time. "Will you make sure I don't kill them?"

"You are going to grow the best tomatoes in Ohio." He patted my hand. "And I'm going to be right there with you picking them."

"Are you two done?" From the front passenger seat, Gus grumbled. "We're on a case here, people, we're not supposed to be talking hearts and flowers."

"It's actually vegetables," I pointed out.

"And we're actually getting close." He had my phone, looking at the map displayed on the Place My Pals screen, and he waggled the phone at me. "You sure this Pal thing is going to show us where the kid is?"

"That's how it's supposed to work."

We careened into the parking lot that served a variety of electronics and home goods stores, and the squad car screeched to a stop. Gus had called for backup and behind us, three more police cars pulled up, lights pulsing. Another two cars from whatever jurisdiction we were now in were already there, and the officers jumped out, waiting for further instructions.

"This is it?" I slid out of the car, stepped onto the sidewalk, and stared wide-eyed at the gigantic red letters over the door and the picture above them of a cartoon mouse.

"What kind of kidnapper goes to Chuck E. Cheese's?"

We were about to find out.

The cops led the way into the restaurant and a second later, I saw Spencer over in the corner munching a pizza. The person who'd spirited him away from his hotel room was there, too, standing next to the table, and the moment she saw us, she burst into tears.

But then, Corrine Kellogg had never been good at much, and I shouldn't have expected her to be much of a kidnapper.

One look at her standing there, glancing at us over her shoulder and everything—Spencer's abduction, the divorce papers, that old photo, and maybe even Meghan's murder—became clear to me.

"I'M STILL NOT convinced." Gus's protest might have been a little more effective if he didn't have a blotch of maple syrup on his tie. He sopped up the last of the syrup on his plate with a bite of French toast and chewed appreciatively. I can't say I blame him. George makes a mean French toast. "We don't usually just let someone out of jail and bring them to a meeting like this."

"But you have to admit, it's the only way we're going to get all the answers we need."

He slanted me a look at the same time he picked up

the coffee cup Inez had just refilled for him. "Thought you had all the answers."

"I think I have the answers. See, it's all about the divorce papers."

Gus managed to wrinkle his nose at the same time he took a slurp of coffee. "Who cares about a divorce that happened so many years ago?"

"Someone cared enough to kill Meghan." I shouldn't have had to remind him. "You've got to give this a try, Gus. If only—"

He held up a hand to stop me. "Gotta admit, when you first suggested this whole thing last night, I thought it was a little loopy. But I spent some time thinking about it. My officers are bringing Corrine Kellogg over here to the Terminal in . . ." He checked his watch. "She ought to be here in just a few minutes."

"And everyone else?" I asked him.

"They've been . . . invited." The way he said that last word made me think it was the kind of offer that cannot be refused. "And if I'm not mistaken . . ." He looked toward the front of the restaurant. "Looks like they're just starting to show up."

From the other side of the front window, Ben Gallo gave us a brusque wave.

I unlocked the door and before he was even inside, he was all over me. Figuratively speaking, of course.

"What is this craziness?" Ben demanded. "I am a busy man. I am an important man. I raced yesterday." He inched back his shoulders. "I won."

"Go on in." I waved him through our waiting area. "Inez will take your breakfast order. As soon as everyone else gets here, we'll get started."

As usual, Ben was dressed casually and elegantly in dark pants and a dusky blue shirt that was open at the neck. The sleeves were rolled above his elbows. "Everyone else?"

He made it sound like some sort of accusation, which is exactly why I acted like it was no big deal.

"Well, we've got some important things to talk about." Because he didn't move an inch, I wound an arm through his and escorted him into the restaurant. "Why don't you sit right there next to Detective Oberlin?"

Instead, Ben took the seat across from Gus at the big round table we'd set up near the back windows.

A minute later, Dulcie Thoroughgood arrived, and she was as jumpy as a june bug. She was followed by the countess Adalina Crocetti, who looked as splendid that morning as all the fashion magazines insisted she was, in a pink sleeveless shift and stilettos high enough that I was tempted to ask her to dust off the overhead fans while she was up there.

She was no more pleased to be there than her husband was.

"This, it is ridiculous." The criticism oozed out of her the moment she set foot in the door. "I am not to be toyed with in such a manner. Police officers at the door of my hotel room! It is an insult. An outrage."

"It won't take long at all," I assured her. "Besides, there's someone here I'm sure you'll want to see."

I escorted her into the restaurant, not so much to be polite but because I wanted to see Ben's reaction when he realized the wife he thought was back in sunny Italy was really in Hubbard, Ohio.

The moment he set eyes on Adalina, he rose to his feet. Okay, so he got points for being a gentleman.

Those sort of got canceled out by the way his jaw flapped and his eyes goggled. "What are you . . . ? Why are you . . . ?"

She tossed her head. Now that she'd gotten rid of the blond wig she wore when she was pretending to be a reporter, her real hair—sleek and dark—gleamed in the early-morning sunlight that washed through the windows. She gave Ben a quick kiss on the cheek. "I am here to see you, of course, my darling. I did not want to distract you before your race yesterday. Today, today, I was going to surprise you. Instead, these people . . ." With one disdainful glance, she took in both me and Gus as well as Inez, who was standing by with the coffee carafe; Sophie, who was seated at a nearby table because she didn't want to miss a moment of what was going on; Dulcie, who was now as starstruck as she was nervous; and Declan, who'd come out of the kitchen just moments before with the poached eggs Sophie had requested.

"They say I must be here." The countess flounced to the chair next to Ben's and sat down. "This, I do not understand. I do not understand it at all."

Since I wasn't prepared to explain quite yet, it was just as well that Wilma and Spencer arrived. To his credit, Spencer didn't look any worse for wear after being kidnapped. But then, according to what the kid told Gus after we'd scooped him up out of Chuck E. Cheese's, he'd pretty much spent the time riding around with Corrine while she mumbled a chorus of "What to do? What to do?" to herself and then finally settled on pizza while she thought about her next move.

"Rabbit?" Spencer asked me when he slipped by.

Was everything okay? I could only smile in a way that told him I hoped so.

Spencer greeted his dad, who nodded in reply, and Wilma and Spencer took seats at the far side of the table.

That left only one person we needed before we began, and Corrine showed up just a minute later, escorted by two police officers and wearing handcuffs. Her eyes were red and swollen. Her nose was red and raw. Her face was red and . . . well, red. One night in the slammer and she was a mess. She should have thought of that before she turned to a life of crime. On Gus's signal, they took off her handcuffs and she sat down, and a uniformed cop would have stood right behind her if I didn't pull up a chair for him.

"So, we're all here." Since Gus and I had discussed what was going to happen, I knew he wouldn't mind that I took the lead. I was less threatening than he was, and I hoped to use that to my advantage. "I know you're all anxious to get out of here—"

"I'll say," Ben grumbled.

"But there are some important things we need to discuss before you all go your separate ways."

"You mean Tina's murder." The coffee cup Dulcie had clutched in both hands shimmied. "You brought us here to talk about Tina."

The countess wrinkled her patrician nose. "Who is this Tina person?"

"Ben?" When he ignored me, I looked to where the cops had seated Corrine. "Corrine? Since you knew her a long time, maybe you're the best one to tell us about Tina."

Corrine gulped and sobbed.

"I'll tell you about her." Dulcie, it seemed, was no shrinking violet. She set down her coffee and propped her elbows on the table. "Tina is Meghan Cohan."

"What?" the countess and Wilma responded in unison.

Dulcie didn't spare them a look. "That was her name," she told them. "Before she changed it. What she didn't change was her personality. She was a grasping, mean, greedy, selfish—"

"We're not here to put Meghan on trial," I butted in. "What matters, of course, is that Dulcie's right. Before she changed her name, Meghan was Tina Moretti, an aspiring actress. Spencer, you wouldn't have known about that, of course, because that was before you were born. Unless your mom told you the story?"

He shook his head.

"And, Countess"—I turned her way—"there's no way you could have known it unless your husband told you."

"He did not." She lifted her chin. "We did not discuss Miss Meghan Cohan. She was a not-so-good memory for my Ben."

"And Wilma?" I asked.

"I had no idea! I can't believe the media never found out."

"It was a well-guarded secret. I don't know why," I added. "You'd think Meghan would have liked the press. You know, kid from nowhere makes good. But that doesn't matter. All that matters is that when she and Ben Gallo were married, she was Tina Moretti."

"Yes, that is true." Ben sat back and gave me a level look. "We were both just starting our careers. She did not change her name until—"

"Until after your divorce was final."

Ben nodded.

"And your divorce was finalized in the state where the marriage had taken place."

"Yes." Ben took a sip of coffee. "Texas."

"And that divorce . . ." I looked at Declan, who'd been holding on to it, and he presented me the divorce papers we'd found tucked in the cookbook.

"That divorce," I said, "is what this whole thing is all about."

"You mean Ms. Cohan's murder?" Wilma asked.

"I mean . . . well, let me set this up for you and if any of you . . ." Slowly and carefully I looked around the table from person to person. "If any of you know I've got this wrong, just let me know. See, Meghan . . . or Tina, as she was then . . . Tina was plenty ambitious. As a matter of fact, she even went so far as to lie to Dulcie here about a screen test."

"You got that straight!" Dulcie crossed her arms over her chest and plumped back in her chair. "That no-good, lousy woman—"

"Took Dulcie's place at the screen test that was supposed to be Dulcie's," I finished for her because really, there was only so much Spencer needed to hear about his mother. "That was the screen test that resulted in her role in *None Are Waiting*."

"Shoulda been my role," Dulcie grumbled. "Shoulda been mine."

"So you see, when I learned that, I naturally thought Dulcie might have killed Meghan."

She sat up like a shot and, one hand in the air, I signaled her to cool her jets.

"But Dulcie has an alibi for the night of the murder. And besides, Meghan's been paying Dulcie off for years to keep the secret of her background. Why would Dulcie want to ruin that?"

"You got that right," Dulcie mumbled.

"So then I wondered about Wilma."

This time, it was Spencer who was about to protest. I mouthed the word *Rabbit*, and the kid settled down.

"You see, Wilma lost a whole lot of money when she invested in a movie Meghan never made. And Wilma, Wilma's got a big heart. She wasn't a fan of Meghan's parenting skills."

"True," Wilma conceded. "Which does not mean that I killed her."

"It doesn't," I agreed.

"And then there's the countess."

"What!" Her Italian ire stirred, she sat up and aimed a look in my direction that was every bit as hot as any fra diavolo sauce. "Why would I—"

"You know what? I don't know. But I thought it was plenty fishy that you just happened to show up here in what I'm sure you consider the middle of nowhere, and in disguise, too."

"Disguise?" Ben could hardly believe his ears. He turned in his seat, the better to see his wife. "Why would you do something crazy like that?"

Her bottom lip protruded. "I had to know. I heard the

news on the television and they said you were here in this silly little town and that this is where Meghan, she was found dead. And I had to know, Ben, I had to know if you still loved her."

"That's why you were asking questions about him?" I could be excused for sounding a little incredulous. "Seems to me if you want to know how someone feels about you, maybe it's just easier to ask them."

"Amen," Declan said from the corner.

I pretended I hadn't heard and instead, went right on.

"And then, of course," I said, "there's our neighborhood kidnapper, Corrine."

We all turned to look her way.

Just in time, too, because she jumped to her feet. "You're right," she said. "I did it! I killed Meghan!"

Chapter 21

That was the whole point of my calling that little meeting, right?

To get our perpetrator to confess?

Then explain to me why I stood there, as speechless and as flabbergasted as everyone else.

One minute melted into two, and two had almost become three when Corrine collapsed like a poorly made soufflé and plunked back down in her seat.

"What! You're not going to tell them it's a lie? You're not going to defend me? You're not going to say you're the one who did it? After all I've done for you?"

She was looking right at Ben.

Ah, now my theory of the case was finally making sense.

I looked at Gus for permission to go on.

He nodded.

"Aren't you going to help Corrine out?" I asked Ben. "After all, you're the one she's been trying to protect this whole time. She's in love with you."

"That's right." Spencer gave his father a narrow-eyed stare. "I heard her talking on the phone yesterday when she was in the lobby of the hotel and she didn't know I was there. I heard her talking to you, Dad. She told you she loved you. She told you she'd done stuff for you and it was time for you to show your appreciation. She saw me. She figured I heard her. That's why she kidnapped me."

"No, no, no." Ben stood, took one look at the cop behind Corrine and the other two who had stationed themselves just inside the doorway of the restaurant, and sat back down. "This is crazy. Corrine loves me? She cannot. And I certainly, I certainly have never loved her."

"It's what you said. It's what you told me. It's why I called you the night Meghan left California and told you where she would be. It's why I followed her here to the restaurant and told you that, too. You said it was so you could get the divorce papers back, the ones you'd fought about the last time you were in California. She . . ." Corrine's voice bumped over the tears that suddenly clogged her voice and she looked my way.

"Meghan wanted to put the papers some place safe. She didn't want Ben to find them, and remember, Laurel, he was in town that weekend. He'd been at the house that afternoon."

"Yes." I remembered now. "And they fought."

"Meghan put the divorce papers in the cookbook and she figured she could retrieve them the next morning but the next morning, you were gone. That's why she had a PI following you. She didn't care where you were, Laurel. Meghan didn't give a damn about you. But she had to get those papers back."

"Because she didn't want Ben to find them." To me, this was the important message in Corrine's statement and I repeated it, slowly but carefully, then pinned her with a look. "Why?"

Corrine gulped.

Ben swore under his breath.

The countess said something in Italian and I was glad I had no idea what it was.

I guessed it was my turn again.

"It seems weird, don't you think, that Ben would be so desperate to get his hands on the papers from a divorce that everyone in the world already knows about? Yet he was. That's why he led Corrine on and that's why she was so angry the night the will was read. Did he finally tell you the truth that night, Corrine? Did he tell you he'd been playing you?"

If looks really could kill, Ben would have been as dead as Meghan, thanks to Corrine's glare.

"We met before we came here for the reading of the will," she growled, "and he told me that I never meant anything to him. He told me he just used me to find out where Meghan was. I was so mad, I could have . . ." She jiggled her shoulders. "That's when I called the countess and that's when she told me she was in town, too, and we agreed to meet. You see, I knew if I could find those papers and get them to her . . ." Her voice hardened. "Well, then, Ben, you'd lose both of us. Just like that."

"That's why you tipped those boxes over on me. You had to get me out of the way to search for the divorce papers. And the terrible thing you told Wilma you did?"

"Getting suckered by him, for one thing." Corrine shot Ben a look. "Everything I did, Ben, it was for you. Always for you."

"Which is also why you lied to Wilma about meeting her at Denny's the night of the murder, right? You wanted Wilma to look guilty."

Corrine hung her head so I went right on.

"And Meghan was so intent on first hiding the divorce papers, then getting them back, she followed me all the way here to Ohio. That's when Corrine told Ben where Meghan was going, where she'd be, how he could find the papers. Am I right so far, Corrine?"

She didn't answer me. I didn't need her to.

"So let's take a look at those papers." In spite of Ben's muffled "No!" I unfolded the papers in front of me. "I've even got an attorney here who can interpret them for us."

Declan stepped forward and read from the papers. "The parties involved are Benito Gallo and Tina Moretti. The marriage took place in Texas and so did the divorce. That date was July 22, 2001."

Dulcie gasped and slapped a hand to her heart. A second later, her expression melted from stunned to *Aha!* I had to give it to Dulcie, she didn't look like the brightest bulb in the box, but she caught on quickly.

Not so much everyone else.

"July 22, 2001," I explained, "was the day Meghan had her screen test for *None Are Waiting*."

"But how could she—" One look from her husband and the countess swallowed her question.

"How could she be in two places at once?" I stared at Corrine. "I should have seen it from the start. You see, Corrine, here, isn't the most efficient personal assistant on the planet. In fact, she's not very good at all. But Meghan never criticized her. Meghan never got rid of her. See, Corrine knew a secret, one Meghan couldn't mess with."

I picked up the photograph we'd found in the cookbook and passed it from person to person.

"That's Dallas in the background, by the way," I told them. "And the woman in the picture—"

"Is Meghan," Wilma said.

"Is Corrine," I corrected her. "Remember, before Meghan had all her cosmetic surgeries, Corrine and Meghan looked enough alike to be mistaken for sisters. So when Meghan . . . or Tina, as she was then . . . needed to be in California for a screen test, but she was desperate to get out of her marriage to Ben and had to be in Texas to sign the papers—"

"She sent this Corrine in her place?" The countess was breathy.

"That's right. She sent Corrine in her place. Declan checked." I gave him a small smile. "Both the parties to a divorce do not have to appear at the same time to sign the papers. Not in Texas. Of course, Ben would have known immediately that it wasn't Tina who signed those papers, but Ben wasn't there."

"And no one else knew Tina," Dulcie said. "If they ever questioned it—"

"They looked enough alike to be sisters," I confirmed.

Ben pounded the table with one fist. "What difference can any of this make now?"

"It made enough of a difference that Corrine would do anything to deflect suspicion from you. That's why you sent me the email implicating Dulcie, right, Corrine? Not that you knew the whole story! You had no idea what Meghan had done to Dulcie, but you knew enough about Meghan's private affairs to know she sent Dulcie a check every month. You figured whatever it was, it must have been something juicy. You thought if we found Dulcie, if we found out about the payments, Dulcie would look guilty."

Corrine didn't answer. She didn't need to.

"Dulcie and Corrine, they were the only ones who knew Meghan was really Tina. Dulcie, Corrine, and you." I turned to Ben.

He kept his mouth shut. It didn't matter.

I shook my head. "Really?" I looked at him hard, but he refused to meet my gaze. "Come on, Ben, you're a smart guy and Meghan knew that. Meghan never signed those papers. Corrine did. The divorce isn't legal."

"What!" The countess rose on shaky legs and when Ben put a hand on her arm, she yanked it away. "Are you telling me . . . ? Does this mean . . . ?"

"I did it for you," he told her. "I had to get the papers back, so you wouldn't know. So our marriage wouldn't be annulled."

"Marriage." She kicked back her chair and marched away from the table. "We have no marriage, Benito. We never have."

With that, the countess stomped out the door.

"That's exactly what you were afraid of, wasn't it?" I asked Ben. "The countess would find out and your lifestyle would go up in smoke. That's why you wanted the papers back. But there has to be a reason Meghan told you about the whole thing in the first place. What did she want from you in exchange for the divorce papers?"

Ben snorted out a laugh. "She told me what Corrine had done, that Corrine had impersonated her and signed the papers. She told me my marriage to Adalina wasn't legal. And the only thing that could get her to destroy the papers would be if I took him to live with me." He slanted his son a look.

Wilma draped an arm around Spencer's shoulders. "And this you would not do?"

"The last thing I need is some stupid kid hanging around." Ben's top lip curled. "I tried to get the papers back myself. When Corrine told me Meghan came here, I knew she must be onto something. I followed her, we fought."

"And you killed her."

Wilma pulled Spencer closer.

Corrine dissolved into a puddle of tears.

And Gus?

He got up and put the cuffs on Benito Gallo.

WITHIN ANOTHER THIRTY minutes, it was all over.

Ben was read his rights and taken to the police station.

Corrine went back to the cell where she'd spent the night.

Dulcie actually thanked us for letting her be part of the whole thing because she said it was better drama than any screenplay she'd ever read.

Wilma and Spencer . . . well, I knew it would take time for Spencer to process everything that had happened. Wilma told me she'd take him back to California, that she'd look after him, and I promised to stay in touch.

As for the rest of us there at the Terminal . . .

It was another busy Sunday and the latest buzz of news—Ben Gallo's arrest—just added to our popularity. By the time we were done for the day, we were all exhausted.

"We're going to need a new waitress," Sophie said, doing the final cash tally for the night. "Too bad, because Dolly was pretty good."

"And pretty desperate." I thought about all those cats. "Gus says it's up to us whether to file charges against Dolly because of the fire. Maybe we don't have to? Maybe we can give her another chance?"

Sophie beamed. "I was hoping you'd say that. And maybe we could help out with those cats of hers, too."

DECLAN AND I stayed behind to lock up.

"No more murders," I told him. "I'm ready for a summer of being nothing but a chef and a farmer and . . ."

We'd already turned off the lights in the waiting area and the evening shadows mixed with the last of the sunlight, slanting over his face. He looked more handsome than ever and I already knew he was the best thing about my life.

"I've been meaning to ask you something," I confessed.

"Well, that's an improvement." He pulled me into his arms and I felt the rumble of his laughter in his chest. "You've been really good about asking for my help lately."

I looped my arms around his waist. "That's because I need your help. I need you. And that's why I have something to ask you. Declan Fury, will you marry me?"

Chapter 22

We waited until fall because by then, we knew we could celebrate our first summer at Pacifique and a bumper crop.

It was a good thing, too. After the church when our guests showed up at the Terminal for our wedding reception, we were ready with the tastiest dishes made from all the freshest ingredients.

There was Irish soda bread, of course, as well as Ellen's Irish stew and a pot of colcannon so big, George could barely get it out of the kitchen.

There was French cassoulet in honor of the farm where Declan and I would spend the rest of our lives.

There was tagliatelle with asparagus and marjoram, and Middle Eastern stuffed grape leaves, and Polish sausage, and pad thai and fried rice.

And there were smiles all around.

"I can't help it!" Sophie, my maid of honor, grinned and cried at the same time. "I'm so happy, Laurel. I've never been this happy in all my life."

I knew exactly how she felt.

Wilma and Spencer were our guests, as were all of our regular customers, all of Declan's huge family, and even Gus Oberlin, who, it turned out, had a wife named Greta who could polka like nobody I'd ever seen.

"It's perfect." Side by side with Declan, I watched our guests dance to the tunes of Luigi Lasagna and his Amici.

Declan slipped an arm around my waist. "You're perfect."

Yes, I know, a wedding day is probably not the right time to correct your new husband, but I couldn't help myself.

"We're perfect together," I told him. "And this is the perfect happily ever after."

Recipes

There's nothing more delicious than Italian food. Here are a couple of recipes passed along from Laurel Inwood Fury and the folks at the Terminal at the Tracks. *Mangia!*

SPAGHETTI FRA DIAVOLO

1 pound of spaghetti
⅔ cup olive oil
10 cloves garlic, sliced very thin or minced
1½ teaspoons crushed red pepper flakes (or use chile de arbol, if you like)
2½ cups tomato puree
½ cup fresh basil leaves, thinly sliced
¼ cup fresh mint leaves, roughly chopped
¼ cup fresh parsley, roughly chopped

2 teaspoons salt
½ teaspoon black pepper

Cook pasta according to package directions. While that's cooking, make your sauce. Heat olive oil in a large skillet over medium flame. Add garlic and cook for 2–3 minutes, stirring frequently, until garlic is fragrant and just starting to turn golden. Add crushed red pepper and stir. Add tomato puree, stir, and reduce heat to medium. Cook for 8 minutes—stirring occasionally—or until the oil begins to rise and separate from the tomato puree. Mix in fresh herbs, salt, and pepper; taste and adjust seasoning as needed.

Once pasta is cooked and drained, add it to the sauce. Reduce heat to low, cover pan, and let pasta cook in the sauce for 2–3 minutes.

Serves 4.

PENNE WITH BACON, TOMATOES, AND SPINACH

1 pound penne pasta
2 tablespoons olive oil, divided
6 slices bacon, chopped
2 tablespoons minced garlic
1 (14.5-ounce) can diced tomatoes
1 bunch fresh spinach, rinsed and torn into
    bite-size pieces

While your penne is cooking according to package directions, heat 1 tablespoon of olive oil in a skillet over medium heat. Place bacon in the skillet and cook until browned and crisp. Add garlic and cook for about 1 minute. Stir in the tomatoes and cook until heated through.

Place the spinach into a colander and drain the hot pasta over it so it is wilted. Transfer to a large serving bowl and toss with the remaining olive oil and the bacon-and-tomato mixture.

Serves 4.

Kylie Logan is the national bestselling author of the League of Literary Ladies Mysteries, the Button Box Mysteries, the Chili Cook-Off Mysteries, and the Ethnic Eats Mysteries.

Ready to find
your next great read?

Let us help.

Visit prh.com/nextread